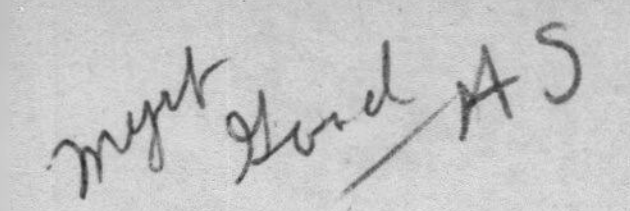

"Do you remember our baby?"

"Our baby?" Emma stared at the man who'd identified himself as her husband. The man with the deep, soothing voice who had whispered to her in the darkness.

"Yes…her name is Carly. Here, I'll show you." Almost frantically he took his wallet from his back pocket, pulled out a picture and handed it to her.

Emma's hands shook as she studied the photo. Grant looked totally masculine, his arm draped around her. She cradled a beautiful infant in her arms.

But it was the tender smile of pride on her face that squeezed at her heart. She really had a child. And she was married.

But she had amnesia.

Dear Reader,

Although we've moved into a new century, I still believe the most treasured days of a woman's life are her wedding day and the day she gives birth to her children. Have you ever wondered what would happen if those precious memories were suddenly taken away? If you met your husband or lover at a different time in your life, under different circumstances, would you fall in love with him again?

While on a romantic weekend getaway with my own husband, I read a magazine article, a true story about a woman who suffered amnesia after a car accident and fell in love with her husband all over again. The story was incredibly sad but very romantic. Thus the seed for *Forgotten Lullaby* was born.

Of course, with my love for mystery and intrigue, the wheels started turning in my mind and I added another layer to the story—instead of a simple car accident, I wondered what would happen if someone had intentionally tried to kill Emma. How would danger and mystery affect her relationship with her stranger/husband? How would Grant feel knowing he and his wife couldn't share memories of their past together? And what would happen to their marriage if Emma never regained those priceless memories?

I hope you are as touched by Emma and Grant's story as I was in writing it. You can write me at P.O. Box 921225, Norcross, GA 30092-1225.

Sincerely,

Rita

Rita Herron

Forgotten Lullaby

Rita Herron

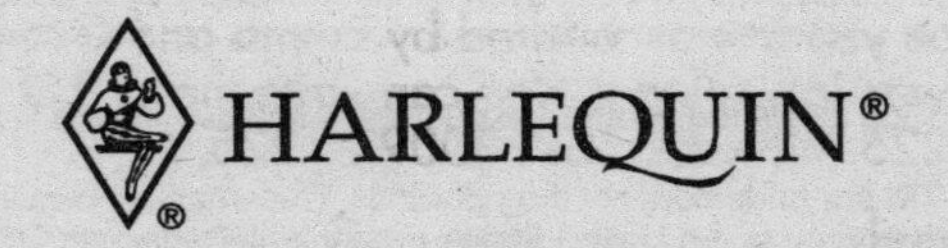

TORONTO • NEW YORK • LONDON
AMSTERDAM • PARIS • SYDNEY • HAMBURG
STOCKHOLM • ATHENS • TOKYO • MILAN • MADRID
PRAGUE • WARSAW • BUDAPEST • AUCKLAND

ISBN 0-373-22556-3

FORGOTTEN LULLABY

This edition published by arrangement with Harlequin Books S.A.

Visit us at www.romance.net

Printed in U.S.A.

ABOUT THE AUTHOR

Rita Herron is a teacher, workshop leader and storyteller who loves reading, writing and sharing stories with people of all ages. She has published two nonfiction books for adults on working and playing with children, and has won the Golden Heart Award for a young adult story. Rita believes that books taught her to dream, and she loves nothing better than sharing that magic with others. She lives with her "dream" husband and three children, two cats and a dog in Norcross, Georgia.

Books by Rita Herron

HARLEQUIN INTRIGUE

486—SEND ME A HERO
523—HER EYEWITNESS
556—FORGOTTEN LULLABY

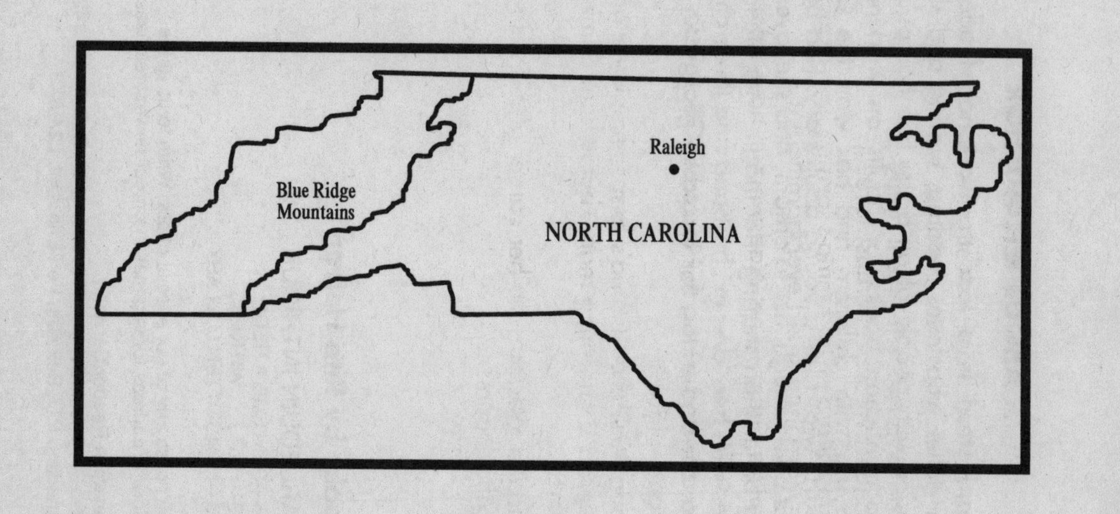
Blue Ridge
Mountains
Raleigh
NORTH CAROLINA

CAST OF CHARACTERS

Emma Wadsworth—A strange accident robbed her of her past; now she must find her future.

Grant Wadsworth—He'll fight for his wife with the strongest weapon he has: love.

Kate Dillard—Did Emma's loving sister like Grant far more than she'd ever admitted?

Martha Greer—The Wadsworths' housekeeper has a dark secret.

Pete Landers—How far would he go to take Grant's place?

Doug McGuire—Emma's former employer and old friend is a charming man—but is he a criminal at heart?

Priscilla Weston—Do her career ambitions extend to after hours?

To my three great kids for all the precious memories:

Adam—I'll never forget the camouflage suit you wore every day to kindergarten, the first time you hit a home run, all the emergency room visits, the teacher who thought you'd be president one day, the day you left home for college and the day you turned my pep talk into a challenge to try something new myself. I did, son—I started writing. Thanks to you.

Elizabeth—I'll never forget racing from the bus stop to the house to get your blanket in kindergarten because you couldn't leave home without it, the day we put the house up for sale and you colored the walls with red crayon, the day you set your first Junior National swimming time and won the State Championship meet, your first Homecoming dance, but most of all, your positive attitude and your never-ending beautiful smile.

Emily—I'll never forget the mustard handprints on the refrigerator, the day the rabbit had babies (when you'd conveniently forgotten to tell us you had bred her), the posters you made when you wanted a big dog, the numerous awards you won in eighth grade, your first soccer goal and most of all, your wonderful independence and drive.

Love always,
Mom

Chapter One

Bright headlights appeared in Emma's rearview mirror, almost blinding her. She sped up slightly, yet the car behind bore down on her tail. Suddenly uneasy, she adjusted the mirror to deflect the light. She hit a pothole and had to brake. Tires squealed behind her, and she clutched the steering wheel, afraid the other vehicle was going to hit her.

She grimaced, wishing he'd back off. The road was deserted, and too curvy for high speeds. Thank goodness she only had a few more miles to go and she'd be home with her baby and husband. Her sister Kate's comments about Grant traveling all the time struck a chord of worry, and she fought the troubling feelings. She and her husband were happy—they were simply going through an adjustment phase with the new baby. All couples went through it. Didn't they?

An image of Grant's chic co-worker, Priscilla, hovered in her mind. So cool and sophisticated, hair perfect, body trim, lips painted a deep kiss-me red, Priscilla wouldn't be caught dead looking as rumpled as Emma had since the baby had arrived. Emma and Grant needed to spend some time alone, quality time without their daughter in tow. Maybe they should hire a sitter, have a romantic evening alone, rekindle their romance—

She swerved to avoid another pothole. The vehicle behind her roared straight over it without even slowing. The woods flanking the road suddenly seemed eerily dark and lonely. A sprinkling of snow dusted the North Carolina highway and dotted the windshield, and tree branches swayed and dipped in the evening wind. She dragged her gaze from the shadowy woods, deciding she'd been watching too many late-night movies while feeding Carly.

Poor baby. Carly had cried with an earache all morning. Emma finally understood how much a mother could hurt for her child. Automatically her hand swept the front passenger seat for Carly's prescription. Instead, she contacted a tube—of lipstick. She gripped the wheel tight with one hand and brought the tube up for inspection. Odd, it wasn't a color she wore. It was red. Priscilla's red. Kate's warnings about men having affairs strummed through her conscience. No, Grant wouldn't—

A horn blasted and the vehicle swerved around her, clipping her rear bumper. Panic streaked through her. She braked again. The guy had been following too close, but this…this was crazy. Was he drunk?

An oncoming set of headlights flashed in the bend of the road. Emma slowed so that the other vehicle—it looked like some sort of SUV—could pass. Instead, he grazed her again, and she skidded sideways toward the side of the road. She clenched the steering wheel as she fought to control the car, her heart pounding. The oncoming vehicle blasted its horn. Oh, God! Her car was going to collide with an eighteen-wheeler!

Emma fought the slide, bringing her Honda back in

the lane. The sports vehicle suddenly slowed, falling in behind her again. The air exploded from her lungs. The oncoming truck passed, a hairbreadth from her bumper, and blared its horn again. Perspiration trickled down her face.

She glanced in the rearview mirror and panic welled inside her when the sports vehicle sped up again. Metal ground against metal as he slammed her from behind. Whoever was driving the car was hitting her on purpose! She began to pump the brakes, but her car skidded off the road.

Burning rubber filled her nostrils. The force of the skid ripped the steering wheel from her hands. She grabbed it again and tried to get control. The SUV sideswiped the Honda once more, this time with such jarring force her car jolted sideways and spun 180 degrees.

The windshield exploded. Shards of glass gouged her arms and face. Pain tore through her head and blood, hot and salty, filled her mouth. As the world went dark, an image of Carly and Grant flashed through her mind. Tears rolled down her cheeks. She should have told them she loved them one more time.

And she should have kissed them both goodbye.

GRANT WADSWORTH stared in horror as rescue workers tried desperately to pry open the door of Emma's small car. She lay inside, unconscious, blood dripping down the side of her face, her skin chalky white. He shuddered, feeling sick all over. A chill engulfed him, not from the cold January wind blowing outside, but from raw stark fear. Another mile and she would have been home, safe and sound with him and Carly. But now...

"Please don't let her die." He choked on the last word.

A police officer stood beside him, one hand on his arm as if he expected Grant to bolt for the Honda at any minute. He would, if he thought he could rescue her without harming her more. Chaos surrounded him. They'd dragged out rescue equipment he'd never seen or heard of. Emergency workers, firefighters, police officers, all racing against time to save his wife. While he simply stood by, helpless.

At last the mangled door was torn off, and two paramedics secured Emma's head and neck, then took her vitals. Another radioed in the information. Their voices and orders faded in and out of his consciousness as he tried to make sense of what was happening.

"Pulse sixty-five, weak and thready, respiration thirty, shallow, BP eighty over fifty...start an IV drip of...let's cut away her seat belt...on three, we'll lift her. One, two, *three.*"

He stared at the dangling seatbelt, now in shreds. Thank God she'd worn it. If only she'd had an air bag. "God, if she dies, I'll never forgive myself." He lunged forward to reach her, but the policeman grabbed his arm.

"Let them take care of her. They need to stabilize her."

Grant collapsed against the side of the police car.

"Are you all right, sir?"

Grant shook his head. "I will be when I know she's okay. I'm not losing her," he said through gritted teeth. "Not now, not ever."

"Looks like there might have been another car involved," the police officer said quietly. "I found two sets of skid marks. And there's black paint chips on the Honda. I'm Detective Warner. My men are questioning the crowd for witnesses."

Grant nodded, confused. So where was the other car? His gaze tracked the parcel of gatherers at the scene. Could someone have seen Emma's accident?

The detective cleared his throat. "How did you make it here so fast?"

Grant's head jerked up at the implication. Or had he imagined the suspicious tone in the detective's voice? "I live about a mile from here. When you called I...I raced right over."

The detective grunted in acknowledgment. "They say most accidents happen within five miles of your own house." He chewed the inside of his cheek. "Doesn't make it any easier, does it?"

"No," Grant mumbled, his gaze on the mangled car. The rescue workers yelled they were ready to go, and he clenched his hands by his sides as he watched them secure Emma onto the boarded stretcher. Panic and guilt clogged his throat. Memories of another young woman floated into his consciousness—*she was bleeding, still and lifeless...he should have done something...* God, no, Emma couldn't die.

He couldn't lose Emma. He moved to her side and took her limp icy hand in his, kissing it ever so gently, careful of the scrapes on her palms. "Hang on, honey, please hang on. I love you. And I need you so much."

"Let's go." The paramedics hoisted her into the ambulance.

He climbed inside and knelt beside her, massaging her hand between his, a sick feeling swirling inside him at the blood matted in her honey-colored hair. "You can't leave us, Emma. Carly and I both need you. We love you, sweetheart."

"We found this in the car," an officer said, holding up Carly's prescription.

"It's for my baby," Grant explained. "She's at home with the sitter."

"I'll get someone to drop it by."

Grant recited his address as he traced a finger over the delicate curve of Emma's chin. The siren screeched and the ambulance jerked into motion. The EMT put an oxygen mask over Emma's mouth and monitored her vital signs, communicating with the hospital staff over the radio. Her face was so pale. Beneath her eyes her skin had turned a strange bluish color.

"I love you, Emma," he whispered again. "Don't you dare die on me." He kissed her hand, memorizing every detail of her face. She had to make it. She had to survive. He couldn't live with another woman's death on his conscience. Especially his wife's.

THE HOURS DRAGGED into days as Grant held a vigil at Emma's bedside, praying for a miracle. But her condition hadn't changed. No news about the person who'd hit her, either.

The steady drip of the IV echoed in the silence of the hospital room, and Grant rubbed his hands up and down his arms, wondering if he would ever be warm again. A few days ago, he'd thought he had everything—a beautiful wife, a new baby, a budding career. If Emma didn't make it…

Emma's sister, Kate, crept into the room. "How is she? Any change?"

Grant shook his head, unable to speak.

Kate folded her arms and sighed. "I tried to call Mom, but she's somewhere en route to Europe. I've left messages to let her know what happened."

He nodded. "Thanks, Kate."

"Did you reach your folks?"

"Yeah." He stood, never taking his eyes off of Emma, and thrust a hand through his hair, not caring that the ends spiked haphazardly. "They don't have the money to fly from Boulder. I offered to pay, even told them the airlines give emergency discount rates, but Dad's job is in limbo already..." Grant hesitated, aware he was admitting his parents' financial circumstances.

"I'm sure they'd come if they could." Kate chewed her bottom lip and he realized he and Kate were actually being civil to each other. They seemed to have called a silent truce in the wake of the accident. Kate stayed with Carly at night. He'd go home long enough to shower and rock his daughter. His stomach twisted painfully as he remembered Carly's tears the night before. She had never been away from Emma for more than a few hours. She missed her mother, and once again he'd felt helpless.

"I'll relieve Martha," Kate said, as if she'd read his mind. Martha Greer was Grant and Emma's housekeeper. "She's been great, keeping Carly all day."

"Yeah." He saw the sympathy in Kate's eyes and felt a ridiculous sense of relief to have her there. "Thanks, Kate."

She gave him a tentative smile, then squeezed his hand. "I love her, too, you know."

Tears pricked his eyes, but he averted his gaze and swallowed the emotion. Kate brushed Emma's hair away from her forehead and placed a soft kiss on her temple. "Get well, sis. I'll treat Carly like she's my own."

Grant flinched at the lone tear that streaked down Kate's cheek. When she closed the door behind her, he slumped in the chair again and took Emma's hand in his, raking his gaze over her unconscious body. The soft gurgle of the humidifier grated on his frayed nerves. Even knowing the equipment attached to her body was meant to help her, he hated that she needed it. He hated the oxygen mask, the IV needle in her arm, the strong smell of antiseptic and other hospital odors that permeated the room.

He was going crazy counting every breath she took. But it was the only way he could make himself believe she was alive. One breath at a time.

A severe concussion, the doctor had said. Possibly brain damage. They were battling a head wound, the most dangerous and least predictable injury a body could sustain. No one would know the extent of Emma's injuries, not until the swelling in her brain went down. But she *couldn't* have brain damage. Not his Emma.

Still, every hour passed in unconsciousness dimmed the outlook. His fingers trembled as he gently touched the bandage on her head. They'd shaved a small area, stitched the head wound and bandaged it. Ugly purple and yellow bruises marred her face, but the scrapes and cuts would heal. She would live, the doctors said—they just didn't know when she would wake up.

A wave of cold engulfed him when he remembered the condition of her car. It was a miracle Emma was alive. When she woke up, maybe she'd be able to tell them what happened. The police had been by to say they'd found a witness, a young boy who'd seen a Jeep sideswipe Emma's car, then saw her veer off the road. He claimed the Jeep's driver had stopped and gotten out to look in Emma's car, then almost immediately driven away. But why would someone want to hurt Emma?

"Please wake up, Emma," he begged as he jolted up

and paced beside her bed. "Why won't you come back to me? Give me another chance."

But she lay still and silent.

DRIP...DRIP....BEEP...beep...beep.

Emma tried to move her limbs, but they felt too heavy. Her body refused to cooperate, even her eyelids. What had happened to her?

A dull low pain throbbed through her nerve endings. Even thinking tired her out. So easy to keep her eyes closed. So hard to open them. The bright light shone in a lone radiant beam that called to her, urging her to lose herself in the calm glow. To be swallowed up, away from the pain. To drift away, at peace...forever.

The constant dripping and beeping in the background faded in and out. The voices. Sometimes a woman's. Sometimes the husky rumble of a man's. Sometimes distressed. Sometimes low and soft. Rolling over the pain and wiping it away. Soothing her into contentment. Drawing her away from the intense pull of the light.

Somewhere in her subconscious, she realized she must be asleep. In a realm so far away no one could reach her. A place where she no longer had to be afraid.

Sometimes the husky voice begged her to stay. Begged her to fight, to come back to him. But she didn't know how. Didn't want to leave the haven where she'd settled.

A sharp grating sound drifted through her reverie, and she tried to turn her head toward the sound, tried to lift her fingers, but again heaviness weighted her down. She strained to open her eyes. Was it the woman's voice this time? Or that calm lulling baritone?

Suddenly her peace was shattered by a shrill eerie voice, "You should have died. You have to die."

Her pulse stirred, her reflexes jarred to life. Not again. No, not again. She tried to run toward the light, strained to hear the other voice, the soothing voice of the man who begged her not to leave. But pain stabbed through her limbs and she couldn't find the other voice. It was dark. Black, suffocating emptiness tried to swallow her. She couldn't breathe. She struggled to move, to twist her head from side to side, to free her arms from their leaden state. But something powerful closed around her neck, trapping her, pressing hard, cutting off her air. And the last sound she heard was another voice, gravelly and low, telling her she had to die.

PANIC BOLTED THROUGH GRANT the second he walked back into the room. "What the hell's going on?" The heart monitor was going crazy. "Nurse, Doctor, hurry! Something's wrong!" Grant squeezed Emma's hand, his heart stopping when he felt her cold clammy skin. Emma's oxygen had been removed, her IV stripped. Blood dotted her arm and the bedclothes, and her pillow lay on the floor.

Two nurses ran in and instantly checked her vitals.

"What happened here?" one nurse asked, looking at the torn mask and blood suspiciously. The other nurse quickly reattached the oxygen tubing, mumbling orders and statistics that set his teeth on edge.

He felt like shaking them. "Is she okay? Tell me something!"

"She's all right," the first nurse stated calmly. "Was anyone in here with her when this happened?" She indicated the torn mask.

Grant shook his head, his heart racing.

"We'll get her IV reconnected in a minute," the other nurse added.

The doctor hurried in. ''Will you wait out in the hall, Mr. Wadsworth?''

''No, I'm not leaving her—''

''It'll just be for a minute,'' the first nurse said softly, coaxing him outside. ''She's all right now.''

He leaned against the wall and was surprised to see Emma's former boss, Dan McGuire, and Martha Greer approaching.

''How's Emma?'' the housekeeper asked, her brows knitted in worry.

He shook his head, too emotionally wrought to speak.

''Did something happen?'' Dan asked. ''Has her condition changed, Grant?''

His breath rattled out. ''The heart monitor went off. And...'' The image of the bloody IV rolled through his head, nauseating him. ''The doctor's with her now.''

Martha and Dan waited silently with him while Grant willed his pulse to slow down. Each minute became an excruciating eternity.

Finally the white-haired physician opened the door. ''She's stable now,'' he announced. ''You can come in.'' He gestured toward Grant. ''Only family for now.''

''Of course.'' Martha patted his arm, her cheeks ruddy. ''You go on and be with her, Mr. Wadsworth. Tell her we hope she feels better soon.''

''Yeah, tell her to get better,'' Dan added as they turned to leave.

''What happened?'' Grant asked the doctor. His blood still roared in his ears as he made his way back to Emma's bed. ''Did Emma pull off her mask? Was she trying to wake up?''

''I don't know,'' the doctor said, studying her chart. ''But her vitals are stable again.'' He listened to her heart, then turned to Grant with a worried expression.

"Mr. Wadsworth, it looks as if someone else removed your wife's oxygen. I don't think she could have torn the elastic or jerked out her IV herself. You should probably talk to that detective about it."

"I will." Grant dropped into the chair beside Emma and clasped her hand. Who would do such a horrible thing? The doctor left, and Grant gritted his teeth in misery. His emotions were on a roller-coaster ride from hell.

The doctor had to be wrong. Maybe Emma had been trying to come out of the coma.

But with Warner's suspicions about Emma's accident, Grant couldn't take chances. He phoned the detective and reported the incident. Warner agreed to come immediately.

Grant hung up and squeezed Emma's hand again. The minutes dragged by, but she still showed no response. "Please, Emma, please, wake up." He closed his eyes, fighting the tears seeping from beneath his eyelids. Desperate, he tried to strike a bargain with God. If Emma woke up, if he had his life back the way it had been before the accident, he'd come home earlier, he'd be a better husband.

All the shoulds and shouldn'ts taunted him. He shouldn't have let Emma go out that night alone. He should have gone to the drugstore, instead. And he shouldn't have stayed at the bar with Priscilla after the business dinner, even if Priscilla had stressed the importance of discussing their client.

He drew a circle around the bandage on her cheekbone. "I need you, Emma. I love you so much. Please open your eyes." Exhausted, he buried his head against her shoulder and gave in to his emotions, letting himself cry, feeling utterly hopeless.

Something brushed his temple. Grant's breath caught. Afraid he'd imagined the slight movement, he hesitated before opening his eyes. There it was again. Feathery soft. So gentle.

He slowly raised his head, his heart thumping like a drumroll. Emma's gorgeous brown eyes were staring directly at him. He muttered a thank-you to the heavens and pushed the call button for the nurse. "Hi," he said, barely able to speak through his tight throat.

"Hello." Emma's strained voice sounded full of pain, as if she could hardly breathe, much less talk. She raised her slender hand to her forehead, then winced in pain.

Grant took her hand in his. "It's about time you came back to us." He gently kissed the tips of her fingers and forced himself to bank his emotions. "I'm so glad you're okay, baby."

Emma's eyes were luminous with moisture, and a tear streamed down her battered cheek. When she finally spoke, her words rasped out, low and broken. "Where...am I?"

"You're in the hospital, sweetheart. You had an accident, but you're going to be all right."

Emma pressed her fingers to the bandage on her head. She glanced at the IV, at their joined hands. Then she frowned, her eyes darkening in pain and confusion. Was she remembering the accident? She pulled her hand from his and simply stared at him, her pale cheeks alabaster in the harsh hospital lights. He didn't understand her withdrawal or the mounting silence.

"Emma..."

Her lip quivered as she finally spoke, and fear laced her soft voice. "Who...who are you?"

Chapter Two

"Amnesia?" A wave of shock rolled through Emma as the doctor's words penetrated the haze clouding her brain. She stared at the man who'd identified himself as her husband. The man with the deep soothing voice who had whispered to her in the darkness. His olive complexion had turned a pasty white, and his smile had disappeared the minute she'd asked his name.

"That's right," Dr. Turner said with a slight nod. "Retrograde amnesia."

"But she knows *her* name." Grant's words echoed with disbelief.

"I even remember my address," Emma said, trying to ignore the blinding pain in her temple. "It's 3551 Summit Trail."

The doctor adjusted his bifocals and glanced at her chart, his brow furrowed.

Grant shook his head. "No, Emma, that's your parents' address. We live on Kingsly."

Dr. Turner scratched his balding head. "Amnesia's not uncommon after a severe head injury. You have a pretty bad concussion, Mrs. Wadsworth." He gave Grant a concerned look. "We can't forget your wife was in a coma for four days. Recovery takes time."

"You mean she will remember?" Grant asked, his eyes brightening.

Emma clutched the hospital sheet with one hand while draping the other across her throbbing head. She felt as if she'd just fallen into the twilight zone. Judging from the strained expression on Grant Wadsworth's face, he wasn't faring much better.

"I mean she *could* remember. It's too early to tell," the doctor answered quietly. "Her memory loss could be due to physical or emotional trauma."

"Are you saying I might not ever remember any more than I do now?" She rubbed her temple and winced, her vision blurring as the room spun around her.

The doctor pursed his lips. "It's possible. We'll have to wait and see."

Grant turned to her. "Don't worry, sweetheart. We'll get through this. I'm just glad you're awake." Emma cringed at the haunted look on his face. Although his voice sounded reassuring, she could still hear his uncertainty.

He raked a hand through his black hair, causing a wavy lock to fall across his forehead. Something about the gesture seemed vaguely familiar, but Emma's mind remained fuzzy. Dozens of questions crowded her thoughts.

Grant's jaw tightened. "Do you remember our baby, sweetheart?"

Fear crawled up Emma's spine, making her voice sound weak. "Our baby?"

"Yes...Carly. Here, I'll show you." The lines around Grant's eyes softened. He reached for her, pausing when she drew back. "Your locket. The one I gave you on our wedding day. It has a picture of the three of us..." His tentative smile faded. "It's gone."

Emma pressed her hand to her throat, her fingers curling around the edge of the hospital gown.

"It could have been lost in the accident," Dr. Turner suggested. "But if your wife was wearing it, the doctors would have removed it when she came in. You can check with the nurses' station to retrieve personal articles."

Grant nodded, then frantically jerked his wallet from his back pocket, pulled out a picture and handed it to Emma. Her hands shook as she studied the photo of the three of them sitting on a green floral-print sofa. Grant looked totally masculine against the country-style furniture. He'd draped an arm around her, and she cradled an infant in her arms. A bouquet of pink balloons danced in the background. But it was the tender smile on her face that squeezed her heart. She really had a child. And she was married.

But she had amnesia.

Grant folded her trembling hand in his and kissed each of her fingers, but Emma instinctively tensed. "It'll be all right, sweetheart," he whispered, pressing her hand against his cheek. "We'll work it out somehow."

The doctor cleared his throat. "Do you recall anything about the accident, Mrs. Wadsworth?"

Emma shook her head. "No, what kind of accident was it?"

"A car accident. You apparently lost control and went off the road."

"I don't remember." The knot of apprehension in her chest tightened. "Was anyone else involved?"

"No, you were alone."

"Thank goodness," Emma whispered in relief. Then she remembered the voice calling to her in her sleep, the voice that told her she should have died. "Was... was there someone else here...in my room besides you?"

"I was here and Kate came to see you," Grant said softly.

"It was someone else, someone who told me I should have died," Emma said. Her hand flew to her throat. "I felt like I was choking."

Grant stroked her hair from her face. "You must have been dreaming." But he exchanged a worried look with the doctor.

"We gave you some medication, Mrs. Wadsworth, and sometimes it plays tricks on the mind. The best thing for you to do is rest," the doctor suggested. "Don't push it. You need time to heal."

"He's right." Grant gave her hand a squeeze. "Why don't you try to sleep for a while?"

Maybe they were right. Maybe it *had* been a dream. But the voice had seemed so real, as threatening as Grant's had been loving.

Weariness settled deep in Emma's bones. She barely managed a nod before her eyelids closed. But the doctor's voice penetrated the haze surrounding her, and the bliss of sleep she craved eluded her.

"Um, Mr. Wadsworth, why don't we step outside and talk," the doctor suggested in a low voice.

Panic rippled through her as she realized the doctor wanted to speak to this man alone. What was the doctor going to tell her...her *husband?* She must have muttered some kind of sound or protest, because Grant clasped her hand again and brought it to his chest where he pressed it against his shirt. She felt the steady rhythm of his heart, warm and full of life beneath her palm. Someone had tried to hurt her, or at least she'd dreamed they had. But not this man. His voice had penetrated her nightmares, had saved her. Hadn't it? Or had she been dreaming that, too?

"I'll be right there, Doctor," Grant said. Emma heard the door close, then studied Grant through heavy eyelids, both relieved and disturbed that he'd stayed with her.

She laid her other hand over her throbbing head, fighting nausea. She couldn't believe it—she was married to this stranger, had conceived and given birth to his child, and she couldn't remember one thing about either of them. She swallowed, trying to hold back a sob, but tears seeped through her now tightly closed lids and rolled down her cheeks.

"Don't cry, honey, it's going to be okay," Grant whispered, his voice tender, comforting. She opened her eyes just as he lowered his head against the side of the bed, his slumped posture at odds with his muscular build. He had to be hurting as much as she was. The scent of his musky aftershave wafted toward her. He was so close his thick hair tickled her arm. Instinctively she reached out to run her hands through the black strands, pushing them away from his wide cheekbones, but when her fingers brushed his stubbled jaw, she pulled away. She couldn't touch this man. She didn't even *know* him.

"I'm sorry…so sorry," she whispered. "Why is this happening?"

"I don't know, sweetheart, but you don't need to worry about it right now. You've been through a lot," he said softly. "Just close your eyes and rest."

He moved to leave. "Don't go," she whispered. "I don't want to be alone."

"I'll be right here when you wake up." Grant pressed a kiss to her hand. "Everything's going to be all right now."

Emma felt another surge of fear. She struggled to look at the man beside her, but fatigue clawed at her. Her eyelids were so heavy. She was so tired...but she needed to stay awake...to find out what was going on....

Grant slipped his hand from hers and left the room, and an emptiness swelled inside her, so deep and powerful it yanked her from the hazy lull of exhaustion. She tried to shove aside her worries, but questions reverberated through her head. She remembered her mother, her father, her sister, Kate. She should have asked Grant about them—was her mother still healthy, did Kate and her husband still live nearby? She remembered high school graduation, going to college.... Why couldn't she remember her own husband? And her little girl?

Hot tears slid down her cheeks again and she pressed her hand to her stomach, a low sob escaping her. What was going to happen now?

She wasn't ready to be a stranger's wife.

WHEN GRANT STEPPED into the hallway, he saw the detective approaching, and his nerves went on alert.

"I came to check out that oxygen mask," Warner said. "The nurses were concerned. They didn't think Mrs. Wadsworth could have removed it and ripped out her IV like that."

Grant leaned against the wall and took a deep breath. Confusion, fear and anger almost overwhelmed him.

"Can I talk to your wife now?" Warner asked. "I need to ask her some questions."

The doctor explained about Emma's memory loss. "You need to let her rest, don't put any stress on her," he cautioned. He excused himself to answer a page.

"Do you really think someone intentionally ran Emma off the road?" Grant asked.

"According to our witness, that's what happened. There were two sets of tire marks. We took samples of the black paint on your wife's car," Warner said. "I was hoping when your wife woke up she could tell us more."

Grant glanced at the hospital-room door in despair. So was he. Instead, Emma didn't even remember their life together. Or that they had a child.

GRANT CUDDLED CARLY close and stroked his finger along her soft creamy skin. "Oh, sweetheart, you miss Mommy, don't you?" He propped her on his shoulder, inhaling the fresh scent of baby powder. She cried more loudly, and he changed positions, awkwardly trying to comfort her. "Honey, please give me a break. I'm not very good at this fatherhood thing yet."

He patted her back and finally Carly's cries quieted as she snuggled against him. "I'm going to take good care of you, you know that? And Mommy's coming home today." *And maybe one day soon that detective will have some answers for me,* he thought in frustration. He'd phoned Warner every day, but still no news. The detective assured him they were doing everything they could to find the person who'd hit Emma. But what if they never found him? And what if someone had tried to hurt Emma in the hospital?

Holding Carly so he could gaze into her face, Grant felt a surge of protectiveness that grew deeper every day. If anyone had told him three months ago he'd be talking baby talk and loving it, he would have said no way. Now he looked forward to time with his daughter, fleeting as it was. And he would get better at handling her, too.

After Carly's birth, Emma had nagged him to spend more time at home. He'd tried to make her understand that he *would,* someday—when he'd earned a promotion and a raise, when he could afford to support them the way he wanted. He'd even hired a housekeeper to help Emma with the daily chores. But since the accident…

Carly whimpered, and he rubbed her back in slow circles the way he'd seen Emma do so many times. "When Mommy comes home, she's going to be tired," he said softly. "But we'll take care of her." He turned his thoughts to Emma's recovery, desperately trying to block the anguish he felt every time he recalled Emma's looking at him as if he was a total stranger. "We'll get through this somehow," he continued, talking quietly. Settling Carly in his arms, he soaked up her innocent features. Big brown doelike eyes, just like her mother's. Tiny button nose. Perfect mouth. Carly cooed, swinging her chubby hands, and he traced his finger down her tummy, smiling gently.

"Mom was hurt pretty badly, Carly. We're going to have to help her out." He kissed Carly's cheek, reveling in her trusting expression. "Right now she doesn't remember us, sweetheart. But maybe when she sees you—"

"I'm still not sure you should bring Emma back here."

Grant gritted his teeth as Kate stepped into the room. With Kate's three inches of extra height, much rounder body and brown hair, instead of blond, no one would ever guess she and Emma were sisters. Apparently the silent truce he and Kate had shared before Emma had awakened had dissolved. He tried to like Kate, but she could be bossy and had a cynical attitude about life. She'd always insinuated he wasn't good enough for Emma.

"I think it's for the best," Grant said quietly.

"For whom?" Kate arched an eyebrow. "You or Emma?"

He frowned. "She's my wife, dammit." Carly squirmed and started to fuss, and he lowered his voice, rocking her gently. "Sorry, sweetheart."

"Have the police found out who hit her?" Kate asked.

"No." Frustration filled Grant's voice. "But I hope they find the creep and lock him up for a long time."

Kate stared at him for a full minute before speaking again. "Emma could come to my house for a while," she suggested. "At least she'd be comfortable there, familiar with things."

He shot Kate a warning look. "Look, we've discussed this before. Maybe if we bring her home, it'll trigger her memory." He could hope, couldn't he?

Kate's brows knit with worry. "What exactly did the doctor say?"

"You want all the medical mumbo jumbo?"

"No, just the truth."

Grant nodded, the haunting diagnosis burned into his brain. "He said memory loss isn't uncommon after a head injury. He isn't sure if the amnesia is a result of physical trauma or emotional trauma. The CAT scan showed she still had some swelling around the part of her brain associated with memory."

"When will he know?" Kate asked.

"If it's physiological, it might be a few weeks. They'll run more tests, do another CAT scan after the swelling goes down."

"And if it's emotional?"

Grant played with the tiny buttons on Carly's sleeper, his chest tightening. He didn't want to think about what would happen if Emma's memory didn't return. "It might be months. Or she might never regain her memory."

Kate sighed. "Did he suggest therapy? Hypnosis?"

"No. Only to be patient, give Emma time. And make sure she rests." He exhaled shakily. "No stress, either."

"She'll need help with the baby." Kate picked up one of Carly's stuffed bunnies, tugged on a floppy ear, then pressed it to her chest in a way that made her seem oddly young and vulnerable.

"I know she'll need help." Grant frowned. "I plan on taking care of her. And Martha comes twice a week. I may have her come every day."

"What about your business trip to Paris?" Kate asked. "I know you postponed it, but have you rescheduled?"

"I'm not going," Grant said, his temper flaring. "I'm going to work at home."

"Well, that's a surprise." Kate folded her arms across her chest.

Grant stopped the motion of the rocking chair and glared at Kate. "What's that supposed to mean? I've been with Emma and Carly every minute I could over the last few days."

Kate shrugged. "I know. But you usually don't let anything keep you from work."

Carly fidgeted, one socked foot slipping out from the

blanket. He tucked her foot back in and struggled to control the tone of his voice. "You really think I'd leave the country with Emma in the condition she's in? What kind of a husband do you think I am?"

A long silence stretched between them, the tension almost palpable. Kate's refusal to answer piqued him even more.

"Look, Kate, you're not being fair. I know you haven't always approved—"

"It's not that," Kate said angrily. "It's just that you've been leaving her alone a lot lately and I figured—"

"You figured I'd bring her home from the hospital and run off to Paris to work?" Grant stood and paced the floor with Carly, shocked at Kate's low opinion of him. "Is it really me, Kate, or do you hate all men?"

Kate winced, ignoring his comment. "Emma has a lot of pride and she's independent, but I can sense she's been lonely lately."

"Emma told you that?"

"No, but I could tell from talking to her." Kate's expression softened. "It's a big adjustment going from working full-time to staying home with a baby."

Grant bit back a retort. How would Kate know? She spent all her time shopping for her beloved antiques and going to the beauty parlor. "Emma wanted to stay home with Carly."

"I know," Kate said on a long sigh. "But that doesn't mean staying home hasn't been an adjustment. Emma was used to being with people all day, taking care of customers, running a business. She enjoyed her job."

"You think she didn't enjoy being home with Carly?"

''No.'' Kate rolled her eyes. ''But it's been a change for her.''

Recent conversations with Emma raced through his mind, especially the one the afternoon before her accident. *I wanted us to have a special dinner tonight,* she'd said. But what had he done? He'd gone to dinner with a client, then stayed for drinks to discuss business with Priscilla. Two days before that, Emma had asked him to meet her and Carly for lunch. Once again he'd been too busy.

But he'd been in meetings, not just dallying around. Emma knew that. She knew he'd been working his butt off to make a good life for both of them. For Carly, too.

''Grant—'' Kate's voice broke into his disturbing thoughts ''—I'm sorry. I was out of line.''

He saw concern written on her usually smug face. ''You think it was my fault, don't you? You think she was unhappy with me and she doesn't remember me because she doesn't want to.'' The idea shook him to the core.

''No,'' Kate said hurriedly, ''that's not what I meant, Grant.'' She walked toward him, holding out her arms for the baby. ''The accident caused the amnesia. You heard what the doctor said.''

Grant barely registered her protests. ''But she remembers you. And her parents. She probably even remembers her high-school boyfriends.'' He hated the desperation in his voice. ''But she can't remember me,'' he finished, feeling defeated.

''Give her time.'' Kate placed a comforting hand on his shoulder. ''I'll put Carly down for a nap while you bring Emma home.'' She squeezed his shoulder reassuringly. ''Maybe you're right, Grant. Emma loves you. Coming home is probably exactly what she needs.''

Grant kissed Carly on the forehead and nodded, his body wound like a tightly coiled spring. *Emma loves me.* At least, she *used* to; now she didn't even *know* him. ''I hope so,'' he said. Once he'd gotten over the shock of the amnesia, he'd realized how frightening the ordeal must be for Emma. She'd not only awakened injured, but she'd lost part of her life.

A fresh stab of pain hit him. Of course, if she didn't remember their marriage, he was going to lose a part of *his* life. The best part.

Chapter Three

Emma took a deep breath and glanced at Grant, hoping to gain strength from his steady calmness, but tension radiated from every pore of his body. Anxiety crawled along her own nerves. She would soon be home, a place she couldn't even remember.

He'd combed his hair away from his forehead, accentuating the hard lines of his angular face. Thick dark eyebrows arched over his tormented blue eyes, and the white shirt he wore contrasted sharply with his olive skin. Dark stubble shadowed his jaw and upper lip, and his sideburns had been clipped high above his ears. She wondered if he had to shave twice a day. *Something I should know, as his wife.*

He glanced over and caught her staring. For a moment their gazes locked. Then the corner of his mouth lifted into a sexy smile and her breath caught as she realized how devastatingly handsome he looked when he lost that tortured grim expression.

He'd been upset when he'd arrived to pick her up, and she'd sensed there was something he wasn't telling her. Had the police discovered what had caused her wreck? "Grant, did you talk to the police?"

Grant's expression became guarded and he kept his

gaze on the highway. ''I talked to Detective Warner, but he said he hasn't found anything yet.''

''I see.'' So that wasn't the problem.

She turned to gaze out the side window, realizing he must be upset about bringing her home. Her stomach drew itself into a tight knot of anxiety. For the past two days he'd been telling her about herself. She dug her fingernails into her palms, stifling the urge to scream in frustration. She'd lost the past four years of her life and had no idea how to get them back.

According to Grant, she'd married him three years ago and they lived in a small Victorian-style house in the middle of a quaint neighborhood in Raleigh, North Carolina. But she couldn't remember any of it. Not even her wedding day or giving birth—possibly the two most important events in a woman's life.

Retrograde amnesia—the words reverberated over and over in her brain, grating on her already frayed nerves like an out-of-tune piano. Only time would tell if her memory would return. And if it didn't…

''We're almost home,'' Grant said in the husky voice that made warmth rush through her. His blue eyes bore into hers, searching, probing, seeking something she might never give. She held his gaze for a brief moment before reality set in. He knew her intimately, but he could have been a stranger on the street to her. She desperately tried to remember some small detail of their life together, some emotion for the handsome stranger, but her mind remained an empty black hole.

''So you're an architect?'' she finally said in an attempt to fill the awkward silence.

''Yes. I've been with this company for three years.''

''Did you design our house?''

His jaw tightened slightly, then he seemed to force it

to relax. "No. It was a resale. It actually needed some fixing up, but we...that is, I planned to do it myself."

"Oh." Emma didn't know why that surprised her. He obviously knew about building houses—probably had redone everything to his own specifications. "I'm sure it's lovely," she said.

Grant rolled his shoulders and tension tightened his shoulders, evident in his rigid posture. "It's nice. But I still haven't gotten around to all those projects yet." He gave her a lopsided smile, an almost apologetic one, she noted, then turned his attention to the road.

Glancing at him once again, she noticed the dark circles beneath his eyes, the way his big hands wrapped around the steering wheel so tightly his knuckles turned white. What kind of a nightmare had they both fallen into? And what about their marriage—did they love each other?

Right now he looked as miserable as she felt. He'd tried to hide it; he'd told her not to worry, that he knew her memory would return once they arrived home. But she saw the fear lurking in his troubled eyes.

She was petrified. What if her memory never returned? Could she stay married to a stranger? Did he want to remain married to her?

"Our cleaning lady came by and straightened up," Grant said, breaking the strained silence. "Her name is Martha. You met her at the jewelry store where you used to work."

"I see," Emma said, hating the formality in her tone.

"And Kate stayed with Carly this morning."

Kate. Emma clung to her sister's name like a lifeline. At least with Kate around, she wouldn't have to face this ordeal alone. Perhaps she could live with Kate for a while. She'd mentioned it to Grant, but had felt his suppressed fury at the idea. Then he'd masked his anger and the doctor had reassured her Grant had a point. Going home might trigger bits and pieces of her memory.

Emma studied her surroundings while Grant steered the Acura down a street lined with ancient magnolias and azaleas. Neat manicured lawns and an array of pastel-colored wooden homes filled the block. Neighbors were out shoveling off the small patches of murky ice and snow from a recent snowstorm, and the trees looked bare and desolate without their leaves. An older woman wearing a blue jogging suit walked along the sidewalk, and two small children raced bikes up and down the street.

"Oh, this is beautiful. I love those weeping willows," Emma said, sitting up to look out the window.

Grant smiled and visibly relaxed. "That's the same thing you said the first time we drove down this street."

A ray of hope darted through Emma. Maybe the minute she saw her home, her past would all come rushing back.

"We looked at that ranch," Grant said, pointing to a redbrick house with green shutters. "But the wallpaper in the kitchen was hideous. Black with these huge orange flowers."

"That sounds awful." Her smile faded, bitterness invading. She couldn't recall how she'd decorated her own kitchen. She liked yellow and rose and green—had she used those colors?

Grant seemed to notice her sudden change of mood, because he reached for her hand and held it. She studied his guarded features and wondered if they were close, if they shared a special bond, the sort she'd always dreamed of sharing with someone. He smelled wonderful, all musky but fresh as if he'd recently showered and put on aftershave. His hand felt warm and big enveloping hers, and Emma took comfort in his presence. He seemed like a kind man. After all, she wouldn't have married him if he hadn't been, would she?

"The Porters live in that house," Grant said, pointing out a gray two-story with a fenced-in yard. "His wife is expecting any day now."

"That's nice," Emma said. "Do we know them very well? Are we friends?"

Grant sighed. "Not really. You wanted to invite them for dinner last week."

"But we didn't?"

"No, I had to work late."

Emma nodded, wondering at his frown. At least she hadn't married a bum. Grant sounded like an ambitious man.

"How did we meet? Through your job somehow?"

He shook his head. "No, we met in college. Kate attended UNC, where I went, and you came up to visit her one weekend. We met at a party after a football game."

"Really? Did we date right away?"

A smile curved Grant's mouth. "You really have forgotten. Sweetheart, you chased me shamelessly."

"What?" Emma's eyes widened. "I...I did?"

Grant laughed softly, a husky sound that warmed her and helped drain some of the tension from her knotted muscles. "You know, perhaps there is an upside to this," he said in a mischievous voice. "You've forgotten all the foolish things I did to win you. I could tell you that you fawned all over me, and you wouldn't know any differently."

Emma shivered at the sexiness radiating from his

teasing tone. ''I may not remember, but I do know I didn't fawn all over you. I wouldn't fawn all over *anyone.*''

Grant's eyes twinkled as he squeezed her hand. ''Can't blame a guy for trying.''

Emma smiled and studied his long tanned fingers, her own hands clammy with perspiration. He seemed to sense her confusion and released her hand. ''So tell me the truth—did I really chase you?''

Grant's tone turned serious again. ''Hardly, sweetheart. It was the other way around. And *I'd* rather not remember those days.''

This time Emma laughed. And she couldn't help the faint stirring of her pulse, the tingle that raced through her body at the humility she saw in his eyes. The passion lurking in the dark blue depths excited and frightened her at the same time.

When he'd comforted her in the hospital, a subtle attraction had strummed through her. She'd been drawn to him, relieved he'd stayed with her. His deep husky voice had called to her when she was in that coma, a heady baritone that had pleaded with her to wake up, not to leave him. He'd saved her life. Now that she knew the voice belonged to her husband, she wanted to remember him. But his face, his smile, his voice—it felt as if she was meeting him for the very first time.

They passed a group of teenagers lounging by a car, the radio blasting. She clung to it as a safe topic. ''It looks like they're having fun.''

''The little redhead, Darlene, offered to baby-sit sometime.''

Questions once again swirled through Emma's mind. She didn't recognize these people, but they would know her. And what about her baby? Could she be a good mother to a child she didn't remember? "Has she ever sat for us?"

Grant's silence lingered a fraction too long for comfort, and Emma raised an eyebrow. "Grant, did I say something wrong?"

"No," he finally said, his voice clipped. "We haven't gotten out much since Carly was born."

"I guess that's pretty normal," Emma said, although at the moment she had no idea what constituted normal.

Finally Grant slowed in front of a blue Victorian house with white-lattice trim. "That has to be our house. I can't believe it. I used to dream about a house like this when I was little."

Grant smiled hopefully and veered the car into the driveway. A neatly weeded flower bed bordered the front of the house. She could easily imagine it with tulips and petunias in the spring. Three ferns hung from the front stoop, and clipped monkey grass formed a border along the sidewalk to the wraparound porch. Blue jays fluttered down and nibbled at birdseed from a tall stone bird feeder in the center of the yard.

"It's beautiful. I can't wait to see the inside."

"It's not all fixed up yet," Grant said, sounding apologetic again.

"I'm sure it's fine, Grant."

"We still have some of the furniture we had when we were first married." Grant shrugged. "We planned to buy a new bedroom suite, but, well..."

Bedroom furniture? Emma paused, gripping the door handle, her pulse accelerating.

Grant rambled on as if he recognized the awkward moment and wanted to smooth it over. Instead, he made it worse. "I mean there's plenty of room, but the furniture's not new."

"It's okay, Grant." Emma took pity on him. Sensing his anxiety, she relaxed, realizing there would be lots of uncomfortable moments ahead of them. She should have asked about the sleeping arrangements before she agreed to move home with him. Surely he didn't expect her to sleep with him.

"We'll redo it sometime," Grant said. "Maybe I'll start a couple of projects right away."

Emma pushed a strand of hair behind her ear. "I don't need everything perfect, Grant." *Just my memory back would do.*

And a separate bedroom for now.

Grant's silent gaze almost unnerved her.

"What is it?" she whispered.

"You told me that the day we moved in, too." A smile crinkled his face, and the cleft in his chin became more pronounced as his mouth widened. He had beautiful teeth, white and straight.

She returned his smile, searching deep inside for courage. "Well, let me go take a look." Her strained muscles protested, and she winced as she tried to open the car door. The smallest movement hurt her sore ribs, and getting out with her injured leg seemed impossible. The reminders of her accident made her touch her face in a self-conscious gesture. She felt like a battered old woman; she must look horrible.

Grant's smile disappeared, and an emotion akin to guilt darkened his eyes. "Wait, Emma. Take it easy and I'll help you."

Emma swallowed. Grant jerked his gaze away from her and opened the door, then stood silently by the car for a moment, his posture rigid as if bracing himself for her return home. Was he glad to have her here? Or did he feel as awkward as she did?

He rounded the car, opened her car door and in one fluid but gentle motion swept her up into his strong arms. "Are you okay?" he asked quietly.

"Yes," Emma said softly. Her heart fluttered as she awkwardly wrapped her arm around Grant's neck. His breath brushed her cheek. His hard chest pressed against her breast. His mouth was so close to hers she could feel the whisper of his breath. He had full lips, and for a second she wondered what it would be like if he kissed her.

"I feel the way I did when I carried you over the threshold," Grant said, moving toward the front door.

Emma strained for the memory to return, but nothing surfaced. Instead, her head pounded in response.

"Relax," Grant said as if he'd read her mind. "Don't try to force it—doctor's orders."

Emma feigned a smile and tried to prepare herself mentally to see her home. And to meet her baby. Her stomach fluttered again when the door swung open.

Her sister, Kate, stood there smiling, concern shadowing her face. "Hi, sis." She motioned toward the couch. "I tried to clear the laundry off the sofa, but Carly can really go through the clothes. The bed's ready, if you need to rest."

The thought of bed immediately sent Emma's stomach into another spasm. But when she gazed into the homey room, she relaxed somewhat, imagining herself choosing the comfortable furnishings. Why had Grant sounded apologetic? The furniture might not be new, but it felt cozy. She immediately noticed a framed photo on the mantel—a picture of Grant, their baby and herself. Her throat closed when she saw the simple wicker bassinet sitting beside the couch. A thick pink baby comforter decorated with little white hearts lay draped over the edge, and a teddy bear sat in the middle, its big button eyes pulling at her heartstrings.

"What do you want to do, Emma?" Grant asked, stopping inside the wide-planked foyer. "I can take you upstairs—"

"No."

"You want to peek at Carly? She's taking a nap. Or you could see the rest of the house," Kate suggested, wringing her hands. Emma tried to ignore the way her sister rattled on like a nervous Nellie, adding to the already tense and awkward homecoming. Emma didn't need spectators to give her pitying looks or watch her reactions to the house. She wanted to explore it alone.

"I'd like to sit in here for a minute." Emma let her gaze sweep the room, hoping memories would flood her mind. Again nothing happened.

"How about the sofa?" Grant asked.

"Great. I've been in bed too long." Grant eased her down and helped her get comfortable. Kate rushed to get a pillow and propped her foot on top of the stool.

"Are you all right?" Grant asked. "Can I get you anything?"

"I made some tea," Kate said. "That spicy kind you like. Or how about coffee? Or I could make hot chocolate."

Irritation filled Emma. "Look, I'm not going to break, so you don't have to hover," she said, picking up a small stuffed lamb and hugging it to her chest as if the child's toy could dissipate her worries.

Grant simply stared at her, his expression more troubled than ever.

Kate shifted uneasily and tugged at the hem of her oversize gray sweatshirt. "I'm sorry. I was only trying to help."

"I know. I'm sorry." Emma heaved a sigh. "Just give me a minute." She searched the room for something familiar. A comfortable-looking armchair that needed recovering sat in one corner. A pine table held a television and CD player. The rose-colored carpet looked fairly new, and an antique white wicker rocker faced the outside window. Solid rose-colored balloon shades allowed the sunlight to filter in while offering privacy.

"You made those," Kate said.

Emma's eyes widened. "When did I learn how to sew?"

Kate laughed. "I couldn't believe it myself. You failed home ec in high school. But when you bought the house, you suddenly turned domestic."

"You signed up for classes at the Decorating Center in town," Grant added.

"I wonder what else I can do," Emma mumbled, her palms sweating as she strained to remember.

Grant gave her an encouraging look. "Don't press it, Emma. We have lots of time to talk about the past."

Kate folded several receiving blankets. "Well, one thing you never learned to enjoy doing was laundry. But with Carly around, there isn't much choice."

Emma laughed and Grant smiled at her, easing the tension. Then he said, "Do you want me to wake Carly and bring her to you?"

"No. Let her sleep. I hate to disturb her." Emma twisted her hands together, wondering if that was a memory surfacing or simply a coping mechanism.

Disappointment momentarily crossed Grant's face as he gestured around the room. "Well?"

Tension crackled between them. Emma met his gaze, unable to avoid the pained hope in his eyes. "No, I'm sorry. I don't remember...anything.'' As her last word broke, a baby began to cry and the sound tugged at something deep within her.

''It's Carly, our daughter,'' Grant said, his jaw tight.

Emma bit down on her bottom lip.

''She's not very patient when she first wakes up. Especially if she's hungry.''

''I'll go get her,'' Kate said, hurrying from the room.

Grant leaned against the brick fireplace, studying his polished shoes. He looked handsome in his pleated khaki trousers and navy polo shirt. Emma suddenly wished he'd brought her something to wear home besides this colorless sweat suit. Surely she had some nicer outfits. Or did she usually wear such frumpy attire?

The baby had stopped crying, and she could hear Kate talking to her softly. Emma glanced at Grant for some clue as to his thoughts. Worry lines creased his face and anguish glittered in his eyes. The enormity of the situation suddenly caved in around her, and all the emotions she'd been trying so hard to suppress welled up, collecting in her chest. Salty tears filled her eyes as she listened to Carly's gurgles. ''Was...was I a good mother?'' She almost choked on the last word, and she buried her face in her hands, unable to look at Grant.

He knelt in front of her, pulling her fingers away from her face, taking her cheeks in his hands, stroking her tenderly. ''Emma, you were...*are* a wonderful mother. The best. You may not remember everything, but don't ever doubt that.''

Emma leaned against Grant, absorbing the strength in his powerful body as he curved his arm around her trembling shoulders. ''This is so hard,'' she whispered. ''What kind of mother can I be now, when I don't remember my own baby? I've forgotten if she even has a favorite lullaby.''

''I know this is tough,'' he said in a rough voice. ''But you are a wonderful mother, and when you hold Carly, all those feelings will come back.'' He gently kissed her temple.

Kate brought the baby in, wrapped in a fluffy yellow blanket. Emma saw two tiny fists waving in the air. She felt a painful tug on her heart. ''She's so tiny.''

''You cried the first time you saw her, too,'' Grant said quietly, brushing her damp cheeks with his fingers.

Emma swallowed, desperately trying to control her raging emotions.

Grant took Carly from Kate, cradling her in his arms. ''How's our little doll?'' Carly waved her hand and smacked Grant's lower lip with her chubby fist.

Emma's clammy hands tightened around the bear. This was her baby. Her little girl. She couldn't let Carly suffer because of her memory loss.

''You want to see Mommy?'' Grant asked. Carly cooed. ''Yes, I know you've missed her. But she's home now.''

''I'll heat dinner,'' Kate said, rushing from the room.

Grant turned to Emma and scooted back against the couch, awkwardly situating Carly in his arms. Finally he angled the baby so Emma could see her face.

Carly's little feet pedaled in the air. Emma's heart swelled. Carly had a small round face with big brown eyes, incredibly long lashes and dimples that appeared as she smiled. Her fair coloring and golden hair resembled Emma's own, but the rest of Carly's face reminded her of Grant. She was adorable.

''Hi there, Carly,'' Emma said, instinctively reaching for her.

"Are you sure you're up to holding her?" Grant asked. "The doctor said you shouldn't lift anything for a few more days."

"I'm still sore, but maybe if you helped me..." She met Grant's gaze. "She's so precious. I really *want* to hold her."

For a brief second she thought moisture glistened in Grant's eyes, but he swallowed, then nodded and lowered Carly into her arms, keeping his hand underneath Carly's body to support her weight.

"She looks like you." Emma pulled the blanket away and studied Carly's fingers. "Did you dress her?"

"I did this morning. But Kate must have changed her into this sleeper. She goes through a million clothes a day."

Emma chuckled and ran her finger over the soft pink terry-cloth fabric, smiling at the little white bunnies on the front.

"She has your button nose." Grant pressed his finger on the top of Carly's nose. "And your long fingers. Maybe she'll play the piano like you."

Emma stroked Carly's hand and smiled, feeling the painful tug on her heart again when Carly wrapped her fingers around her own. "Does she like it when I play?"

"She loves it. Especially 'Twinkle Twinkle Little Star.' I swear she gurgles the minute you start playing." He stroked her hand tenderly. "And her favorite lullaby is 'Hush Little Baby.'"

Emma smiled, her vision blurring as she hummed the song. Grant tucked his hand over hers and she stared at their fingers, splayed over Carly's small ones. Grant gently brushed his other hand along Emma's cheek, his eyes filled with emotion. Emma tensed, unsure about the intimacy of their connected hands and the hunger in his dark gaze.

"Do you want dinner in here?" Kate asked, interrupting the moment.

"Sure." Suddenly nervous about being alone with Grant, Emma hoped Kate would stay in the room. "Thanks, sis."

Grant threaded his fingers through his hair again and shot Kate an agitated look. "I'm not very hungry. I'll wait till later."

"Okay, Emma and I can eat together and talk," Kate said. "Just like old times."

Her college days flashed into Emma's head. She smiled at Kate again, thinking of the fun they'd had. "Are you going to tell me about all your old dates?"

Kate laughed. "You wish."

The doorbell rang and Grant got up to answer it. Seconds later, he returned, a tall blond man by his side. "You remember Detective Warner from the hospital, Emma?"

"Yes." Emma's fingers tightened around Carly as she stared at his uniform.

"Sorry to interrupt your homecoming, ma'am." Emma shrugged, and the young detective shifted on one booted foot, refusing a seat when Grant motioned to the chair. Carly whimpered, prompting Kate to ease her from Emma and thrust a bottle into her mouth.

"Did you find the car that hit Emma?" Grant asked.

"Not yet," the detective replied in a thick New York accent. "That's what I wanted to talk to you about."

Grant angled his head toward the kitchen. "Maybe we'd better talk alone."

Emma's heart pounded as the officer glanced back

and forth between her and Grant. "Is there something you're not telling me?"

Grant stared at the policeman, then cleared his throat and looked at Emma. "It's nothing you need to worry about, sweetheart."

Emma's fingers curled into fists in her lap. "Look, Grant, Detective, I'm the one who had the wreck. If you've learned something about it, I want to know."

"Emma, don't get upset." Kate patted her shoulder. "The doctor said it's not good for you."

"Stop it." Emma frowned at Kate. "I was injured, but I have a right to know what's happening. This is my life we're talking about here."

The silence in the room seemed deafening. "Grant, please be honest with me. What's going on?"

Grant exhaled, his eyes troubled. "There was a witness to the wreck. A young boy." He paused, tunneling his hair with his fingers before he met her gaze. "He said somebody ran you off the road."

Emma's heartbeat picked up.

"He said it looked intentional, Mrs. Wadsworth," the detective added.

"But...why would someone intentionally hurt me?" Emma asked, the strain pounding at her temples.

Warner rolled onto the balls of his feet. "I was hoping you folks might be able to tell me that."

"I don't understand," Kate said. "I thought some nut hit her, then freaked and ran."

Warner made a noncommittal sound. "The witness said he thought the person might have been drunk and lost control the first time, but then he backed off, sped up and rammed her car again and again until she went off the road."

Emma realized by the look on Grant's pale face that

he'd known about the witness all along. Only, he hadn't shared the information with her. ''Why didn't you tell me, Grant?''

''Because you've had enough to deal with lately, sweetheart. I didn't want to upset you any more,'' Grant said, his voice apologetic.

Carly began to fuss. ''I'll go change her diaper,'' Kate offered, slipping from the room.

''And the incident at the hospital, it draws more suspicions,'' Warner added.

''What are you talking about?'' Emma asked.

Grant explained about the oxygen mask and IV.

''So I was right. Someone was in my room.''

''It's possible. With all the hospital staff around, we couldn't pinpoint any prints.'' Warner paused. ''Did anyone visit Mrs. Wadsworth at the hospital besides you, Mr. Wadsworth?''

''Kate, Emma's sister.'' Grant frowned. ''Her former boss and our housekeeper stopped by, but they didn't go into Emma's room. Only family members were allowed to visit.''

''See any strangers hanging around her room?''

''No,'' Grant said. ''Of course, other patients had visitors. You don't think one of them could have snuck into Emma's room, do you?''

''It's too early to tell.'' Warner shrugged. ''Have you remembered anything about that night, Mrs. Wadsworth?''

''No, nothing.'' Emma pressed her fingers to her forehead.

''You and your wife need to make a list of any enemies you might have,'' Warner said.

''Emma doesn't have any enemies,'' Grant declared. ''She's a housewife and mother, for God's sake.''

''It may seem like she doesn't have enemies,'' the detective said, raising a brow, ''But someone *did* try to hurt her. And I have to investigate.''

Emma felt the air whoosh from her lungs.

Warner's gaze swung to her. ''That voice you said you heard in the hospital—was it a man or woman's?''

Emma massaged her temple, trying to think. ''I...I don't know. I was so tired and disoriented. But I remember feeling as if I was being suffocated.''

''You didn't receive any threats or notice anyone following you before the accident?'' the detective asked.

''I don't know,'' Emma said quietly.

''She didn't mention anything to me,'' Grant added with a worried frown.

''All right. But make that list for me,'' Warner snapped his notepad shut. ''And, ma'am, if you do remember anything about that night or the voice you heard, let me know. Even the smallest detail could help. Think about work, your friends, anyone you've angered in the past, any confrontations you've had, that sort of thing. Make a list of all your friends, co-workers, business acquaintances—''

''But how can I do that when I don't remember the last few years of my life?''

''Stay calm, Mrs. Wadsworth,'' the detective said gently. ''If you can tell me where you worked, I'll start there. Your husband can probably fill in the rest.''

''She managed a small jewelry store named Sentio's, but she hasn't worked since Carly was born,'' Grant interjected. ''And like I said, Emma doesn't have any enemies.''

''Hmm. Sentio's. That's a nice, upscale place.''

''Emma practically ran the place by herself,'' Grant added. ''You really think someone would try to hurt her because they weren't happy with a piece of jewelry she sold them?''

Warner scoffed. ''Sounds a little farfetched. What about the owner?''

''Dan McGuire travels a lot, goes on buying trips around the world. But Emma's known him since high school.'' Grant noticed Emma give a start when he said Dan's name.

''I've heard of him,'' the detective said with a scowl. ''Anyway, like I said, call me if you remember anything else, Mrs. Wadsworth.''

''I will,'' Emma said quietly.

''And you'll let us know what you find out?'' Grant asked.

''Of course,'' Warner said. ''And send me that list ASAP.''

Grant nodded, then showed the officer to the door.

THE TENSION GREW THICK as Emma listened to the heated whispers between Grant and the detective at the door. Kate lay Carly in the small bassinet beside the couch and put her arm around Emma. ''It's going to be all right, sis. They'll find the creep who did this.''

Grant appeared in the doorway holding a manila envelope. ''What's that?'' Emma asked.

''Some of your personal things the police found in the car.''

The paper rattled as Grant pulled out a small wallet-size purse. Dry-cleaning receipts. A tube of lipstick. ''I can't believe it,'' he said, sounding irritated. ''I was hoping they'd find your locket.''

Kate picked up the lipstick. ''That's odd. I've never seen you wear red before, Emma.''

Emma narrowed her eyes, instinctively touching her

lips. "I usually wear plum shades. Or at least I used to."

"You still do," Kate said, giving Grant an accusatory glare. "Do you know who this lipstick belongs to?"

Grant shook his head. "How would I know? I don't buy lipstick or use it."

"Perhaps one of your business associates wears red," Kate said in a snide voice.

"I told you I don't know whose it is," Grant said. "Besides, it was in Emma's car. I haven't driven the Honda in weeks."

"You two, please don't argue." Emma massaged her head again, wondering about Kate's suggestion, but the air stilled, hot and stale, and the room spun.

Grant and Kate both quieted as Grant hurried to help her sit down. "I'm sorry, Emma," Grant said immediately. "I don't know what got into us."

"I guess we're a little on edge," Kate added hastily.

Emma sighed, letting out a shaky breath. "It's okay. This is hard for all of us. Could we just relax, please? I'm really tired."

"Sure. I'll fix you some tea with dinner," Kate offered.

Grant pulled his keys from his pockets, the metal jangling. "Since you're here now, Kate, I need to go to the office for a while. I have to pick up some work to bring home. I won't be gone long."

"Sure." Kate patted Emma's shoulder. "I won't leave Emma."

"I'm not leaving her," Grant said through clenched teeth. "But I've fallen behind at work the past few days. I want to bring some files home to finish while I help with Carly."

"Stay as long as you like," Kate said, patting

Emma's back. "Emma and I are going to reminisce about old times, anyway."

"I'll be back soon." He gently brushed the side of Emma's face with his fingertips. His thumb stroked the sensitive skin at the base of her throat, and for the longest moment he looked down at her, caressing her with his eyes. "Are you all right, sweetheart?"

Emma nodded, her throat clogged with emotion. "I'm tired. I think I'll rest a bit."

Grant wove a strand of her hair around one finger. She thought he was going to say something else, but instead he leaned over and dropped a kiss on her temple, then kissed Carly on the cheek. "I'll be back in a little while, girls."

Kate cleared her throat. "I'll make up the guest room for you, Grant."

Grant faced Kate, anger evident in his glittering blue eyes. "Maybe you should go home when I get back, Kate. I think I can take care of my wife."

"I told you I'm not leaving."

"But—"

"I want her to stay," Emma said, cutting off Grant's next words.

If possible, Grant's rigid posture stiffened even more. He gave her a hard, almost hurt look, then left without saying another word. Whereupon Kate mumbled something about not trusting men, and Emma wondered if she was talking about Grant.

Chapter Four

Grant screeched into the parking deck and slammed out of his car, then strode toward his office building, his mind a blur of frustration. He couldn't stand having Emma look at him as if she didn't know him when once she'd looked at him with love, as if he were the only man in the world. He wanted her to love him again.

They'd been intimate for three and a half years. He'd seen every inch of her glorious flesh and tasted it, too. He'd buried himself so deeply in her sometimes he thought he'd lose himself. And he wanted to do so again. Soon.

Guilt nagged at him for running out on her right after she'd come home. Especially after that detective had upset her. Then at the door the detective had asked him where he'd been the night of the accident, as if he suspected Grant might have hurt his own wife. Dear God!

What if the cop was right? What if someone had been after Emma? If the person who'd hit her didn't know about her amnesia, they might be afraid she could ID him. What if there had been someone in her hospital room?

His body broke out in a cold sweat. He balled his hands into fists, his heart pounding so fast he could hear the blood roaring in his ears. If he ever got his hands on the SOB who'd run her off the road and left her to die, he'd kill him.

When the cop left, Grant had wanted to comfort Emma. He'd needed to feel her in his arms. But Kate had been there. Emma hadn't needed him. She and Kate were going to reminisce about old times. They would talk about old high-school dates, none of which would include him.

He knew he was acting selfishly, but the realization hurt. There had been a time when Emma would have easily chosen him over Kate, but now... The past week had been pure hell, and he wanted to be alone with his wife. *But she doesn't want to be alone with you,* a dark voice whispered.

She'd jumped right in, asking Kate to stay. And separate bedrooms... He hadn't planned that far ahead. He'd thought—what? He and Emma would pick up like husband and wife? Not yet. But separate rooms...

He entered the building, stepped into the elevator and punched the button for the eleventh floor, grateful to have a few seconds to clear his head before facing his co-workers. The elevator dinged. The doors swung open, and he walked down the hall as if he'd been sent to face a firing squad.

"Hi, Mr. Wadsworth." His secretary, Bernice Weaver, glanced up from her computer and gave him a sympathetic look over the rims of her glasses. "How's Emma?"

Grant tried to sound calm. "She's okay. Her sister's with her now."

Bernice clucked, her gray curls bobbing as she shook her head. "I'm so sorry to hear about her accident. I'm glad she's all right."

"Thanks," Grant said, shoving his hands into his pockets. Having amnesia wasn't exactly being "all right," but he didn't say so. He wasn't sure why he hadn't told his co-workers about Emma's condition. Maybe he was hoping Emma's memory would return and nobody would have to know. "I came by to catch up on some paperwork."

Bernice handed him a thick stack of pink message slips. "Call Jonathan Ferguson as soon as you can."

Grant flipped through the messages. He'd missed work, too. The activity, the challenge, the blueprints, even the boring meetings. "Where's the boss?"

Bernice pointed to Carl Rodgers's door. "He's in a meeting with Ms. Weston and Mr. Landers."

"Pete?"

Bernice nodded as her fingers started flying over the computer again. She didn't even break speed as she spoke. "Yes, I believe they're discussing the Paris trip."

"I thought Carl postponed the meetings in Paris."

Bernice nodded. "I guess he changed his mind. I made the flight arrangements for them this morning."

Grant gritted his teeth as he hurried to Carl's office. That little twerp. Pete's title as assistant didn't give him as much clout as he thought. Grant hadn't invested three years with this company to be pushed aside by a twenty-five-year-old playboy who'd barely learned to draw to scale, much less engineer a project the size and magnitude of the Paris one.

After a perfunctory knock on Carl's door, he stepped into the office. Carl, Pete and Priscilla sat huddled around the coffee table, deep in conversation. He cleared his throat.

"Grant, we didn't expect to see you." Priscilla

quickly rose and greeted him with a warm smile. *Thank goodness,* someone *was glad to see him.*

''Obviously.'' Grant watched Carl hastily light a cigarette, his gaze drifting down to the papers on his lap. Pete leaned against the dark leather sofa and smiled, his perfect teeth flashing as he nodded to acknowledge Grant's presence. Grant disliked everything about Pete Landers, from his manicured nails and expensive clothes to his neatly clipped dark hair.

''How's Emma?'' Priscilla asked, patting his arm.

Grant could read Priscilla like the *Wall Street Journal.* She intended to smooth things over. ''She's resting,'' he said, still directing his gaze at Carl. ''I came for some paperwork to take home.''

Carl tapped his cigarette ashes into the ashtray. ''I thought you'd need some time off.''

''I do,'' Grant said. ''We discussed postponing the Paris trip until I could reschedule.''

''Yes, we did. But my wife and I have been planning a trip around the world. I've decided to take a leave of absence, and since you're having problems, I'm placing Priscilla in charge. Everyone will be answering to her on this deal.''

Priscilla grinned, obviously pleased with the power she'd been assigned. She folded her arms across her hunter-green suit, the hem of her skirt rising to give Grant a lengthy view of her legs. He averted his gaze, only to catch his boss glancing back and forth between him and Priscilla. The eyebrow lift that followed shook him. Did his boss think that something was going on between him and Priscilla?

''I talked to Atkins yesterday,'' Carl continued. ''The company wants us to visit their international subsidiaries. The Thorpe group is placing a bid on the account. We have until Friday.''

''If we can design the Paris facilities for Comp. Link, it would be a big coup for us,'' Pete interjected. ''They're planning to expand into every major city in the world.''

Grant ran a hand through his hair, debating. He'd have to give points to Pete for doing his homework—the little backstabber.

''You know I'd like you to be on this, Wadsworth,'' Carl said. ''You and Priscilla make a hell of a team. But time is money.''

Right. Grant had heard his boss say it a million times. And he'd always agreed. But this should be *his* deal, dammit, not Pete's.

''If you can wait a couple of days, maybe I can work it out,'' he said. Maybe it would be best for him to go. Emma might be more comfortable with Kate. She hadn't exactly begged him to stay. In fact, she'd looked relieved to see him leave for a while. And the police were investigating the accident, so there was nothing he could do to help there.

''That would be terrific, Grant,'' Priscilla said, her voice bright with enthusiasm. ''You're already familiar with Atkins's little quirks.''

''I'll need to know by tomorrow.'' Carl stabbed his cigarette in the ashtray.

Priscilla caught Grant's upper arm and rubbed it in a comforting gesture. ''Listen, Grant, if there's anything I can do to help, let me know. I hate what you're going through. And you know I want you assisting me on this.''

Grant nodded, catching Pete's angry glare out of the corner of his eye. Pete would be tripping all over himself to please Priscilla. It was a cutthroat business, and he refused to allow Pete Landers to rob him of the partnership he'd been working so hard to obtain.

Then he remembered Emma's fragile condition and his adamant *I can take care of my wife* statement to Kate. If someone had intentionally run Emma off the road and had tried to kill her at the hospital, she could still be in danger. He couldn't possibly leave her. He'd have to think of a way to stall Priscilla.

Pete trailed him to his office. "You know I can handle this, Wadsworth. You're not the only man around here who can land this account. You should stay home with your wife."

"I think you should mind your own business," Grant snapped.

"That's exactly what I'm doing—taking care of business," Pete said with a smirk. "And you should take care of your family."

Grant's temper soared. "What would you know about family? You're out with a different woman every night."

Pete's voice became lethal. "You're right. What would I know?" Then he stormed off, his anger lingering as if he'd left it smoldering in Grant's office.

Grant barreled around his desk, swept up a stack of files, crammed them into his briefcase, then flew out of his office. He had twenty-four hours to decide what to do—or rather, to decide how to convince Priscilla to postpone.

Ten minutes later Grant climbed onto a barstool, his pulse still racing with anger. He had to get his emotions under control before he went home. The doctor had warned him that stress would only make things worse for Emma. She'd already suffered enough. He certainly didn't want to add to her anxiety by taking his work problems home. Or by making her uncomfortable because he was there. Would she be relieved to see him go? The bartender slapped a napkin in front of him. "What'll you have, mister?"

Sweat had beaded on his forehead and Grant wiped it with his hand, Emma's battered face flashing before him. Two weeks ago he'd thought he had it all. Now all he had was trouble.

"Scotch on the rocks. Make it a double."

The bartender grinned and reached for the bottle. "Got problems, buddy?"

"You wouldn't believe it if I told you," Grant said. He and Emma had truly been thrust into a bizarre situation. He'd thought amnesia only happened in the movies. Now it was destroying his well-planned orderly life. And Emma's, he amended, realizing he sounded selfish.

A white-haired man across the room sat necking with a girl half his age. An attractive redhead in a short black dress flounced onto the stool beside him, the taut material clinging to her silicone-enhanced breasts. She offered him a come-hither smile. The sound of liquid splashing over the ice cubes soothed his nerves, and he immediately directed his attention back to the bartender, giving the woman the brush-off.

"Here you go, pal. Enjoy."

He glanced at the time as he swirled the glass. Four o'clock. Cursing silently, he stared at the dark rich color of the liquor. He'd always made it a point never to drink before five.

"Oh, well," he muttered, raising the glass to his mouth. "It's five o'clock somewhere in the world." He wondered what time it was in Paris.

FOR THE FIRST TIME since Emma had woken up in the hospital, she felt the tension dissipate slightly. Carly was sleeping soundly in her crib. But she remembered the policeman's words and shivered. He had to be wrong—someone wouldn't intentionally try to hurt her. And if they had, she wouldn't have forgotten it.

Or would she?

Maybe it was some anonymous weirdo who'd run into her, some psycho with road rage. Or a drunk.

She twined her fingers together, her pulse beating out of control. Could someone hate her enough to want to kill her? Maybe she'd done something cruel to someone—

"Don't look so worried, Emma," Kate said, scooting onto the sofa beside her.

"But what if that policeman was right? What if someone meant to hurt me, Kate?"

Kate twisted her mouth in thought. "I can't think of a single reason anyone would want to hurt you."

Emma tugged her robe, clutching the lapels. "You mean that, Kate?"

Kate chuckled. "You won Miss Popularity in high school, didn't you? I was so jealous I couldn't stand it."

Emma smiled slowly. "You were popular, too."

"I had to work at it," Kate said, settling an afghan around Emma's shoulders.

Emma shook off the disturbing thoughts as Kate continued, "Remember the night we threw that wild party when Mom and Dad went to Germany and Roy came over?"

Emma nodded, munching on the buttery popcorn Kate had made. "How could I forget? It took us days to clean up."

''Roy got pretty sick, didn't he?''

''It's a wonder he survived.'' They both laughed, and Emma clutched her sore ribs. ''Whatever happened to him, anyway?''

Kate held up three fingers. ''He's on his third wife. Maybe I'll be number four.''

Emma laughed. ''Right. Todd would go crazy.''

Kate grew quiet.

Emma read the strange look in her sister's light-green eyes. ''What is it, Kate?''

Kate picked at the unpopped kernels of corn. The kernels were her favorite part. At least Emma remembered that. ''Todd and I are divorced.''

''What?'' Emma leaned back against the sofa and stared at her sister in shock, her good mood fading. ''But...I don't understand. You two had the perfect marriage.''

Kate snorted. ''Yeah, until I found out he'd been cheating on me.''

Emma fingered the gold wedding band on her left hand, studying the diamond. ''I'm sorry, Kate. I didn't—''

''It's okay,'' Kate said, flipping her hair over her shoulder. ''It happened over two years ago. I'm fine. *Really.*''

Emma swallowed, the reality of her amnesia returning. How many more times would she put her foot in her mouth?

The telephone jangled, breaking the awkward moment, and Kate tucked it under her chin. ''Hello.'' A long pause followed. ''She's fine, Mom. Do you want to talk to her?''

Emma frowned and waved her hand no, but Kate

jammed the phone in her hand. "Go on and get it over with, sis."

"Emma, how are you, darling?" her mother said cheerily. *Great. Her mother hadn't lost any of her stuffy charm.*

"I'm a little sore, but other than that, I'm fine."

"I'm so sorry I didn't make it to the hospital," her mother said. "But Joel and I were en route to Europe, then we went yachting and it took them days to find us."

Joel? He must be the new man of the month. Emma wound the phone cord around her fingers. Since her father's death, her mother traded travel companions as often as she traded cars. Emma and she had never been close. If Emma had to forget something, why couldn't she forget that part of her life?

"Is it true, dear—you've lost part of your memory?"

"Yes," Emma said slowly, realizing her mother sounded more embarrassed than worried. "I remember Kate and high school and you and Dad." *And the awful divorce before he died.* Instinctively Emma knew she never would have entered into marriage lightly; she had always promised herself to take commitment seriously.

"Emma? Are you all right?"

Emma sighed. "Yes, Mother, but I don't remember anything that's happened in the last few years." *And I have no idea why someone would want to kill me.*

"What a shame," her mother said. "After the way you pitched a fit to marry Grant, now you can't even remember him. That seems odd, doesn't it?"

Emma bristled at her mother's condescending tone, wondering why her mother didn't approve of Grant. "I'm sure it'll come back to me," she said in defense of Grant. ''The doctor said the concussion probably caused my memory loss.''

''I see,'' Mrs. Baker drawled. ''Well, dear, how are you and Kate getting along?''

''Great,'' Emma answered.

''Really? Hmm.''

''What is it, Mom?''

''Oh, nothing, dear. Sometimes you and Kate, well, you haven't always been amicable. Sibling rivalry and all that.'' Her mother was right. She and Kate had fought over the same boy in high school several times. Kate had been jealous of her; she'd always wanted the guy Emma was dating, no matter who it was. But she and Kate were older now, more mature. Surely Kate had changed.

''Mom, all sisters have squabbles.''

''Well, yes. I hope you're both putting that money thing behind you.''

''What money thing?''

''Oh, dear, that's right. I forgot you have amnesia.''

''Mother, what are you talking about?''

''It's nothing, dear. You and Kate had a small spat about some of your father's inheritance, but maybe it's a blessing you've forgotten. You and Kate shouldn't allow a little argument to come between you. Now I'll say goodbye.'' Almost as an afterthought she added, ''That is, unless you want me to come there.''

''No,'' Emma said immediately. ''Kate's being great.''

''I could hire a nurse to care for you and the baby. I know Grant can't afford it.''

''No,'' Emma repeated more forcefully this time, knowing instinctively Grant wouldn't appreciate the gesture. ''I'll be fine. Besides, Grant hired a housekeeper to help out. I just need to rest.''

''Okay, well, Joel's arranged a five-day cruise for us. I'll call you when we dock.'' Her mother hung up, leaving Emma confused. Although she didn't remember Grant, she'd felt compelled to stand up for him. The feeling was strong, as if she'd done it before.

''She offered to come?'' Kate asked in a bewildered tone.

Emma nodded. ''I don't think she really would have, but you know Mom—always does the socially acceptable thing.''

Kate chuckled. ''Well, you haven't forgotten *everything.*''

''I lost my memory, not my mind.''

Kate laughed. ''I wish I had the nerve to talk back to her the way you do. She's pressing me to go to New England on a buying trip.''

''You can go, Kate.''

''Are you kidding? I dread it, meeting with all those stuffy old dealers, digging through dust and cobwebs to find an old piece of furniture to resell.''

''If you hate it so much, why don't you quit?''

''I'm considering it.'' Kate patted Emma's hand. ''But I'm not leaving until you're comfortable with Grant. It must be really weird not remembering him or Carly.''

''It is.'' Emma stared at the bassinet. ''Kate, when I was talking to Mom, I had this feeling I should defend Grant to Mother. Have Mom and I had a falling-out or something?''

''Let's just say you speak your mind, and Mom wants docile and obedient.''

''I guess I'm not docile or obedient, huh?''

Kate laughed. "You've got your pride. And you've always been...well, independent. Except where Grant's concerned."

Emma massaged her leg. "You mean I don't stand up to Grant."

Kate simply shrugged. "Every couple has their differences, Emma. Heaven only knows, after my catastrophe of a marriage, I'm no expert."

Emma frowned, sensing Kate knew something more. "What do *you* have against Grant, Kate?"

Kate's eyes widened in surprise. "Nothing," she answered quickly. "I think he's a great guy. But I think every man should respect a woman's independence."

"Did we...did Grant and I get along, Kate? Were we having problems?"

Kate chewed her lip and Emma thought she wasn't going to answer. "You've been a little frustrated since Carly was born." She shrugged. "Probably normal postpartum stuff. Grant was spending a lot of time at work, having a lot of dinners with clients and Priscilla."

"Priscilla?"

"She works with Grant. They studied architecture together, then she hired on at the same firm."

"I was upset about Grant working with her?"

Kate hesitated again, fidgeting. "Look, Emma, you were lonely. Staying home with a baby was an adjustment. It would be for anybody."

Emma wondered if there'd been other problems. But fatigue was settling in. Her leg throbbed, her muscles ached, and her eyelids felt heavy again. She leaned her head back and sighed. "Kate, why can't I remember Grant?"

"Give it time, sis. The doctor said to relax, not to push yourself."

Emma pressed her fingers to her temple. "I know. Every time I try to think about it, my headache comes back. It's pounding like a drum right now."

"Then don't think about it," Kate said. "Think about that precious little girl you have in there. You're married, you have a baby—"

"But I don't remember Carly, either." Emma could barely force the words out as fresh tears stung her eyes. "What kind of wife and mother am I?"

Kate grabbed Emma's hand and forced her to look into her eyes. "You're a great mother and wife. I envy you. I married Todd because he was in banking, traveled in the right circles, and Mom approved of him. But you went after what you wanted. Even when Mom didn't approve."

"Like when she didn't want me to marry Grant? What does she have against him, anyway?"

Kate paused. "You know how Mom is—he didn't come from the right sort of family and all that rubbish."

Emma sighed. "I've always thought her notions about people's backgrounds were ridiculous."

Kate laughed. "That's exactly what you told her on your wedding day."

Emma chuckled. "I bet she loved that."

"Almost as much as your not having a big wedding."

"Did we elope?"

"No." Kate said, "You were married at this quaint little chapel in Raleigh. You thought Grant and his parents would feel more comfortable with that."

"Why would I think that?"

"Well, Grant's parents are more…you know, lower class." Kate twisted her hair around one finger. "It turned out to be a lovely wedding. Simple, but elegant."

"And you—what do you think of Grant?"

"There's no denying Grant is attractive. A woman would have to be blind not to think so. But..." Kate hesitated.

"But what?"

Kate unwound her hair and finger-combed it. "It's nothing. Besides, I really don't want to interfere, Emma."

Earlier Emma had sensed tension between Grant and Kate. Now she knew she was right. What was Kate hiding from her?

"HOW ABOUT ANOTHER SCOTCH? That one's getting watery."

"No, thanks." Grant pushed away the nearly full drink and tossed a five-dollar bill on the bar. One sip had been all he could stomach. He didn't want to get drunk; he wanted to be home with Emma. The heady sultry taste of the scotch had only fired his need for his wife. Dammit, he refused to let Kate run him out of his own house. Emma needed him now. And he needed to be with her, to see for himself she was safe.

Whether or not she remembered the details, she had promised to love, honor and cherish him and he'd made the same promise to her. They'd squabbled over her sister before, and if he had to, he'd remind her of the devious things Kate had done in the past. Like the fact that Kate had frivolously spent her inheritance, then hounded Emma for money, even forged Emma's name on a couple of checks. She'd even had the audacity to argue when Emma refused to cover for her.

Yeah, Kate had her secrets, and she hadn't always been so buddy-buddy with Emma. In fact, she'd been openly jealous. Now she intended to take advantage of

Emma's amnesia to worm her way back into Emma's good graces. But he'd stop her.

If he had to, he'd remind Kate that he knew about a few of her underhanded tricks and he'd tell Emma the truth about her. He climbed in his car and headed home. He'd do anything to keep his wife safe, anything at all. Even if it meant keeping her away from her own sister.

"I FEEL MUCH BETTER," Emma said after a bath. She relaxed on the couch, her hair wrapped in a towel. Kate brought her a comb and Emma worked through the tangles, sweeping her honey-golden strands over her shoulders.

"Okay, now for the surprise." Kate popped a video in the television, adjusted the volume and settled down beside Emma. Within seconds soft piano music filled the room. Emma covered her mouth in astonishment as she recognized the wedding march. She was watching her own wedding.

She leaned forward, soaking in every detail. She wore a beautiful ivory antique wedding dress that swept the floor with its scalloped train. An antique-style hat trimmed in lace adorned her head, and she carried a bouquet of white roses and peach-tipped carnations in one hand. Kate was dressed in a peach-colored tea-length dress with baby's breath and tiny peach carnations tucked in her shoulder-length brown hair. Emma's uncle escorted her down the aisle, and even though she couldn't remember it, she knew she'd been missing her father that day. She'd always dreamed of him walking her down the aisle. Her wedding day must have been a bittersweet time for her.

She recognized other family members and a few friends. Still, several strangers sat interspersed among the crowd. Frustration clawed at her. Were those people she knew but couldn't remember?

She refocused on the wedding scene. As she watched herself near the end of the chapel aisle, the camera zoomed in on Grant.

What a handsome man. So tall and impressive. His black tuxedo framed his broad shoulders and accentuated his dark hair. Pleated dress pants enhanced his muscular build, making him look dark and rakish next to her petite feminine body. The contented expression on his face tore at her heart. A dimple appeared in his left cheek and he winked at her as she walked down the aisle, his deep-blue eyes dark with desire—for her.

An ache settled in her chest as his gaze raked over her. Passion and heat burned in his hungry eyes. She was mesmerized as the camera returned to her, and the photographer captured the radiant glow in her smile as she looked at Grant.

"We were really in love," she said in awe.

"Yes."

Emma glanced up at the sound of Grant's voice. How long had he been standing there?

He walked slowly over to the sofa and stared at the TV. A muscle worked in his jaw as he watched the video.

"I'm going to bed now," Kate whispered, tiptoeing from the room. "I'll sleep on the cot in Carly's room."

Grant gave Kate an odd look, seemingly surprised at her retreat, then lowered himself beside Emma, his knee brushing her leg as he sat down. They watched the remainder of the video in silence. When the minister asked them to repeat their vows, Grant took her hand in his and declared his love with such tenderness that moisture pooled in her eyes. Emma repeated the vows in a voice filled with emotion.

While Grant slipped the wedding ring on her finger in the ceremony, Emma fingered her wedding band, admiring the small tear-shaped diamond and the thin gold band.

"I wanted to buy you a bigger stone," Grant said. He took her hand and pressed it over his heart.

"This is lovely," Emma whispered.

Tenderness softened his features, and he gently reached out to cup her face in the palm of his other hand. "I promised to love, honor and cherish you, for better or worse," he said huskily.

"I think these past few days have probably been the 'worse' part," Emma said quietly.

"For better, for worse, *forever.*" Grant traced her lip with his fingertip, drawing circles around her mouth. Then he touched the bruise on her cheek and planted a soft kiss on the tender spot. A mixture of emotions welled up inside her.

"I must look terrible." Emma lowered her head, but Grant cupped her face in both hands this time.

"You're beautiful. You can't imagine how I felt when you had that accident. I was so afraid when I saw you trapped in that car."

His warm strong hands caressed her jaw. Emma felt protected and needy, as if she wanted to crawl in his arms and let him hold her until everything was normal again. His breath feathered against her cheek, and his masculine scent wafted around her as his body drew closer to hers. She recognized the faint scent of liquor, but found it oddly stimulating.

He lowered his head and with a rough sigh touched

his lips to hers. "I've missed you so much, Emma. I'm glad you're home." He drew her close, brushed his mouth over the seam of her lips, pressed his hand against the small of her back, then moved his lips softly over hers, down the side of her face, down the column of her neck. She arched her back and groaned, shocked at her own response. Her mind whirled with misgivings while her body screamed with desire. He deepened the kiss, his hands inching up her spine, caressing, stroking, until his fingertips curved underneath her breast. His tongue probed her mouth, urging her to open it, and Emma did, almost succumbing to the pleasure, but then a sharp pain shot through her chest and she winced. Her sore ribs served as a definite reminder that she'd been in an accident—and that Grant was a stranger.

Grant plundered her mouth for several seconds before he realized she'd stopped responding. He stilled, then raised his face to search her eyes. "I'm sorry, I got carried away."

"No, I'm sorry," Emma said, hating the uncertainty in her voice. "But it's..." She struggled for words. "I can't do this. I...barely know you."

Grant automatically dropped his hands, the desire on his face fading into disappointment. "I forgot. I'm a stranger to you." Emma drew back, her lips trembling. "But I know you, Emma. I know you and I miss you. And this is damn hard," he finished in a strangled whisper.

He pushed himself up from the sofa and stood, putting some distance between them. Emma clenched her hands by her sides, trying to steady her breathing. When Grant faced her, he squared his shoulders, his expression unreadable. ''Do you want me to help you to bed now?''

Emma shook her head, avoiding his hard perusal. ''No, I can manage. If you'll hand me those crutches, I'll check on Carly and go to bed.''

''You're my wife, Emma. I'm going to help you.'' Grant grabbed the crutches, curved his arm around her waist and lifted her to her feet. Emma clung awkwardly to him for support, her insides quivering again as she felt his heart beating beneath her hand. His chest was warm and solid, his shoulders broad, his arms strong. But his face looked utterly tormented.

''I won't touch you again,'' Grant said, his calm voice belying the turmoil in his expression. ''Not until you ask me.''

''I'm sorry,'' Emma whispered, her heart in her throat. ''I'm so sorry.'' Then she turned and hobbled off to bed.

GRANT GRIPPED THE SOFA edge and closed his eyes. He'd acted like a jerk. What had come over him? He'd kissed her as if he couldn't get enough. He'd hoped that she'd feel the passion they'd once shared, that she'd remember him. But she hadn't.

That damn video. He'd been shocked to see Kate showing it to Emma. Was Kate actually trying to help Emma remember him?

After seeing the sentimental reminder of their wedding, he'd inhaled the sweetness of Emma's flower-scented shampoo, and it had reminded him of their honeymoon night. Carnations always reminded him of Emma. She liked roses, but she said carnations were heartier, they lasted longer, just as she wanted their marriage to last a long time.

He'd thought it would last forever. Now he wasn't sure.

When he'd seen her wearing that silky blue robe with her golden hair curled around her shoulders, still damp, her eyes glued to the video of their wedding ceremony, her fingers touching her wedding ring, desperation and desire had overwhelmed him. After almost losing her, he needed to hold her, needed to feel her come alive in his arms, needed to reassure himself he hadn't lost her. He'd wanted her as badly as he had the first time they'd made love. Maybe more. But she didn't want him.

A sickening pain churned through him—disgust at his own impatience, disappointment for what he'd lost, fear that he'd never have her again. First the accident, then amnesia, now problems with his job. Last week he'd been on the top of the world. He'd thought he had everything. A beautiful wife, a darling daughter, a pathway to partnership. Now his whole life was falling apart. No matter what he did, his dreams were crumbling right in his hands. He'd promised to provide for Emma and Carly, to give them the best. He'd silently vowed never to let his family suffer the way his own father had allowed him to. It took hard work to make a good life. Even with insurance, he'd have medical bills to pay, and possibly therapy if Emma's condition stemmed from emotional trauma.

He picked up a sofa cushion and crushed it in his fist, his temper flaring at the whole situation. The doctor had told him to be patient. He'd agreed, at the time not realizing how difficult it would be to have his own wife push him away. How could he live here with Emma and not touch her? How could he bear for her to treat him like a stranger?

And how could he sleep in the guest room, knowing her warm body lay in the next room, the same body that had tantalized him into ecstasy so many times before? He didn't think he could. He pictured her in the long ivory gown she'd worn for the wedding so demure yet so sophisticated—then saw her after she'd changed into that hot-pink nothing of a teddy when they'd gotten to the hotel. Her passion had shocked him. She had been his—totally unequivocally *his.* And he'd thought it was forever.

Another image flashed through his mind: Emma wearing the silky black nightie the weekend they'd been in the North Carolina mountains and gotten snowed in. They'd watched old comedy movies, cooked steaks over the fire and had wild wonderful sex. He'd never seen Emma so uninhibited. They'd also conceived Carly that weekend.

He stared down the hallway, his gaze lingering on the door to the guest room where he'd be sleeping alone. He hoped it would be temporary, but what if it wasn't?

Could he stand it if he lost Emma for good?

Hell, no, he couldn't. And he couldn't go flying halfway around the world after the detective had implied she might be in danger.

Gritting his teeth, he reached for the phone. Carl had said to let him know his answer about the trip in the morning. He didn't have to wait until morning. He'd already made up his mind. Somehow he was going to have to make Emma remember their love. He'd start tomorrow. He'd send her a gift, some reminder of their past.

But before he had a chance to dial, the machine whirred in his hands. He picked up the handset. ''Hello, Wadsworth residence.''

Thick heavy breathing filled the line. ''You will lose everything,'' the voice rasped, sending a cold chill slithering up Grant's spine. ''Because next time Emma will die.''

Chapter Five

Something was wrong.

Emma paused at the doorway to the den and gripped the doorjamb for support, her gaze riveted on her husband as he clutched the phone in his hands. He sank against the arm of the chair, his eyes tormented.

The phone receiver clattered into its cradle, a morbid sound in the silence of the cozy room. She heard her breath escape in a gust of nervous tension. Grant looked up and met her gaze, his olive skin a sickly shade of white.

"What's wrong?"

His jaw tightened and he averted his gaze. He wanted to spare her. The realization struck a tender chord of understanding, a need to comfort him mellowing her own fear. "Grant?"

"It's nothing." He studied his neatly clipped fingernails. "I thought you were in bed."

She moved toward him, limping but determined to know the truth. He instantly rose to help her and she smiled, deciding her husband had been bred a Southern gentleman through and through. Not only was he protective, but he had impeccable manners.

She accepted his outstretched hands and stood in

front of him, her eyes resting at his chest level so she had to look up into his face. "Tell me," she urged quietly. "I can see something's wrong by the expression on your face. Who was on the phone?"

His breathing hissed out and his nails dug into her hands, but she ignored the sting and simply tightened her hold on him. "Grant, who was on the phone?"

"I don't know," he said with an edge to his voice that alarmed her. "But I think I should call Detective Warner."

"Why?"

He shook his head and she tugged at his fingers. "If it was about me, I told you earlier I wanted to know."

His blue eyes turned violet. "The caller made a threat," he said hoarsely. "I don't understand why or who would do it, but somebody was warning me, warning us..."

Emma fought the tremor rushing through her at the reality—her accident might not have been an accident at all. Maybe she hadn't *imagined* someone in her hospital room. Maybe someone *had* come in and tried to smother her.

"What exactly did the caller say?"

Grant suddenly swept her in his arms, clinging to her as if afraid to let her go. He nuzzled his face into her hair and she felt his warm breath bathing her neck, then looped her arms around his waist. "They said next time you would die," he finally whispered.

His voice was so rough she almost didn't understand him. But in spite of her resolve to be strong, when his words sank in, she sagged against him. "I don't understand," she whimpered. "Why would someone want to kill me?"

"I don't know, but I intend to find out," he said, his

voice firm with determination. He coaxed her to the sofa, then picked up the phone and dialed the police. Emma twined her hands in her lap and memorized the hard planes of his back and shoulders as he spoke to the detective. Seconds later he turned to face her.

"He's going to put a tracer and caller ID on the phone."

Emma nodded, wondering what else they could do. Especially since she couldn't remember anything. Then Grant's warm hands enveloped hers. "I'm sorry, sweetheart."

"They'll find whoever's doing this," Emma said with as much conviction as she could muster.

He nodded, a lock of dark hair falling across his forehead. "I just hope the police find the creep soon. I don't want you to have to go through anything else."

Emma reached up and thumbed the lock of hair away from his face, amazed at the tenderness she saw in his eyes at her gesture. "You used to always do that," he said in the husky voice she recognized from the hospital room.

The lull of intimacy and their earlier kiss suddenly shattered through the tension, and Emma wet her lips, her heartbeat speeding up for a whole different reason. "I wish I could remember."

He couldn't stop himself from asking, "Emma, I thought you were going to bed. Why did you come back?"

"I just wanted to thank you."

He lifted his hands in a questioning gesture. "For what?"

A smile curved her lips. "For the wedding, the house, our daughter. They're all beautiful and they're all things we did together."

Grant pressed her hand to his chest for a moment and Emma's gaze focused on the movement, then she brought his hands to her mouth and kissed them. His dark gaze was loving and kind, and she felt a thread of hope. Then she saw his desire and panicked. She'd hobbled off to bed to avoid falling into this man's arms and into *his* bed, and she had to find the willpower to do it again. Because she absolutely could not sleep with a stranger.

So she gently released his hand and rose. Then she made her way to their bedroom and crawled into bed alone.

EMMA'S RETREAT SERVED as a painful reminder of the threat to her life and the chasm between them. Grant wanted nothing more than to hold her safe in his arms. Damn the accident that had robbed him of her!

Fatigue tugged at his limbs, tightening his neck muscles. He needed to go to bed, but the prospect of sleeping alone held no appeal. When Emma had been in the hospital, he'd counted the hours until she woke up, then until he could bring her back home. He'd dreamed of taking her to bed and showing her how much he loved her.

Now he couldn't even sleep with her. At least in the hospital he could sit in the chair beside her bed. Exhaling in frustration, he decided he needed that drink now. He poured himself a scotch, trying to make sense of everything. Violence had no order or system about it, he decided. Because there was no logical reason for anyone to harm or kill his wife.

He tossed down the drink, grateful for the sharp sting in his throat, then scraped the chair back from the desk, remembering the information the detective wanted.

Yanking a legal pad from his briefcase, he began listing everyone he and Emma knew. Business acquaintances, their friends and neighbors—and family? Surely no one in the family would want to hurt Emma. Then, remembering Kate's penchant for money and the fact that Emma had refused to part with her own inheritance to help Kate, he included Kate's name on the list. But Kate had been in Carly's room when he'd gotten tonight's phone call. She couldn't have made the call. Or could she? She had a cell phone...

No, Kate might be greedy but he'd seen her tears, *honest* tears when Emma had lain in the hospital in a coma. And she'd been wonderful with Carly. Besides, what would Kate gain by harming Emma? Emma had put her inheritance money into a trust for Carly, so there was no way Kate could get at the money. No. He scratched through Kate's name. His sister-in-law didn't warrant being on the list.

He added the name of Emma's former boss, Dan McGuire. Then he folded the paper, stuffed it in an envelope and put it in his briefcase. Tomorrow he'd make sure that Detective Warner received the list, that he investigated every person on it. And he'd make sure Emma wasn't left alone, not for any reason. If the psycho was looking for a way to get to her, Grant would make sure he didn't have the opportunity. And if he did come after her, he'd have to deal with Grant first.

THE NEXT MORNING Emma slipped from the comfort of her brandy-colored sheets and dark-green comforter, inhaling Grant's musky scent in every corner of the bedroom. She hadn't thought she'd be able to sleep in a strange place, especially after that threatening phone call, but the accident had definitely left her weak and exhausted.

Odd how the bedroom seemed to fit her tastes, felt warm and cozy and safe, but radiated Grant's masculinity at the same time. Had Grant helped her select the color scheme? Or the black iron bed and that handsome oak wardrobe?

She could almost see him sprawled across the thick comforter, his long legs crossed at the ankles, his head propped behind his hands, the cleft in his chin widening with his sexy smile. Judging from the five-o'clock shadow of his beard the evening before, she wondered if he had a lot of hair on his chest. She should know this, she thought in frustration. After all, he'd seen every inch of her and probably remembered it in vivid detail. He'd probably seen the slight stretch marks, but would he be dismayed at the scars she had now?

Was the erotic image of him a fleeting memory trying to surface, or simply her imagination conjuring up the man as some kind of subliminal reminder of his sex appeal?

Dismissing the confusing thoughts, she listened for the baby. Did she normally check on Carly during the night? Then she remembered Kate had slept in the room with Carly and decided she'd probably rested so well because Carly was safe with Kate.

She hurriedly bathed, wishing she was free of the awkward bandage, then dressed in a long loose peach sweater with a pair of sweatpants she found in the closet. Evidence of the man who claimed to be her husband filled the bathroom, and she paused to study his toiletries, feeling almost as if she was invading his privacy. She needed to become familiar with him. Hopefully seeing and touching his things would jog her memory.

The minty aroma of his cologne swirled through her senses, reminding her of walking in the rain. He'd arranged his other toiletries on the shelf beside the sink, with the exception of a deep maroon tie he'd discarded haphazardly over the counter edge. A pair of men's slippers peaked from underneath the vanity and a large navy terry-cloth robe hung on a brass hook over the back of the door. She ran her finger over the soft fabric and imagined Grant rising from the sunken tub and slipping into it. Mirrors banked the walls surrounding the oval rug, and she swallowed, wondering how many times she and Grant might have shared a bubble bath. And if they'd ever made love in front of the mirrors.

Disturbed by her lascivious thoughts, she hurried awkwardly from the bathroom and collided with Grant in the hallway. He looked sexy and rumpled, but shadows darkened his eyes as if he hadn't slept well. Her heart went out to him. And when his hands touched her arms, her skin tingled with sensations so alive it startled her.

"Good morning," she whispered.

"Good morning, Emma," he said in a troubled sexy rumble.

The need to comfort him rose strong in her chest, but she fought off the urge to tell him everything was fine. Because she knew it wasn't. She still didn't remember him.

Besides, the turmoil in his eyes disturbed her deeply. She refused to placate him with false promises. He didn't deserve lies. Not when he'd stayed by her bedside and brought her back to consciousness with the pulsing need in his deep husky voice. And not when they had a child together. Her heart squeezed and she wondered again if she could have done something awful to bring this danger on herself.

GRANT STARED at his beautiful wife, afraid that if he blinked, she might disappear from his life forever. At the sound of her door opening, he'd halted in the hallway in the midst of rushing through his morning routine, a difficult chore since most of his toiletries remained in the bathroom adjoining the master bedroom where Emma slept. The bedroom they'd once shared.

To give her some privacy, he'd showered and dressed in the guest bathroom, wanting desperately to be able to go in and wake her up with a kiss the way he used to. And wanting even more to find that she'd regained her memory, that once again she loved him and wanted him in her bed. The past five months without sex had been a strain. First, the trouble with her pregnancy and then the problems with nursing.

The past few weeks, they'd had no time together. He hadn't been exactly attentive, either. He'd been too wrapped up in work, he thought with a surge of regret. He only hoped it wasn't too late to make up for the time he'd missed.

She gave him a tentative smile. Suddenly overwhelmed by the stirring of his pulse, he smiled in return, grateful to see his wife gazing at him with an emotion other than fear or shock. Something akin to affection, or at least warmth, radiated from her lovely brown eyes. It was all he could do to keep from sweeping her into his arms and showing her how much he loved her. Dare he hope she remembered him?

Then he saw the reserve in her expression, a flicker of the sorrow she felt over not remembering tainting her smile, and he realized the truth: she still had amnesia. He swallowed back his hope, fighting a wave of despair. He wouldn't settle for her pity. Not when he'd once had her love.

"Are you feeling all right this morning?" he asked.

"I'm fine," she said softly.

"How did you sleep?" He remembered the disturbing phone call the night before. That and visions of the last time they'd made love had kept *him* awake most of the night.

"Pretty well." She ran her hand through the damp strands of her honey-kissed hair, a sign of nervousness. He wanted to touch her so badly he ached.

Instead, he rubbed his hands down the sides of his khaki slacks. "I called Warner. I'm going to drop off that list he wanted."

The calmness he'd seen in her face disappeared. "I suppose that's a good idea. Can I see the list?"

He nodded. "And I have to meet Pete and Priscilla—"

"You're meeting Priscilla this morning?" Grant spun around to see a bright-eyed Kate, Carly in her arms, coming out of Carly's room. She gave him a scathing look.

"I'm bringing them my designs for the trip," Grant said, gritting his teeth.

"Why don't you ask your friend Priscilla about that lipstick?" Kate asked snidely.

"Kate," Emma gently chided.

"It can't be Priscilla's," Grant snapped. "She hasn't ridden in Emma's car." Carly cooed and he softened his voice. "Hey, sugar, how's our little girl this morning?" He reached for her and cradled her in his arms.

Emma instantly moved closer to him, stroking Carly's blond curls.

"Hi, sweetie," Emma said softly. "Did you sleep well last night?"

"She slept all night," Kate said. "She must have known you were home, Emma. While you were in the hospital, she woke up every hour."

"She always wakes up a lot when she has an earache," Grant explained, not wanting to heap guilt on Emma.

Carly gurgled and swiped at Emma's gold loop earring. "I suppose you're ready for breakfast, aren't you, Carly?"

"I'll go heat her a bottle," Kate offered. "And stir up some of that nasty baby cereal she likes to throw everywhere."

Emma laughed softly and Grant felt some of the tension dissipate. "And what about you?" Emma asked, turning to Grant. "Do you want something for breakfast?"

Yes, you. Grant bit back the words. A meal with Emma and Kate would be torture, especially when he wanted to send Kate home and have breakfast in bed with Emma. Alone. Like they'd done so many times before Carly was born.

"I've already had coffee," he heard himself say. "I'll pick up a bagel later. I want to get this list to that detective so he can solve this case."

"Sure," Emma agreed. "Maybe he'll figure out who made that call last night."

"I hope so. I'm going to ask him to send a guard to the house."

"Do you really think that's necessary?"

"I'm not taking any chances on losing you." He

couldn't resist her any longer. He brushed a strand of her dewy hair away from her cheek, a tingle of awareness streaking through him at the familiar feel of her satiny skin. "I want you to be safe. Then we can both sleep better tonight."

Emma nodded, her eyes luminous with the recognition of his desire, but he forced himself not to push her.

"I want you to look at the list, too, Kate. See if there's anyone you'd add."

Emma and Kate followed him to the table. While they studied the names, Grant called the police, and Warner agreed to send a patrol car over to watch the house. Kate didn't have any names to add to the list, so when he saw the patrol car pull up, he kissed Carly goodbye, brushed a soft kiss on Emma's cheek, then headed to the police station. Yeah, he'd sleep better once the police found the creep who'd hurt Emma.

"KATE WAS WRONG, Carly. You don't like to throw that cereal, you like to spit it everywhere." Carly cooed and blew bubbles. Emma laughed as she wiped a blob of the sticky rice cereal from her hair, trying to forget about the police car outside her house. She and Kate had both checked the windows and doors to make sure they were locked. "I'm going to need another bath when we finish breakfast."

Kate poured them a cup of coffee. "She really missed you when you were in the hospital."

Emma glanced at the bouquet of carnations that had arrived from Grant. She and Kate had both been wary when the florist had rung the doorbell, then she'd seen the truck and relaxed. "Kate, I've been thinking about the accident." Her fingers trembled. "Could I have done something to make someone hate me?"

Kate's eyes narrowed. "Heavens, no. What would make you ask something like that?"

Emma shrugged. "I was just thinking about what you said about me and Grant, about him working a lot." She paused. "You don't think I would have had a..."

"A what?" Kate asked.

"An affair." Emma whispered.

Kate set her cup down with a thud, laughing wryly. "Heavens, no, Emma. You were so devoted to that man it was sickening."

Emma's heart fluttered in relief. "I was?"

"Yes, Emma, you were." Kate gestured toward Carly. "And you completely turned into Mother Knows Best, too."

Emma sighed and wiped Carly's face with a damp cloth, mesmerized by the way Carly's eyes lit up when she smiled at her. "I wish I could remember her." She angled her head at Kate. "That sounds awful, doesn't it? I'm her mother and I don't remember holding her before last night."

"Stop beating yourself up over it," Kate said. "Everything will probably come back to you soon."

Emma nodded, praying Kate was right. Carly bounced her legs playfully in the baby seat and Emma tilted her bottle, letting her drink the rest of the milk while Kate cleaned up the breakfast dishes. When Carly finished, Kate carried her into the den and changed her diaper. Emma lay beside Carly on a bright yellow quilt on the floor and played with her. Circus animals created a hodgepodge of colorful funny scenes on the blanket, and Carly seemed fascinated with it, batting her hand at the animals and kicking her feet in excitement. When she began to fuss, Kate laid her in Emma's arms and Emma rocked her to sleep.

Eventually, Kate took Carly from her and moved down the hall to the nursery, Emma following.

"Are you getting tired, too?" Kate asked, as she settled the baby in her crib.

Emma looked down at her sleeping child, guilt clogging her throat. "A little."

"Why don't you rest a while?" Kate suggested. "I can throw something together for dinner."

Before Emma could reply, the doorbell rang. She and Kate exchanged questioning looks and walked out of the nursery together.

"It might be one of your neighbors checking on you," Kate suggested.

"Grant said we weren't really close to anyone."

"Well, maybe it's one of your friends."

Somebody I won't recognize, Emma thought with a twinge of panic. *And what if it's the threatening caller?*

Kate started to open the door, but Emma checked the peephole first and was surprised to see the deliveryman from the florist again.

Kate opened the door with a bright smile. "Looks like your hubby's planning to woo you with flowers and gifts all day long." Emma signed for the carnations, noticing a small package attached, and Kate tipped the deliveryman.

Slowly Emma slid her fingers underneath the seam of the wrapping and pulled it apart. Black tissue paper filled the box. She lifted the paper away, her fingers fumbling through the tissue until she contacted something hard. It felt like metal. A shiny flash of silver flickered through the black paper, and she finally unearthed the object, a silver locket etched with fine black lines—was it the locket she'd been wearing at the time of the accident? Had Grant found it or retrieved it from one of the nurses?

No, that didn't make sense. Then she noticed the mangled condition. Dirt and soot stained the edges, probably from the accident. But who would have sent it to her wrapped like a gift? Surely Grant wouldn't...

"Oh, my goodness!" Kate gasped. "The locket Grant gave you on your wedding day."

Emma's fingers trembled. "He said I wore it all the time. But I didn't have it on in the hospital."

Kate's voice squeaked in affirmation. "I know. Grant was really upset. He asked all the nurses about it."

Emma fumbled with the clasp, working furiously to open it, anxious to see the family picture Grant had been so eager to show her in the hospital. But when she pried open the dented heart-shaped locket, her chest constricted. She immediately saw the picture of Grant and Carly, but her photo was missing.

"There's a note," Kate said in a low voice.

"What does it say?"

"I can't read it out loud." Kate's hands trembled as she handed the neatly typed message to Emma.

Emma's breath became lost somewhere deep in her chest as she read the warning: *Your perfect family is falling apart. Soon it will be destroyed.*

GRANT WAS FRUSTRATED with the police and their lack of clues. His day deteriorated even more when he walked into the office and saw Pete, ready to go to the airport.

"You have the perfect family," Pete said. "Take care of them while we're in Paris, and we'll take care of this deal."

"I am taking care of my family." Grant studied Pete,

wishing he hadn't confided in Priscilla. She'd obviously told Pete about the threats.

Priscilla leaned up and kissed his cheek. "Take care of yourself, Grant. You look exhausted."

Grant ran a hand through his hair. "I'm fine. I just want the police to find the person who hurt Emma."

Pete straightened his tie. "Do they have any clues?"

Grant shook his head. "Not yet. This morning I gave the police a list of everyone we know so they can start checking around."

Priscilla gasped. "You don't really think it's someone you know, do you?"

Grant shrugged. "I hope not. Detective Warner's hoping someone might have noticed a stranger hanging around outside the house lately."

"You think someone was stalking her?" Priscilla asked.

"She didn't mention anything before the wreck."

"Well, don't worry," Priscilla said. "I'm sure the police will figure it out."

She checked her watch and indicated it was time to go. Grant said goodbye and watched Pete and Priscilla head to the waiting taxi. A surge of resentment swept over him. He should be the one closing this deal, going to Paris and showing off his designs, not Pete. Once Emma regained her memory and the creep who'd caused her accident had been caught, their lives would return to normal. He wanted to take care of his family financially the way he'd always planned. He sighed and thought about Pete's high ambitions and cutthroat tactics. He just hoped that by staying in town to protect his wife he wasn't kissing his career goodbye.

Then shame hit him for thinking about his job.

Emma's safety was the most important thing in the world. And he couldn't forget it.

"DID YOU PAGE GRANT?" Emma asked, still shaken by the locket and the note.

Kate nodded. "Three times. But he hasn't called back yet."

"Ma'am, I'll have this dusted for prints. I've phoned the florist to see if they know who sent it."

Emma twisted her fingers in her lap, her gaze straying to the box. Who was doing this to her, and why?

The phone jangled and she jumped, then snatched up the receiver. "Hello?"

"Kate?"

"No, it's me, Emma," she said, relieved at the sound of Grant's voice.

"What's wrong? You paged me?"

"Yes," Emma said softly. "Can you come home?"

She heard his breathing falter. "I'm on my way. What's wrong, Emma?"

"I received a package today. A box with that locket in it."

"The one I gave you?"

"Yes, but there was a message inside," Emma said shakily. "A threat."

He muttered a curse and Emma waited, winding the phone cord around her fingers.

"I'm calling Detective Warner—"

"We've already talked to that officer outside. He's here right now."

"Good. Tell him to stay there until I get home."

Emma agreed, then hung up the phone and glanced at Kate. Earlier she'd felt awkward with Grant. Now she couldn't wait to see him.

GRANT'S HANDS TIGHTENED into fists as he read the threatening note. Rage unlike anything he'd ever experienced balled in his stomach. He wanted to crush the note and tear it into shreds to purge his anger, but the police officer had warned him not to touch the box or its contents. So he dug his nails into the palms of his hands and silently cursed. Something about that phrase *Your perfect family*... It seemed familiar, but why?

Then he glanced at Emma and saw the vulnerable, half frightened, half courageous look in her dark eyes, and guilt overwhelmed him. Without hesitating to contemplate his actions or the fact that she didn't remember him, he dragged her into his arms and held her. He was an architect, not a he-man or a cop or a bodyguard; he'd never been anybody's hero. But he'd damn well protect her with his life if he had to.

Emma's soft curves pressed into his chest and he nearly moaned aloud at how wonderful it felt to have her back in his arms. At first she seemed tense, uncomfortable with their bodies pressed together, but he whispered soothing words in her ear, and finally she relaxed against him. He brushed a kiss across her temple and banked his temper and sexual desire, hoping to win her trust, wanting to be her savior. Lord knows, he hadn't been able to keep her from being hurt so far.

"What do you make of it, Detective?" he heard Kate ask.

"We'll check the box and the contents for fingerprints. Maybe we'll get lucky. But even the craziest people usually wear gloves. Damn TV's taught everyone how *not* to get caught."

Grant glanced over Emma's shoulders and saw the officer studying him, his eyes narrowed. "This is the locket you gave your wife, huh?"

He nodded.

"You two having any marital problems?"

His shoulders went rigid and Emma tensed in his arms again. "No, Detective, we weren't." Surely this man didn't suspect him. Couldn't he see how much he loved his wife?

Emma searched his face and he wondered if Kate had been feeding her some cynical gossip.

"Any ideas who might have sent this, Mr. Wadsworth?" Warner asked.

"If I did, I'd be on my way to kill the SOB right now," Grant said, his calm tone lethal.

Warner raised a brow. "That so?"

"Yeah, that's so."

Carly stirred in the background and Emma hurried to the nursery to get her.

"I've put a tracer on the phone," Warner said. "From now on, if you receive any packages, tell your wife to wait and let an officer open them."

"Did you talk to anyone at the drugstore the night of the accident?" Grant asked.

"The pharmacist had a record of your wife picking up the prescription. One of the clerks also saw her leave, but said he didn't notice anyone following her." Warner frowned. "'Fraid it was a dead end. But we did find something interesting about your wife's former boss."

"Dan McGuire?"

"Right. He has a prior arrest record."

Grant gripped the arm of the chair, stunned. "But Emma's known Dan since high school. She never mentioned it."

"He was arrested for selling stolen goods a year ago, but the charges didn't stick." Warner scratched his balding head. "No charges for violence or assault, though."

Warner stepped into the alcove, his voice hushed, his gaze scanning the outer premises. "Have you considered taking your wife away for a while?"

"I thought about it, but the doctor thinks being home might jog her memory," Grant said. "I'm installing a security system as soon as possible."

"Good idea, Mr. Wadsworth. And you might want to get an unlisted number, too. Just to be on the safe side."

Warner glanced at Kate. "You're Mrs. Wadsworth's sister, right?"

"Yes."

"Ma'am, you and your sister get along all right?"

Kate's eyes narrowed. "Of course we do. What are you implying?"

Warner chewed his cheek. "Nothing, ma'am. Just doing my job. I need to account for everybody's whereabouts the night of the wreck." He looked almost apologetic. "Can you tell me where you were about ten o'clock that night?"

Kate's mouth tightened. "I was at my apartment."

"Can someone verify your story?" Warner asked.

"No, I'm afraid not. I'd just come home from a trip and I was tired, so I turned in early." She glanced hastily at Grant. "I was asleep when Grant called me from the hospital. You know, Grant, you woke me up."

"That's right," Grant said.

Warner nodded. "I've been checking your list. So far, your boss, Carl Rodgers, and your housekeeper, Martha Greer, have alibis. Mrs. Greer spent the evening with her daughter. Got her daughter's message machine, but she's out of town right now, so we'll check with her in a couple of days.'' Warner ran his thumb down the names on his notepad. ''Still need to talk with the people you work with, particularly Priscilla Weston and Pete Landers.''

Grant told Warner about their trip to Paris as he walked Warner to the door. ''Mr. Wadsworth, I hate to ask you this again, but it's important I know. Were you and your wife having marital problems? Were you having an affair?''

''I told you no,'' Grant said. ''I love my wife.''

Warner studied his boots for a long minute. ''Could Mrs. Wadsworth have been seeing someone?'' He paused. ''Say, maybe her boss?''

Fury streaked through Grant. ''No, I don't think so,'' he said between clenched teeth.

''That's ridiculous,'' Kate added. ''Emma would never be unfaithful.''

Warner stared at them. ''Then your wife might have stumbled onto some illegal business while she worked with him. McGuire might have tried to kill her to keep her quiet. I'll check it out.''

''I hope you make it fast,'' Grant said. ''I don't want anything else to happen to Emma.''

Chapter Six

Emma tried to relax on the sofa while Carly cooed and batted her hands from her baby swing, obviously enthralled by the soft litany of children's music floating from the CD player. But Grant was making arrangements for a security system to be installed, a reminder of the horrible threats on her life. And since coming home hadn't triggered her memory, she wondered again if she should stay at Kate's.

Only, Kate's constant worrying was driving her crazy. In addition, her sister had made male-bashing her favorite pastime. Had Kate always disliked men so much? Or was her animosity for the opposite sex due to her recent divorce? And if Kate thought Emma and Grant had a good marriage, why did she seem hostile toward him?

Emma bit her lip in frustration, the trauma of the last few days taking its toll. She thumbed through one of the photo albums of Carly. She seemed like a happy well-adjusted baby. Would Emma's amnesia affect her child adversely?

Shortly after the detective left, Kate decided to run some errands. Martha Greer had arrived with a homemade pound cake in one hand and a dust rag in the other. Although Emma didn't remember the older woman, Carly seemed to adore her, so Emma assumed she must have liked her, too.

"Hi there, precious," Martha said to Carly as she dusted the coffee table. "You getting your exercise this afternoon?"

Carly gurgled as she bicycled her legs, her pudgy cheeks glowing pink, and Emma's heart contracted.

"How about you, Mrs. Wadsworth? You feeling all right?"

"A little tired, but I'm okay," Emma said, resting her leg on a pillow. "And please, call me Emma."

"Okay, dear. Now you let me know if I can do anything for you while I'm here." Martha stuffed her dust rag into her apron pocket and straightened the magazines on the table. "Mr. Wadsworth asked me to come every morning for a while to help out. Is that all right with you?"

"If it fits with your schedule," Emma agreed. "With Carly here, I'll feel more comfortable having some help, that is, if it's not too much work for you."

"Mercy, no." Martha grabbed Carly's finger and wiggled it. "I don't clean the jewelry store till the evening after it's closed."

"Grant said that's where we met. I don't recall working there. Did you baby-sit for us before?"

"Every now and then." Martha smiled and tickled Carly under the chin. Carly giggled and swung her legs playfully. "This little angel makes my day. I don't mind sitting with her while you nap, either."

Emma propped herself up, grateful she and Grant had chosen such a loving woman to help out. "Do you have any children or grandchildren of your own, Martha?"

"I have a beautiful daughter," Martha said, a distant

expression in her hazel eyes. ''She's about your age now, pretty and sweet as a picture.''

''Spoken like a true mother,'' Emma said with a laugh.

''We talked about her last time I saw you. She's gonna have a baby soon herself.'' Martha's gray eyebrows creased together. ''They say you have amnesia? You really don't remember anything?''

Emma pulled at a loose thread on the afghan beside her. ''No, I'm afraid not.''

''That's a shame.'' Martha shook her head. ''Must be awful to forget your own family.''

''It is,'' Emma said, shifting restlessly.

Carly whimpered and Martha made a silly face at her, momentarily pacifying her. ''My girl married and moved to Atlanta, has a fancy big house in Buckhead, got herself a nice-paying job in one of those executive offices. Her bosses think the world of her.''

''Atlanta's not too far,'' Emma commented. ''Do you visit her often?''

''Not as often as I'd like. 'Course, you don't know what that's like now, but one day you will.'' She jiggled Carly's nose, bringing another giggle from the baby. ''Seems like one day you're holding your baby in your arms, and the next day they're grown up and gone. Time just flies.''

A wave of nostalgia hit Emma. She already wondered where the time had gone. She'd missed the first few months of Carly's life.

TIME DRAGGED BY. Knowing Martha was taking care of Emma and Carly gave Grant enough peace of mind to actually work at home for a few minutes, but every second he spent in limbo, not knowing if Emma would ever remember him, seemed like an excruciating eternity.

After Warner left, Grant had arranged for a security system to be installed. Then Priscilla called from Paris. She and Pete had plans to have drinks with the president of Comp. Link that night. Grant should be ecstatic, but he felt edgy and tense, wondering if Pete would represent *his* ideas effectively. Would Pete give Grant the credit or steal it to further his own career?

Forcing his mind back to his work, Grant drew up a projected schedule for the new building project he'd been assigned on the outskirts of Raleigh. The complex would provide office space for more than five thousand people and include recreational facilities, food courts, a day-care center and a three-acre park.

At least working had momentarily distracted him from the Paris deal and his family problems, he thought as he finished the draft. But Emma never strayed far from his mind. And neither did the threat to her life.

The doorbell dinged and he checked the peephole. Emma's former boss, Dan McGuire, stood on the porch stoop.

"Hi, I came to see Emma," McGuire said in a thick voice.

Grant instantly recalled the detective's suspicions about McGuire and the fact that he and Emma had dated in high school. "What do you want?"

McGuire's tanned face blushed against his white-blond hair. "I brought her a get-well gift."

Grant's gaze flew to the package in the man's hands. He'd always thought McGuire was an okay guy, the bodybuilder type that some women liked. Did a violent criminal mind lurk behind his innocent-charmer act?

"Is she available?" McGuire asked. "'Cause we

miss her at the store and I wanted to tell her we're all thinking about her."

"She's in here," Grant said, gesturing toward the den. Martha waved from the hallway, cradling Carly in her arms.

"Hey, Ms. Martha. How're you doing?" McGuire asked.

"Fine, Dan. I'll be over at the store around six to clean. I'm going to give this little one a bath."

McGuire nodded and Martha went into the nursery. McGuire followed Grant, ducking his head and fiddling nervously with the package in his hand.

Emma's eyes widened when she saw her former boss and classmate approaching. Grant chewed the inside of his cheek at the bright smile she offered him. Emma remembered Dan, but not him. He hadn't thought about how much that would hurt, but it did.

Kate suddenly bustled in with a bag of groceries, narrowing her eyes at McGuire. Did Kate know something about McGuire she hadn't told him? Or was she being her normally cynical self?

"Hey, there, Emma, Kate." McGuire's wide grin surprised him, made Grant wonder if McGuire had been interested in more than a working relationship with Emma. She'd mentioned going back to work right before her accident, but he'd passed it off as just a whim. Maybe…

"I heard about your accident, Emma, and wanted you to know how sorry I am." McGuire shrugged. "So I brought you something. I hope you like it."

Emma smiled hesitantly. "Thanks, Dan, that's so sweet. I'm sorry I don't remember working for you."

McGuire handed Emma the box, and Grant rubbed his chin with a finger, studying the man. Kate left the groceries in the kitchen, then returned, perching on the sofa beside Emma like a protective mother hen, irritating Grant more.

Emma's fingers trembled as she ripped the gold wrapping paper. Grant eased over beside her and watched as she lifted the lid off the little white box.

"Oh, my," Emma whispered.

"It's beautiful." Kate glanced up at McGuire with a touch of admiration. "I've never seen a piece like this. It must be early eighteenth century."

"It just arrived," Dan said. "I bought it from an estate in England."

Grant clenched his jaw as Emma removed the delicate antique heart-shaped necklace from the box. Suspicions fueled his quick temper. "Why did you choose a locket, McGuire?"

McGuire ran a hand through his short wavy hair. "Kate told me Emma lost hers in the accident, so when this one arrived, I thought Emma might like it as a replacement."

Kate's startled gaze shot to Grant's. "I didn't know I wasn't supposed to tell him. You seemed so upset about the necklace, Grant, I asked Dan if he had something similar to replace it."

"This is really sweet, Dan," Emma said. "And there's no harm done, Grant. The necklace is lovely." Emma opened the clasp and gestured for Kate to fasten it around her neck. "I'll find a picture to put in it right away."

Grant's breath whistled out between his teeth. He couldn't help but wonder if there was more to McGuire's motives than he was letting on. And if he and Emma had been involved, Emma wouldn't remember, but McGuire would. "I would have replaced the necklace," Grant grated out.

Emma and Kate both looked at him with puzzled expressions. He hadn't shared the detective's information about McGuire with them yet, so they had no idea what he was thinking, that perhaps McGuire already knew about the locket before he talked to Kate, that he could be the one who'd run Emma off the road and taken it. And now McGuire was pretending to be nice to her to get close to her, so he could… No, Grant could hardly bear to think it.

McGuire's nice-guy act just didn't cut it—he didn't trust the man for a minute. And he'd be sure to caution Emma as soon as McGuire left.

EMMA TRIED TO SHAKE OFF the tension pervading the room as Grant escorted her former boss to the door. Why had Grant acted so uptight around Dan? Dan had always been such a sweet guy, even back in high school. She was certain she had enjoyed working for him. Was Grant jealous of Dan? And if he was, why? Had she given him some reason?

Did they have marital problems? How had their love life been before the wreck? Did Grant enjoy making love to her? Was he missing it? Did *she* enjoy it?

She must, she thought, her fingernails curling around the afghan. Because every time he walked through the door and his blue eyes searched her face, she thought about being close to him. What it would be like to be loved by him. To be possessed by the heat in his body and the passion in his eyes.

Kate brought a tray of tea and snacks to the table, and Grant came in with a scowl on his face, his tall sexy form appearing in the doorway. "I need to talk to you about McGuire."

"What is it?" Emma asked.

Grant's eyes grew shuttered as he walked over and sat down beside Emma. Her nerves tingled with anxiety at his forced calmness, and when his leg brushed hers, a feeling of sexual awareness settled in the pit of her stomach. Jealous or not, this man radiated an enticing aura of masculinity. Then he gently covered her hand with his, and the warmth from his fingers sent desire pulsing through her. Stranger or husband, friend or lover, his gaze was almost hypnotic.

Making love with him would probably be powerful.

"Warner told me that McGuire has a prior arrest record."

Emma swallowed, unable to fathom Dan involved in any criminal activities.

"What were the charges?" Kate asked.

"Selling stolen goods," Grant answered. "The detective's still checking into him."

"Was he convicted?" Emma asked.

"No. But who knows what happened." Grant shrugged. "The guy could have bought his way out or gotten off on some technicality. Happens all the time."

"Or he might be innocent," Emma said quietly.

Grant's slight scowl made her uneasy, but his voice remained level when he spoke. "You're always so trusting," he said gently. He brought his hand up and rubbed a strand of her hair between his fingers. Goose bumps shimmied up her arms. "But you can't trust anyone, Emma."

Including you? She bit back the words, afraid to ask. His look was dark, dangerous, protective. Predatory.

There were lots of ways to be afraid, she decided.

And she was definitely afraid of Grant Wadsworth. Afraid of never remembering him. Afraid of the way he made her feel.

Afraid she'd fall into bed with him in total abandon, even though he was a stranger.

GRANT TRIED TO IGNORE the momentary look of desire sizzling in Emma's eyes. She was vulnerable and scared. She didn't remember him as her husband. And the look had only been fleeting.

But he wanted her, anyway.

He hadn't meant to make Emma more nervous than she already was by telling her about McGuire, but she wanted him to be honest, and he'd never forgive himself if he hadn't warned her about Dan's past.

He'd failed to keep her safe once. What if he let her down again?

"I'm about to serve dinner," Kate announced. "Grant, will you put Carly in her playpen while we eat?"

"Sure," Grant was tired of Kate ordering him around in his own home, but he didn't want to upset Emma's fragile state by making waves with her sister. He gently reached for Carly, giving Emma a heartfelt smile. She pressed a kiss on Carly's cheek and a streak of tenderness swept past his anger toward Kate.

"She looks so content in your arms," he said, his voice thick with emotion.

"She's precious." Emma's dark eyes searched his face for reassurance. "She doesn't really understand what's going on, does she?"

"I don't think so," he said, hoping to alleviate a little of her worry. "She knows you, though, Emma." He cradled Carly in his arms, tucking the soft blanket around her tiny feet, then gazed lovingly at Emma. "She knows your smell, your touch, your gentle voice." *Just like I do.*

Emma smiled warmly and touched his hand, her fingers brushing lightly over his knuckles. "She knows you, too. You're a wonderful father, Grant."

He swallowed, wondering if she'd say the same thing if she could remember the past few weeks. The days and nights he'd abandoned the two of them for his job. And the night she'd had her accident, when he should have been home, instead of out with a client. And Priscilla.

EMMA FORCED HERSELF to eat, hoping to regain her energy, but the tension between Grant and Kate tied her stomach in knots. She either had to go to Kate's or send Kate home. Kate's negative attitude about men grated on her nerves. How badly had Kate taken the divorce? Maybe Kate needed counseling. Or maybe she'd already seen a counselor, Emma thought, irritated at all the missing details of her life.

The doorbell rang and Grant excused himself to answer it while Kate cleared the dishes. Seconds later he returned with a bouquet of fresh daisies.

"They're beautiful," Emma said, sniffing the sweet fragrance as Grant placed them on the table. "Who sent them?"

Grant checked the card. "They're from my folks. They've called every day to check on you."

"How sweet." Emma unfolded the pale yellow stationery and read silently.

Our dearest Emma,

It broke our heart to hear about your terrible accident. Grant explained to us that you lost your memory. Things in life don't always go as planned, such as your surprise pregnancy, but remember that Carly is a symbol of your love.

We hope you'll be able to accept Grant's love and hold him to your heart now, because we know he needs you, dear, just as you need him. Doctors have all kinds of cures for things these days, but only a strong love like the one you and our son share can heal a troubled mind.

Willene and Ed Wadsworth

Emma swiped at the tears streaming down her cheeks, touched by the handwritten letter. When she glanced up at Grant, tenderness warmed his eyes. He stroked her cheek with the back of his knuckles. ''Don't cry, sweetheart,'' he said in a low voice. ''My mom wouldn't want to upset you. She loves you.''

''It's so sweet of them,'' Emma said. *I wish I could remember them. And you.*

''You've always loved my parents,'' he said as if he'd read her mind. ''But my mom can be kind of long-winded.''

She nodded. ''She sounds wonderful.'' *Not like my mother.*

''I finished the dishes,'' Kate said, interrupting the moment.

Grant's smile faded automatically, and Emma tried to keep her fragile control, disappointed at the sudden tension in the room.

''You want to watch TV?'' Kate asked.

Emma shook her head, aware Grant was watching her. ''I'm feeling stronger this evening, Kate. I'm sure you're ready to be home, so you can leave anytime.''

Kate's surprised expression took Emma off guard. "But I told you I'd stay and take care of you and Carly."

Emma patted Kate's hand affectionately, uneasy at the suspicious look Kate shot Grant. "I know and I appreciate it, sis. But it'll probably do me good to be here with Carly and Grant." She forced a smile. "The doctor said a normal routine might trigger my memories."

"And I'm not going anywhere tonight," Grant added in a voice that warmed Emma all the way to her toes.

Kate frowned, then began to gather her things. "Okay, but call if you need me, sis."

When Kate closed the door behind her, Grant slipped his hand over Emma's. "Thanks, Emma. It'll be nice, just the two of us tonight."

"You mean the three of us," Emma said with a slow smile, gesturing toward Carly's room.

"I mean the three of us," Grant said with a wink. "But right now Carly's asleep and I have you all to myself."

No, she wouldn't go to Kate's just yet, Emma decided. She'd stay here and get to know her husband again. And she'd try to make their marriage work.

The phone rang, waking Carly, and Emma went to her. Detective Warner's booming voice filled the line. "Did you find something?" Grant asked without preamble.

"Nothing specific yet," Warner said. "At least not enough to make an arrest."

"Is it about McGuire?"

"No, haven't found out anything else on him. But I've been checking on the other people on your list."

Grant's fingers tightened around the phone. "Yeah?"

"The boy who witnessed your wife's accident said the Jeep he saw was a dark color. That guy, Landers, who works with you owns a black Jeep. It just so happens that Landers's Jeep is in the shop, having some bodywork done."

Pete? Grant's heart stopped, the memory of his last encounter with Pete flashing through his mind. Pete had been more than ready to take over the Paris project for Grant, and he'd been agitated when Grant had contemplated going on the trip and leaving Emma. It was obvious Pete wanted the job promotion at work. Would he stoop to desperate measures to obtain it?

Chapter Seven

Grant's voice dulled to a low rumble, and the hair on the back of Emma's neck rose. Then Grant hung up the phone, hesitating before he looked at her, and her nerves stretched thin.

"What was that all about?" Emma asked.

"It was Detective Warner. He says the boy that witnessed your accident described the car that hit you as a dark Jeep."

Emma searched his face, wondering if he was keeping something from her. "Did he say anything else?"

Grant shook his head. "He didn't learn anything more about McGuire."

"You don't really think Dan had something to do with my accident, do you?"

Grant shrugged. "I don't know what to think, Emma." He looked at Carly. "Is she sleeping?" Grant asked quietly.

Emma kissed the top of Carly's head. "Yeah. She dozed off again."

"I'll put her in her crib." Grant smiled as he gently curved his hand under Carly's bottom and lifted her to his chest. Carly seemed so fragile and small next to his broad chest that Emma's heart squeezed with emotion.

He returned a few minutes later, running a hand through his hair. ''Are you ready for bed?''

An image of Grant carrying her to bed sent a sliver of awareness up her spine. But the tightness in his voice alarmed her.

''Grant, was there something else you wanted to tell me about the call from the police?''

Grant shook his head, averting his gaze. ''No, nothing else.'' He offered his hand and helped her stand. ''Come on, let's get you to bed.''

Emma hobbled, feeling awkward and nervous. She wanted to alleviate the troubled look on Grant's face, but she didn't know what to say. He turned down the covers for her, then jammed his hands into his pockets.

''Can I get your gown for you?''

The huskiness of his voice sent a tiny thrill running through her. At the same time the intimacy frightened her to death. ''I can manage,'' Emma said quietly.

Their gazes locked, questions lingering in the air. Heat sizzled between them, the master bedroom simmering with lost memories, nights of lovemaking, a reminder of the vows they'd spoken and the life they shared, the marriage she'd completely forgotten.

Finally Grant backed toward the door, disappointment drawing his thick dark eyebrows into a V above the bridge of his nose. ''Will you call me if you need anything?''

''Y-yes.'' Emma winced at the uncertainty in her voice. He nodded, a frown tightening the fine lines beside his gorgeous blue eyes, then left. She hated causing him so much grief. He honestly seemed to care for her and for Carly. And if he was a faithful husband, the kind of soul mate his mother had described in her letter, this separation had to be torture for him. But what if

Kate's comments about not trusting men weren't based solely on her own experience? What if Kate knew something about her marriage she was afraid to tell her?

Their lives were suspended in space and time, and Emma realized she held the key to all the answers, locked somewhere in her mind. The question remained, haunting her day and night—would the answers be lost forever?

Emma huddled beneath the covers, staring into the darkness as she listened to the sound of the shower running. Knowing Grant was naked fueled fantasies she wasn't prepared to act on. Would she normally strip her clothes and join him? Would they make love with the warm water sluicing their backs and faces?

Switching on the bedside lamp, she lowered the covers and lifted her loose cotton gown to examine her bruises. Purple and yellowish marks streaked her pale skin. The small cuts and scrapes still hadn't healed. A jagged scar ran the length of her red and bruised thigh to her waist. Not exactly a sexy sight. No, even if she had her memory back, Grant probably wouldn't want to see her naked right now.

He was handsome and masculine, his body almost perfect, or so she imagined from the way his broad shoulders and muscled body filled out his clothes. And her body was...damaged. Flipping off the light, she wiped a tear from her eyes, refusing to dwell on her imperfections. If her memory returned and they found out who was doing these awful things, then she'd worry about letting her husband see her flawed body. But for now, being with him intimately was not an option. She might not remember the past four years of her life, but she knew she had scruples. And making love to someone had always meant *love* in her book. Love, honor and marriage.

The peal of the phone startled her and she reached for it, knowing Grant couldn't hear it from the shower. ''Hello.''

A raspy whisper echoed over the line and Emma froze, barely able to make her voice work. ''Who is this?''

A soft hiss filled the silence, then the low voice mumbled, ''You'd better be careful. The people you trust are exactly the people who will hurt you the most.''

Emma clutched the sheet to her chest, her heart thumping with panic. ''What are you talking about? Who is this?''

''You think your friends and family are perfect, but they're not, Emma.'' The sound of labored breathing rattled over the line, sending her nerves screaming. ''Everyone has secrets. And those secrets will destroy you.''

A shudder coursed through Emma. ''Why don't you tell me who you are? And why you're doing this!'' But the phone clicked into silence. Emma dropped the receiver onto the cradle and stared at the closed door, her chest heaving.

Only the hallway separated her from Grant. She started to go to him, to ask him to hold her, to ask him what the caller could be talking about. But the eerie rasp of the caller's words made her pause. If the person had meant to frighten her, he'd succeeded. He'd warned her she shouldn't trust her friends or her family. Dan. Kate. Grant.

Grant obviously didn't trust Dan. She was surprised about Dan's arrest record. And her mother had hinted she and Kate hadn't always gotten along, but Kate wouldn't hurt her. Would she? And what about Grant? Was their marriage as wonderful as he'd said, as his parents' letter had implied? Had she done something to bring this on herself?

She shivered, angry at the distrust the anonymous phone caller had wreaked in her mind. No, she wouldn't go to Grant just yet. Not until she discovered who she could trust. And if the people closest to her had secrets they were keeping from her. Dark, silent secrets that might cost her her life.

GRANT PACED the hospital's waiting room, hoping the doctor would have some encouraging news about Emma's condition. She'd been acting strangely all morning, elusive and quiet. Almost withdrawn. As if her fears had taken an unnatural preoccupation in her life. After she'd read his mother's letter yesterday, she'd relaxed around him and sent Kate home, a sign she trusted him enough to be alone with him. Even though he hadn't told her everything about Warner's phone call, he'd gone to the guest room with a tiny ray of hope bubbling inside. But every time he'd touched her this morning, she'd stiffened and pulled away.

He checked his watch, removed his cell phone, then called the hotel where Pete and Priscilla were staying, hoping the time change didn't interfere with his reaching them.

Priscilla answered on the third ring. "Hello."

"Priscilla, it's me, Grant. How's it going?"

"Oh, wonderful, Grant. It's so good to hear from you."

"Fill me in on what's happening there," he said, anxious to know about the deal.

"We met with Davis yesterday and he liked the preliminary sketches you did. He wants detailed cost analyses and bids from contractors before he'll decide.''

''How many firms does he have bidding on the account?''

''Three. But he says he's impressed with our firm and really likes your style.''

''And yours, too,'' Grant said with a tight smile. ''You have a way of working the clients, Priscilla.''

Her laughter rang through the line. ''Are you saying my design skills are less than par, darling?''

''Not at all,'' Grant said, annoyed by the fact that he had to answer to Priscilla. ''But your charm goes a long way, especially in enticing the male clients.''

''I'm going to take that as a compliment,'' Priscilla said in a soft silvery voice. ''Now tell me how you are, Grant. I miss you here, you know.''

Heat warmed Grant's neck. ''Thanks, Priscilla. I miss being there.''

''How's Emma doing?''

''She's okay. She's with the doctor now.''

''Grant, I know this is difficult on you. You're always taking care of everyone else, and I worry so about you.''

Grant rubbed his hand over his face. ''I'll be fine, Priscilla. I just want Emma safe.''

''I know Emma was bugging you about spending more time with her before the accident, but don't let that guilt trip keep you from coming back to work.'' Priscilla's voice dropped to a soft whisper. ''We need you, too. Your wife doesn't understand how valuable you are to the firm.''

Uncomfortable with Priscilla's praise, Grant's jaw snapped tight. He *was* feeling guilty, but he didn't want to discuss it. And he didn't intend to indulge in Priscilla's flirtatious games to win his promotion. Damn

Carl for putting her in charge. "Priscilla, tell me how Pete's working out?"

She sighed. "He's doing fine. A little overzealous, but I'm keeping him in line."

"By the way, Priscilla, do you know anything about Pete's car being in the shop?"

A clock chimed in the background. "No, I don't even know what the man drives. Why?"

"No reason," Grant hedged. "I think I received a message on my voice mail meant for him. Something about bodywork being done on his car."

"I'll ask him about it if you want. He probably needs to call the garage."

"Probably. And Priscilla, keep an eye on him, will you?" Grant said, more serious now.

"Why, darling? What's wrong?"

Grant knew he couldn't accuse Pete of doing something unless he had concrete details. "I guess I'm just being paranoid, that's all. Be careful, Priscilla."

"Honey, I'm always careful. I can take care of myself," Priscilla drawled with a touch of sexual innuendo in her tone. "And when I get back in town, I'm going to take care of you, too. You sound dreadful. Maybe I'll buy you dinner."

"Dinner? Maybe," Grant said, not wanting to commit because of Emma. "Call me when you get back and we'll set a date."

When he hung up, he turned and saw Emma standing in the doorway. His heart lodged in his throat. She was watching him with a look of distrust in her eyes.

EMMA TRIED TO SQUELCH the feeling of hurt over hearing Grant laughing and talking with another woman. And that he'd used the word *date* in his conversation.

Her earlier doubts were compounded by her memory loss and, she admitted reluctantly, by her own vanity regarding her physical scars. And that phone call the night before...

"How are you feeling?" Grant asked hesitantly.

"Fine." Emma leaned on her crutches. "The doctor wants to talk to us together."

Grant nodded and followed Emma back into the office.

"I suggested your wife use these crutches or a walker to help her get around until that leg gets stronger," Dr. Dunlap said, gesturing as Grant helped Emma settle into a chair. "She's going to need some physical therapy to regain her strength."

"I'll make sure she receives therapy," Grant said. "Should she come here or do we need a referral?"

"I gave her the name of a physical therapist to work with—my nurse will set it up. The therapist can show Emma some exercises to do at home, also."

"Great. I'll help her if I can," Grant offered.

"I can handle them," Emma said in a tight voice, hating feeling so helpless and dependent.

"Emma still doesn't remember anything about the accident," Dr. Dunlap said. "I know you're probably both frustrated, but it hasn't been that long since the wreck. Physically she's healing fine." He gestured toward her leg. "We can perform plastic surgery later to mend her scar."

Emma's eyes burned with misery and she avoided Grant's gaze, wondering about his thoughts.

"Could we try hypnosis?" Emma blurted.

"Are you ready for that?" Grant asked.

Emma opened her mouth to tell him she'd do anything to remember her life and get out of limbo, especially after that disturbing phone call, but the doctor cut her off.

"I think it's too early for hypnosis," Dr. Dunlap replied. "You need more time to heal, both physically and mentally, Emma." He steepled his hands on top of his desk. "Once you're feeling stronger, you may remember on your own."

"But what if I don't?" Emma asked, panic tingeing her voice.

Dunlap shrugged. "Then we'll try hypnosis. But it can be stressful, so I really want you stronger first. Once you recover physically, your memory may come back and you may not need to be hypnotized."

"I suppose he's right, Emma," Grant said quietly, a concerned look in his eyes. "We'll have to be patient, sweetheart."

Emma's throat clogged with unspoken words. She hated not knowing whom to trust, and she didn't know if she could afford to be patient. Finding out the truth might be dangerous, but *not* finding out could cost her her life.

GRANT WORKED AT HOME all afternoon, designing plans for a shopping mall to fit into the Bronson account, the city within the city he'd been working on earlier. At least with work he was accomplishing something. As for resolving the crisis in his home life, though, the answers remained aloof.

It was so damn frustrating. *Be patient,* he'd told Emma. But being patient was the hardest thing he'd ever done in his life.

He stretched his stiff neck muscles and removed his reading glasses, placing them on his drafting table as he listened for Carly—she might be waking up from her nap. Emma had been tired when they'd returned from the doctor and had immediately lain down to rest. Carly was napping and, thank God, Kate had had an appointment. So he'd retreated to his home office, the only place he felt vaguely in control of his life at this point. That is, as long as he didn't dwell on Pete Landers and the Paris account.

Unable to bear the silence any longer, he opened his office door and spotted Martha bringing Carly from the nursery. ''I'll take her,'' Grant offered, crossing the room in quick easy strides.

''She had a good nap,'' Martha said, patting Carly's hand.

''Come here, sweetie pie.'' Carly grinned at him, and his mind must have turned to mush, because he heard himself babbling baby talk that would have had the people at the office rolling on the floor with laughter. But Carly loved it. She swiped her fingers at his chin and latched onto his earlobe, tugging it.

''You're pretty strong for such a tiny thing,'' he said, nuzzling his face in her terry-cloth sleeper.

''She sure is,'' Martha said.

''I appreciate your watching her while we went to the doctor, Martha.''

''It's my pleasure,'' the housekeeper said, beaming.

''Martha, how well do you know Dan McGuire?''

She looked puzzled. ''He's a kind employer. Personally I don't know him all that well. He seems real nice, a charmer with the ladies.''

''Yeah, I got that impression.'' *He certainly tried to charm mine.* ''Did he...did he and Emma have any... problems?''

Martha's forehead wrinkled. ''Not that I knew of. He was usually leaving when I arrived.''

''Right,'' Grant said, remembering Martha cleaned the store after hours. ''Well, thanks again for watching Carly.''

''Nonsense.'' Martha waved him off and gathered her things. ''I love Carly.'' She gave Carly a last kiss and left.

Carly began to fuss and Grant prepared a bottle for her. Carly latched onto the bottle just as the phone rang. He started to reach for it, but the sound died and he realized Emma must have answered it. Probably Kate, he thought, since she hadn't been by. Let Kate and Emma talk for a while, he decided, wiping a drop of formula off Carly's chin.

Then he remembered the threats to Emma and reached for the portable phone.

THE CALLER WAS THE SAME, Emma realized with a dull panic that knotted her insides. The same hushed whisper, the same heady warning that had made chills sweep up her spine.

''I warned you before. *The people you trust will hurt you the most.*''

The hateful words sounded even more horrible the second time. And the dead silence on the other end of the line when the caller hung up hit her with a wave of nausea.

''What did he mean he warned you before?''

Emma nearly jumped off the bed when Grant's husky voice sounded from the bedroom doorway. But the calm resonance held an unleashed fury almost as potent as the rage in his eyes.

''Someone called last night,'' Emma murmured, brushing her tousled hair over her shoulders. ''Do you think they were on long enough for the police to trace it?''

''No.'' Grant moved into the room, his tall frame outlined faintly by the late-afternoon sunshine streaming through the blinds. ''Why didn't you tell me?''

Emma shrugged, biting down on her lip. Feeling vulnerable in the darkness, she flipped on the Victorian lamp on her nightstand. Hurt simmered below the surface of his anger, she noted, when he stepped into the circle of light.

''Why, Emma?'' he asked again.

''I don't know,'' she said, trying to formulate a reasonable lie. ''You were in the shower.''

His hand shook as he ran it through his hair. Then he closed the distance between them and stood over her, so that she had to look up to see his face. His hands sought her shoulders, rested gently on the top, but she could feel the trembling in his muscles as he fought to control himself. ''You could have called me, Emma. I would have been here in a second.''

Remorse tightened her chest. ''I'm sorry, Grant. Really. I...didn't know what to do. I was scared.''

He tenderly thumbed the outline of her sweater along the shoulder, then traced a line up her cheek. ''You didn't trust me?'' he asked, hurt coloring his quietly spoken words.

Emma hesitated, knowing her actions had already answered his question.

''That's right, you don't remember me,'' he said tightly. ''I guess you're not even sure if I've told you the truth about our marriage.''

She lowered her eyes, hating the anger and truth in his accusation. But he tipped up her chin, forcing her to face him. "I really am sorry, Grant," she whispered. "I'm so sorry for all of this."

"What else did he say?" he asked, his expression clouded.

She strung together the first conversation verbatim, watching the muscles in his throat work as he swallowed.

Grant ran a hand through his hair again. "The caller ID simply said Raleigh. It could be a cell phone anywhere."

Emma nodded, her fingers tracing over his knuckle. He followed the movement, his eyes darkening. Emma shivered, looking into the distance. "Where's Carly?"

"In the playpen. She's fine."

Emma slumped, exhausted and scared. "Why is this all happening?"

"I don't know," Grant said, pulling her to him. "But it's beginning to sound more and more personal."

Emma leaned against him. "You're right. It's almost like the person knows me. And my friends and family."

Grant's blue eyes darkened with uncertainty. "And you're wondering if there's some truth to what the caller said. You're making a list in your head, wondering who you should trust and who you shouldn't." A deep labored sigh escaped him. "And since you don't remember me, I'm at the top of that list."

"I never said that." Emma's voice quavered.

Grant exhaled loudly. "Kate's been telling you awful things about me, telling you all the reasons you shouldn't trust a man."

Emma's fingers tightened on the edge of his shirt, Kate's cynical comments reverberating in her head.

"Kate's marriage failed, so now she wants to destroy

ours,'' Grant continued. ''Her husband cheated on her, so she assumes all men are cheaters.''

''Maybe she does think that, but Kate wouldn't do all this,'' Emma argued. ''She'd never threaten me or hurt me.''

''But she's making you doubt me.''

''I overheard you making a date with Priscilla,'' Emma admitted.

''That call was business, Emma. Business, nothing more.'' He closed his eyes and dropped his hands to his side. ''Kate's wrong about me, Emma. Maybe I haven't always been the perfect husband or the greatest father, but I do love you and Carly.'' His voice became a pained whisper. ''I wish you'd believe me.''

Emma's heart lurched at the sincerity in his voice. She reached for him, but the doorbell rang and he went to answer it. She limped to the living room as the detective came in.

''Did you find out something new?'' Grant asked.

Warner nodded. ''I'm afraid so.'' His gray eyes flitted over Emma, then Grant, his expression serious. ''I need to ask you some questions about your past, Mr. Wadsworth.''

Grant's dark eyebrows arched in surprise. ''What's this about, Detective?''

''It's about Faye Simmons.''

Grant jammed his hands in his pockets, tension radiating through the room.

''You remember her, Mr. Wadsworth,'' Warner said, his voice level. ''The girl you dated in college, the one who died in a car accident.''

Chapter Eight

Blood thundered in Grant's ears. This couldn't be happening. Faye's death had haunted him for years and now, when his wife was in danger, the police wanted to dredge up the past. Why? What could Faye's death possibly have to do with the threats to Emma?

"I don't understand, Detective," Grant said. "Faye died five years ago. She has nothing to do with Emma, so why bring it up now?"

Warner shot Emma a look of regret, rubbing one hand over his balding spot. "I understand you were questioned about the Simmons girl's death."

Grant sat down beside Emma and gestured toward the opposite chair for the policeman. "Yeah, everyone at the homecoming party was questioned."

"But Ms. Simmons was driving your car when she wrecked. She ran the car off into the river."

Grant shuddered. He remembered the scene too vividly. The broken bridge, his car nose-dived into the muddy banks of the river, Faye's limp bloody body, her tangled wet hair, the cold iciness of her skin when he'd touched her.

Grant forced the images to the back of his mind and

glanced at Emma, wondering how the detective's questions would affect Emma's already shaky trust in him.

"Mr. Wadsworth?"

"Sorry," Grant said. "I don't understand what that accident has to do with Emma. Besides, the police covered this years ago."

Warner cleared his throat. "Yes, but with your wife in danger, we investigate all the family."

"Including me?" Grant asked.

Warner nodded. "Everyone. As a matter of fact—" his direct gaze was intimidating "—most times the spouse is the prime suspect. The fact that Ms. Simmons was killed in an automobile accident seems a little coincidental in light of your wife's suspicious accident."

Grant bolted off the sofa, his anger boiling through his veins. "I don't like what you're implying, Detective. I asked you to help find the person threatening my wife, and you come into my house and insinuate it's me!"

Emma's shaky breath filled the strained silence. Warner linked his hands together, his face rigid. "I told you, Mr. Wadsworth, we have to look at every angle. Now I'm not saying you're guilty, but it would help clear things up for me if you'd simply answer my questions."

Rage still tore through Grant, but he took a deep breath, gauging the strength of Emma's doubts by the wariness in her eyes. Or was it sympathy?

"All right," he finally said, settling back on the sofa. "I went over this a dozen times as I'm sure you read in Faye's file, but what do you want to know?"

The detective removed a small notepad from the pocket of his denim shirt and flipped it open. "I believe the report said the accident happened around midnight."

"That's right," Grant confirmed. "I lent her my car to drive home."

"How did you plan to get home?"

Emma was watching him with avid curiosity. Of all the details he'd like to share with Emma about his life, this particular evening's awful events were not among them.

"Mr. Wadsworth?"

"I was going to get a ride with one of the other girls at the party."

"I see. You had a date other than Ms. Simmons?"

"That's right," Grant explained. "She and I were acquaintances..." He shrugged. "Friends, but that's all."

"So you didn't have a sexual relationship with her?"

"No," Grant said, his voice clipped. Emma's big dark eyes revealed none of her thoughts, but she'd clenched her hands on her knees and scooted to the far end of the sofa as if she didn't want to touch him, even accidentally.

"And why did Ms. Simmons borrow your car? Didn't she have her own transportation or date?"

Grant frowned, trying to remember the details of the evening. "She came to the party late with a girlfriend. She was upset when she arrived. She'd had a fight with some guy she'd been seeing."

Emma's eyes remained glued on him. He softened his tone, wanting her to realize he'd been sensitive to Faye's problems. "Anyway, she said the guy had ditched her earlier and she wasn't in a partying mood. But she didn't want to spoil her friends' night."

"So you gave her your keys?"

Grant bristled at the implication. "Sure, I felt sorry

for her—she was crying. I let her drive my car. She claimed she was going back to the dorm.''

''But she didn't return to the dorm, did she?''

Her blood-splattered face flashed through his mind. ''No, she didn't,'' he said in a low voice. He studied his fingernails, fighting the sense of guilt that tugged at him every time he remembered that night. If only he'd offered to drive her home, insisted she stay and talk things through. If only she hadn't just discovered she was pregnant...

''You had no idea she'd taken sleeping pills before she got behind the wheel of the car?''

''No,'' Grant said emphatically. He gave Emma a beseeching look, praying she believed him. Her dark lashes fluttered over creamy cheeks, and his gut clenched. God, he didn't want his wife to doubt him. And he didn't want her to end up like Faye....

''You didn't see anyone slip drugs into Ms. Simmons' drink that night?''

Grant shook his head. ''We partied, but none of us were into that kind of stuff. We didn't do drugs, Detective. Just had a few beers, a little cheap wine.''

Warner nodded, then snapped his notebook shut. ''And you told the police everything you knew about that night, right?''

''That's right,'' Grant said, his voice stronger.

''You admitted you knew the girl was pregnant?''

A soft gasp escaped Emma's mouth. He fought the instinct to touch her and reassure her. ''Yeah, she told me about the baby,'' he said, his voice strained.

Warner arched a gray eyebrow. ''You weren't the father?''

''No, I told you we weren't sexually involved. We were just friends.''

Warner cleared his throat, his gaze never wavering. "Didn't she tell you who the father of the baby was?"

Grant swallowed his emotions, then answered the same way he had three years earlier, hoping the detective would let sleeping dogs lie and move on with the search for the person after his wife. "No, she never told me."

Emma listened to Grant's comments with an uneasiness that threatened to break her calm. Her palms were perspiring, and she brushed them on the side of her sweats, her insides quaking at the desolate expression on his face. She noted the fine tremble of his fingers, the way his chin quivered slightly when he spoke, the way his hands started to move toward her, then retreated to fists at his sides. Either Grant was telling the truth or he was a great actor.

But why was the detective so curious about this young woman's death? Had she also known this girl named Faye?

"Mrs. Wadsworth, you still haven't regained your memory?" Warner asked.

Emma bit down on her bottom lip. "I'm afraid not. I don't remember anything of the past four years."

Warner made a clicking sound with his cheek. "What about this Ms. Simmons? Did you know her?"

"No, she didn't," Grant answered automatically, earning a suspicious look from the detective.

"I don't remember if I knew her or not," Emma said, her own patience flailing with the strain of the inquisition.

"Emma and I hadn't started dating yet," Grant clarified.

"Had the two of you met?" Warner asked.

Emma shrugged, feeling helpless. She would have to

rely on Grant to fill in the detail—and trust him to tell Warner the truth.

"We met through Emma's sister, Kate, a year later. She attended UNC. Kate and I had a couple of classes together."

"Hmm," Warner mumbled. "Did you ever date Emma's sister?"

Grant shook his head. "Not really. We went to a couple of movies together, a few ball games, but we didn't really date."

"You went out with Kate?" Emma asked in surprise.

"Not on a date. A whole group of us hung around together," Grant explained.

"So Emma's sister introduced you and Emma?"

"Yeah. Emma came to visit for the homecoming weekend." Grant tilted his head back in thought. "But Kate wasn't too keen on me dating Emma at first."

"She didn't want us to go out?" Emma asked.

"Did she have a crush on you, Mr. Wadsworth?"

"You've got to be kidding. Kate like me?" Grant laughed wryly. "She didn't think I was good enough for her—or you, Emma."

"You don't remember any of this?" Warner asked, his face angled toward Emma.

Emma shook her head, frustration pounding at her temple.

"And nothing about the accident?"

"She already answered you," Grant barked.

"You seem agitated, Mr. Wadsworth," Warner said, narrowing his eyes. "Is there some reason you don't want your wife to remember the past?"

Grant's expression turned thunderous. "Of course I want her to remember. But I don't like the way you're making her doubt me! I'm her husband, for God's sake.''

The pain in Emma's head intensified. She rubbed at her forehead, spots dancing before her eyes, then sighed when Grant's broad hand cupped her neck, massaging the tense muscles. ''Are you all right, sweetheart?''

''I'm getting a headache,'' she whispered, noticing he'd lowered his voice to a soothing pitch.

''Detective, I think we've had enough,'' Grant said calmly. But Emma saw his shoulders go rigid. ''Now, did you find anything on McGuire?''

''Nothing. So far his business looks legit.''

Emma remembered the strange phone calls. ''Detective, there is something else I need to tell you.'' She explained about the phone calls, relaying the message word for word.

''I heard him,'' Grant assured Warner. ''He called a few minutes before you arrived.''

''So the voice was definitely a man's?''

Emma hesitated, searching her memory. ''I'm not sure. The voice sounded very hoarse and faraway.''

''She's right,'' Grant said. ''I thought at first it was a man's voice. But when I think about it, it was so muffled it could have been a woman's.''

''Well, we should have the voice on tape. We'll have it analyzed. Should be able to at least tell if the voice belonged to a man or woman.''

Emma blinked against the pain in her temple and lay her head back.

''I hope you find the creep who's doing this soon,'' Grant said.

''I'm working on it. That message may be our best clue so far.''

''What do you mean?'' Emma asked.

"Whoever's doing this may be someone close to you, Mrs. Wadsworth. Someone who has a personal problem with either you or your husband." He glanced at Grant. "And for your wife's sake, Mr. Wadsworth, I hope you're telling the truth." Then he strode toward the door and let himself out.

Grant swung around and faced her, studying her for so long she began to tremble. His voice was hoarse when he spoke, anger burning his cheeks red, "Emma, you don't think I would do anything to hurt you, do you?"

EMMA'S SLIGHT HESITATION slashed into Grant's hopes like a knife tearing through his skin. He sank down beside her on the sofa, despair filling him. "Emma?"

"No, I don't think you would hurt me," she finally said, her voice a throaty whisper.

His breath tumbled out and he cupped her shoulders with his hands, then pulled her to him. "You can't imagine how bad I felt when that girl died. She was driving my car. I kept thinking if only I hadn't lent her my car..." He dropped his forehead against hers, his breathing labored as the memory of Faye's dead body and Emma's injured one mingled in his mind. Thank God Emma was alive. "I've wished a thousand times that I could go back and change that night, that I'd offered to drive her..."

"Shh, it's okay," Emma whispered against his neck. "It wasn't your fault, Grant."

Grant squeezed his eyes shut, the guilt he'd thought he'd buried long ago erupting. "I should have offered to take her home. I knew she was upset. She shouldn't have been driving, just like I should have been driving the night you had your wreck—"

Emma pressed a finger to his lips. "Grant, you couldn't have known she'd taken some pills or that she was going to have an accident." Then she gently lifted a lock of his hair from his forehead, an intimate gesture that pained Grant, for he remembered all the other times she'd completed the same sweet loving gesture and knew she did not. "And you couldn't have known I was going to have a wreck, either."

Grant shook his head miserably. "I would have died before I'd let you get hurt," he said in an anguished whisper. Then realizing she was in his arms, knowing she'd offered him comfort, he couldn't resist having her, if only for a moment. He had to taste her, to know she was real, still alive in his arms, still his wife.

He swept his hand gently down her back and around her waist, then lowered his mouth and sipped at the rose-petal corners of her lips, tasting, teasing her until she parted her lips and let him inside. Tenderness, passion, raw heat swirled through his body, dancing through his fingertips as he massaged the curve of her hip and felt her subtle response become bolder.

He asked and she gave, she moaned and he nearly came apart, devouring her hungrily, making love to her with his mouth. Her hands found their way into his hair and he groaned, the tender way she drew his head down for more plundering exciting him beyond reason. Then he threaded one hand into her silky gold mane and sank into oblivion. He tilted her head back and nibbled at her ear, tasting the sensitive skin on her neck, laving her with his tongue.

She clung to him, her hands digging into his arms, her small moans encouraging him to do more. He accepted her invitation and kissed her neck, brushed her face with gentle but hungry kisses, her shoulder, then lower until he nuzzled his face in the crevice of her breasts. Her nipples puckered and hardened beneath her light cotton sweater, and his hand inched beneath the fabric, moving slowly upward until he connected with bare skin. She groaned and cupped his head with her hands, her breathing shallow and unsteady. He curved his hand over the fullness of her breasts, aching to do more, but an image of her in the mangled car tore through his need and he was afraid he would hurt her. He gently flicked his thumb over the nipple while he angled his mouth and kissed her again, whispering sweet nonsense words of yearning to her as he loved her.

Unable to stand the torture, he lowered his head and nibbled at her breasts through her sweater. Slowly he pushed up the fabric and sought her with his mouth. Easing the edge of her lacy bra away with his teeth, his tongue flicked over her nipple, and she groaned, dropping her head forward and hugging him to her.

''Grant, no...'' she whispered.

He suckled the rosy tip, then nipped at her other breast. His groin surged with desire, his lips gorging themselves on her warm delicate flesh.

Emma's hands wrestled in his hair. ''No, Grant, please, we have to stop.''

Her soft plea invaded his urgency, and he paused, his hand gripping her sweater with trembling fingers, then smoothing it back in place. God, what was he doing? Acting like a sex maniac.

Or like a husband who wanted his wife. Emma had once welcomed his hungry sexual advances, but now...now she wanted him to stop.

''I'm sorry,'' she said in a tear-filled voice. But instead of pushing him away, she hugged him to her breasts. "I'm so sorry, Grant. I need more time."

He let his hands linger at her waist, then lifted them to stroke her arms, his face buried against her. "Shh, it's okay. I shouldn't have rushed you." Then he lifted his head and saw the misery in her eyes, the confusion, and his heart nearly broke. She needed more time. He'd have to give it to her. He'd do anything not to make her cry. So he raised his finger and wiped at her tears, then said good-night.

THE NEXT FEW DAYS, tension hung in the air, blanketing Emma with a weariness she couldn't escape. Grant wanted more. She could see the yearning in his eyes every time they passed in the hallway, shared a meal or simply cared for Carly. When their hands brushed or he kissed her good-night, sensations stirred within her, making her want more, but a dull ache settled in her chest when she thought about the threats to her life. The calls had continued to come, more of the same, never long enough to trace, never offering more information, just menacing enough to keep her on edge. Each time she told Grant about one of them, his jaw tightened and his blue eyes flickered angrily.

But Grant didn't press her for sex, and she grew more anxious about her memory loss, frustrated that she hadn't even had a small glimpse of her former life. Kate came daily and drove her to therapy. Martha baby-sat Carly so Grant could work at the office a few hours a day. She wondered if he spent more time working simply to avoid her.

Her physical progress had been steady. She had finally graduated from crutches to a cane, and the doctor had said she could drive again when she was ready. To an outsider her family routine might appear normal. She and Grant shared a home, a child, and were cordial with one another. But Emma sensed their relationship was a time bomb, ready to explode at any second. Emma patted Carly's back, humming the lullaby Grant had said was Carly's favorite. She loved her baby. Whether she remembered her or not, the sweet precious child in her arms had stolen her heart. But Grant?

She wasn't sure how she felt about him, she thought, as she carried Carly to her crib and tucked her in. She wanted to be the woman Grant loved. But she still couldn't remember him or their relationship, and her physical therapy served as a definite reminder that she wasn't the same woman he'd loved before the accident. With each passing day her doubts escalated. She watched the videos of their wedding and a few of their family excursions over and over, hoping to trigger her memory. Each time she was touched by the scenes, but nothing clicked in her mind. She'd looked naive and young and sweet in the pictures. She wasn't that innocent young woman now. She had scars, both inside and out, and she was afraid she would never be the same.

At times she saw pain lingering in Grant's eyes, and she wondered if it was fair to stay here in this house with him as his wife when she couldn't truly be a wife to him. Was he simply staying with her out of loyalty?

The telephone rang and she started, then stared at the machine, her heart thumping. Was it the threatening caller?

Angry with herself for letting the calls upset her, she reached for the phone, preparing to tell whoever it was to bug off. But a woman's lilting voice sounded on the line.

"Hello, Emma?"

"Yes, who is this?"

"This is Priscilla—I work with Grant."

Emma wound the phone cord around her fingers. "Yes, he's mentioned you."

"He has?" Priscilla sounded surprised.

"Yes, he told me about you and Pete Landers and the trip to Paris."

"Oh, yes. The trip went great. We missed having Grant along, but the company loved his work." Priscilla paused. "Is Grant there?"

Emma frowned in confusion. "No, I thought he was at work."

"He was," Priscilla quickly said. "But after lunch I had another appointment and when I returned to the office, he was gone."

"I see." Emma shifted onto her uninjured leg, keeping the weight off her sore ankle. "Do you want to leave a message?"

"Yes, if you see him, tell him we're meeting with Mr. Bronson this afternoon. He wants to discuss the designs Grant drew up for him."

Emma twisted her mouth in thought. "I'll tell him, but he'll probably go to the office first. He isn't driving me to the doctor until three."

Priscilla's loud sigh wreaked with agitation. "Can you arrange for someone else to drive you? This is a very important meeting, Emma."

Emma stiffened at Priscilla's condescending tone. She knew Kate would drop her at the doctor's office, but Kate had an appointment later and couldn't stay.

"I realize you've had a hard time lately, Emma, but you really need to be supportive of Grant," Priscilla chided. "He's worked so hard to make a name for himself, and right now he needs to put everything he has into the company. He might be promoted. That would mean major money and status with the firm.''

''I understand,'' Emma said, rubbing her hand along her thigh. ''When he comes in, tell him Kate will take me to the doctor, but he'll need to pick me up at five.'' Priscilla agreed and hung up. Emma's leg was aching, so she hobbled over to the couch and propped it on the ottoman, then lay her head back and sighed. She was letting Grant down by not remembering her marriage. After talking to Priscilla, she wondered if she'd failed him in the past, as well, by not supporting his career.

Too tired to think, she closed her eyes and drifted off. But several minutes later she woke up with a start. Even in her sleep, questions plagued her. She was a burden to Grant, she was sure. And she had to do something about it.

She pushed herself up, grabbed her cane and went to the bathroom to freshen up before her session. She was going to talk to the doctor about running some more tests. She needed to find out if her memory loss was due to physical trauma or emotional stress. And if the results showed emotional stress, she'd arrange for the hypnosis. And if the tests showed permanent physical damage, she needed to know that, too. Then she and Grant could move on with their lives, one way or another.

GRANT HURRIED BACK into his office to retrieve the files he'd left behind, anxious to get home to Emma and Carly. Each day he told himself to be patient, that one day Emma would wake up and remember him. But each time he saw the listless look in Emma's eyes, he knew she hadn't. It was eating at her, as well. He recognized the tension radiating between them.

''I can't believe you, Wadsworth,'' Pete said, almost accosting him in the hallway.

''What is it now, Landers?'' Grant asked, mentally counting the number of times Pete had chastised him for coming in to work and leaving his wife. ''Going to lecture me again about how I should go home?''

Pete's nostrils flared with anger. ''I decided that wouldn't do any good, you're so hardheaded. But how dare you insinuate to the police that I might have hurt your wife!''

''What?'' Grant paused over the papers on his desk.

Pete exploded. ''They came to my office and questioned me about my Jeep. Just because it was in the damn body shop, they accused me of running your wife off the road!''

Grant exhaled noisily. ''Look, Pete, I had nothing to do with that.''

Pete folded his arms, his expression furious. ''Really? They said you gave them my name.''

''I did,'' Grant said, forcing a calm into his voice before they had the entire firm wandering in to witness their confrontation. ''I had to give them a list of everyone Emma and I knew, all our friends and family, and the people we both worked with. It was a formality.''

The angry splash on Pete's neck faded slightly. ''I know you don't like me, Wadsworth, but I can't believe you think I'd hurt your wife. What reason could I possibly have?'' Grant's silence seemed to fuel Pete's temper again. ''The job?'' Pete asked in disbelief.

''I never accused you of anything,'' Grant said.

''You think I'd stoop to murder to beat you out of a promotion?''

''I didn't say that,'' Grant replied quietly. ''And I'm sorry if the cops bothered you. They're only doing their jobs.'' *They even questioned me,* he thought, remembering how angry he'd been with the detective's insinuations.

Pete's voice dropped an octave. ''You just don't get it, Grant. Some things are more important than your job.'' Then he spun around and exited the office in a gust of anger.

Priscilla nearly bumped into Pete as she entered. She arched an auburn eyebrow. ''What's going on with him?''

Grant relayed the argument. Priscilla simply clucked, dismissing Pete's problems with a wave of her hand. ''Don't worry about him, Grant. You have enough on your mind.''

A muscle twitched in his neck and Grant rubbed it, rolling his shoulders to relieve the strain. Before he realized it, Priscilla had slipped behind him and pressed her fingertips to his sore neck and begun to massage. He dropped his head forward, unable to resist the tension release as she kneaded his aching muscles.

''I know you're having a rough time at home. Pete should cut you some slack.''

''I don't blame him for being angry,'' Grant said. ''But he never did say what happened to his Jeep.''

''He told me somebody hit him in the parking lot. Didn't even leave a note.''

''It's possible,'' Grant agreed, rotating his shoulders in the opposite direction.

''You need to concentrate on the Bronson account right now,'' Priscilla said. ''Not Pete. Bronson called and wants us for cocktails at four, then an early dinner.''

Grant sighed. ''I can't, Priscilla. I have to take Emma to therapy.''

"It's all right—I talked to Emma. She said to tell you her sister's taking her."

"Oh," Grant said, feeling as if Emma had once again chosen Kate over him.

Priscilla leaned over his shoulder, her perfume wafting around him. "Bronson wants you to build a scale model of the city within the city."

"Great," Grant said, slightly uneasy when Priscilla's hair brushed against his collar. He leaned forward, expecting her to release his shoulders, but she ran her hand over his arm and squeezed his bicep.

"Are you feeling more relaxed, darling?"

"Yeah, thanks." He straightened his tie and turned to face her, surprised she hadn't moved.

She brushed a piece of lint from his jacket, her hand lingering at his collar. "I really am worried about you, Grant," Priscilla said softly, her ruby lips curving into a sensuous smile. "You've been under a lot of stress lately. If you ever need to talk or...anything else, let me know."

Grant swallowed. With Kate's undermining him with Emma, Emma's reluctance to let him touch her and Pete's antagonistic attitude, he should be flattered to have someone think about him for a change, but Priscilla's catlike eyes seemed to be suggesting more than comfort.

Or maybe he was so desperate for physical attention he was reading more into her gesture than she meant. Whatever her motive and no matter how tempting the idea of leaning on her, he couldn't possibly have a personal relationship with Priscilla without seeing Emma in his mind. Only Emma didn't want him.

Priscilla's hand feathered over his arm, her touch

light, almost provocative. "You will let me know if you need anything, won't you, Grant?"

He caught her hand in his and squeezed it, then angled his head toward the phone. "Yes, thanks."

Priscilla's smile widened. "Good. I'll make the reservations and confirm with Bronson." She sashayed toward the door, then glanced at him over her shoulder. "We make a great team, Grant, don't you think?"

His fingers tightened around the phone as he nodded. *Yeah, but it's only business,* he thought, stifling images of what she'd seemingly offered. The diamond chips in his wedding ring sparkled as they caught in the light, and he forced his mind back to business.

"I'LL LET YOU KNOW the results of the test next week," Dr. Jacobs said. "Until then, go home and rest. You look exhausted, Mrs. Wadsworth."

"It was a long therapy session," Emma said. "But I'm feeling stronger every day." She settled her cane on the carpeting and stood, steadying herself. "Thanks for working me in for those tests."

Jacobs checked her chart. "Most of the swelling around your brain tissue has gone down. We should get a better indication of your condition from these tests."

"I want to try hypnosis if we find out my amnesia's due to emotional stress," Emma said.

Jacobs nodded. "Let's take it one step at a time, Emma. For now, that means go home to your family and rest. And try not to worry." Jacobs opened the door for her to leave.

"I'll try. Now I'd better get going. My husband's supposed to be picking me up."

Emma was surprised to see that Grant wasn't in the waiting room. She made her way down the hallway and into the elevator, her muscles aching from her therapy session. Although her gait was still awkward, she *was* getting stronger every day, she reminded herself. And the threatening phone calls had petered off; she hadn't received one all day. Of course, Grant had changed the phone number to an unlisted one, so perhaps they would end entirely.

The office complex was shutting down, most of the offices empty. Maybe Grant was running late and had decided not to park. He'd probably be outside, she thought, making her way to the front door. The sun had set, dark skies hovering over the horizon. The gusty winter wind sent a chill through her spine as she looked out at the nearly deserted parking lot.

She didn't see Grant. She pulled her jacket around her more tightly and awkwardly searched the front of the building, then slowly walked around to the side parking lot. Shadows loomed from the corners, whispers of indistinguishable sounds echoing off the concrete. Tension fluttered through her—a product of seeing too many women attacked in parking garages on TV, she thought wryly. Her gaze automatically surveyed the vacant lot and she reached in her purse for the cell phone. Suddenly frightened, she turned to go back to the front. There was a noise behind her. The thump of shoes on the pavement. She glanced over her shoulder and saw a shadow at the edge of the building. Someone was following her.

Panic hit her. She stumbled forward and tried to run. But someone grabbed her shoulder and pushed her to the ground.

Chapter Nine

Emma screamed as she pushed up and tried to run. She wielded her cane like a weapon, swinging it wildly. A cab rolled up and parked at the street corner, and she ran toward it, stumbling in the dark. The hands clawed at her again, but she dodged her attacker, almost losing her balance when her foot slid off the sidewalk.

She screamed again and darted into the street, dodging an oncoming car. The car blasted its horn and careered on. Then a muffled popping sound rent the air. A gunshot?

She lunged toward the taxi, swung open the door and collapsed into the back seat.

"Take me to the police station," Emma shrieked, scanning the street. "Someone just tried to shoot me."

AS GRANT REFILLED Adam Bronson's glass in preparation for a toast to their business deal, a tremor rippled up his spine. Something was wrong.

Priscilla automatically lay her hand on his thigh to get his attention, but he quickly removed it, his anxiety intensifying. Not only had Priscilla been late, she'd come in looking flustered and shaky.

"Won't you share the toast?" Bronson asked, his graying eyebrows arched.

"Of course we will," Priscilla said, glossing over the moment with her usual feminine ease. She refilled her glass, as well as Grant's.

"To the most ingenious architect I've had the pleasure of meeting in a long time," Bronson said. "And to Little Raleigh, the city within a city that is going to be the next wave in development."

Priscilla smiled flirtatiously at Bronson, and Grant swallowed the wine, then checked his watch. He couldn't focus, couldn't get Emma off his mind. How had her doctor's visit gone? Had she and Kate made it back all right?

"Grant does have wonderful ideas," Priscilla boasted with a wink. "And the best part is, he always follows through."

Bronson slapped him on the back. "That's what I want to hear. How soon can you have this scale model completed?"

"When would you like it?" Grant heard himself ask woodenly.

"Three weeks—is that doable?"

"Of course," Priscilla agreed smugly. Once again she slid her hand over his thigh, patting it as she grinned at Bronson. "If we have to work together day and night, we'll have it finished for you, won't we, Grant?"

"Um, yes." Grant set his glass down. "Excuse me, please. I have to make a phone call. I need to check on my wife."

Priscilla caught his wrist. "Oh, dear. Grant, I forgot to tell you, Emma wants you to pick her up after her appointment."

"What time?"

Priscilla cut into her cheesecake and offered him some. ''I think she said around five.''

Grant glanced at his watch in a panic. ''Five. It's nearly six now.''

''I'm sure she won't mind if you're a few minutes late,'' Priscilla said lamely.

He clenched his jaw, his anger at Priscilla almost overwhelming. ''She shouldn't have to wait.''

Bronson eyed him speculatively. Grant muttered a brief explanation, reached into his jacket for his keys, then headed to the exit. His beeper went off just as he climbed into his car. He checked the number, his anxiety level rising when he spotted the detective's number. His heart racing, he punched the numbers on his cell phone.

''Mr. Wadsworth, I think you'd better come to the station.''

''What is it?''

''It's your wife.''

''Emma? She's at the doctor—''

''No, she's here. She isn't hurt, but she's pretty upset. She said someone tried to shoot her outside the doctor's office.''

''I'll be right there.'' Grant slammed down the phone and pressed the accelerator, cursing a blue streak. This was all his fault. Damn Priscilla. He could strangle her for not giving him Emma's message. And he wouldn't believe Emma was all right until he saw her himself.

EMMA SIPPED THE TEA one of the officers had given her, trying to warm her hands and steady her nerves. Warner had assured her they would check the parking lot for a bullet. And Grant was on his way. When she glanced up and saw him enter the office, his face was a mask of misery. ''Emma?'' he said in a rough whisper. ''Are you okay, sweetheart?''

Her resolve instantly crumpled and the tears she'd tried to hold at bay erupted, streaming down her cheeks. He was beside her in a second, his big strong arms enveloping her as he rocked her back and forth. ''Shh, honey, it's okay. I'm here. I'm not going to let anyone hurt you, not again. Not ever again.'' He crooned soft words of comfort and stroked the hair from her face, his broad shoulders cradling her against him.

''I thought someone was following me at the hospital,'' she whimpered. ''I heard footsteps and it was dark and I saw shadows,'' she said, pouring every ounce of strength she had left into telling him the details of the night. ''Then he grabbed me.''

''Oh, God, baby, I'm sorry, I'm so sorry.'' He cocooned her in his protective embrace and Emma clung to him.

''I thought you were going to be there.''

He pulled her back and cupped her face in his palms. ''I should have been there, I would have, but Priscilla didn't give me the message. I thought Kate was with you.''

Emma searched his face for the truth. ''But I told her Kate couldn't bring me home.''

His jaw tensed. ''I'm sorry, she didn't tell me until we were in the middle of dinner.'' He ran his hands over her face, her hair. ''I swear she didn't tell me or I would have been there, Emma. I never would have left you alone, not with all that's been going on.''

''Mrs. Wadsworth,'' Warner said, sidling into the office. ''One of my men just called. He said he found a slug from a .38 in the parking lot.'' He frowned at

Emma. "I guess you were right. Someone did shoot at you."

Emma shivered and felt Grant tremble against her.

"We'll have it analyzed. We're questioning folks to find out if there were any witnesses."

"You have to find this maniac," Grant said, clutching Emma to him. "Don't you have any ideas yet? What about the florist? Did you find out who sent the locket?"

Warner shook his head. "The florist said it was dropped off by an independent service with a request to be sent to you with the flowers. Cash in an envelope." Warner gestured toward a chair. "But there's something else. You might want to sit down."

Grant coaxed Emma back into the wooden chair and pulled another up beside her. "What is it now?"

Warner leveled his gaze at Grant. "We did some further checking on Pete Landers, the guy who owns the black Jeep."

"Yeah?"

"Found out some interesting things about his past. How well do you know Landers?"

Grant shrugged. "As well as anyone knows a coworker, I guess. We work together, attend general meetings, sometimes have lunch with a group of clients. We're definitely not buddies."

"Ever socialize with him or his family outside the office?"

"No." Grant's curiosity was piqued. "What are you getting at, Detective?"

"So you didn't know Mrs. Landers?"

Grant frowned. "There isn't a Mrs. Landers, at least not that I know of."

Warner cracked his gum. "You're right, there's not

anymore. But Landers was married. His wife died about a year ago,'' Warner continued. ''In a car accident.''

Grant's jaw went slack.

''That's terrible,'' Emma said in a low voice.

Warner nodded. ''Worst part was that his wife was pregnant at the time. Baby didn't have a chance.''

A fine sheen of sweat dampened Grant's neck. ''Pete never mentioned it.'' He thought back over the past year. When had Pete come to work for the firm?

''Records show Landers signed on with your company right after his wife's death. Other company he worked for said he went berserk after the accident. They encouraged him to seek counseling, but he refused. Said he got volatile, almost went off the deep end.''

''What a tragedy, losing both his wife and baby,'' Emma added quietly.

''I had no idea,'' Grant said. His gaze shot to Warner's. ''But I don't understand what this has to do with Emma.''

''Maybe nothing,'' Warner said. ''But a shock like he suffered can make some people go crazy. I was thinking about the threats Mrs. Wadsworth's received. Seems sort of eerie, kind of parallel. The car accident. You have a baby, he lost his. If Landers has something against you, maybe he snapped and wants you to hurt like he's been hurting. Sounds like a motive to me.''

''He wants the promotion I'm up for.'' The threats flashed through Grant's head. *I lost my loved one and so will you. The broken locket and missing picture. Pete's chastising him about staying home with his family.* Could Pete's ambition and grief drive him to such cruel acts?

EMMA CLUTCHED Grant's hand the entire way home, comforted by his presence. Warner followed them, wanting to confer with the officer stationed outside.

"How's Carly?" Emma asked the moment she stepped through the door.

"She's sleeping," Kate said. "We went to the store earlier to buy diapers."

"You took Carly out alone?" Grant asked.

Kate bristled. "I didn't know I wasn't allowed to go to the store with her."

"It's okay, Kate," Emma said. "We're both on edge right now."

Grant explained about the shooting.

"Oh, my God!" Kate exclaimed. "I can't believe it." She gestured toward Carly's room. "You don't think this crazy person would hurt Carly, do you?"

"I don't know, but we're not going to take any chances," Grant said firmly.

"That's right," Warner cautioned. The detective had come in before he left, saying he had a few more questions. "If anyone comes to the door, calls, whatever, I want to know about it."

Kate gestured toward a long white box on the dining table. "That box was on the back doorstep when I arrived."

They all moved toward it hesitantly. Warner slowly lifted it and listened, took it to the kitchen sink and slowly undid the ribbon, then opened it. He carefully removed the tissue, and Emma gasped when she saw what was inside.

"Oh, my," Kate said, pressing her hand to her cheek. "Dead roses."

Emma's gaze rested on the enclosed card. *Roses are red, violets are blue. I lost my family, and so will you.*

Her stomach heaved when she saw a snapshot of

Grant, Carly and herself underneath the note. The picture had been cut into a dozen tiny pieces.

"Damn." Grant's eyes darkened. He started to pick up the butchered photograph, but Warner ordered him not to touch anything. He rubbed his neck, then turned away, his hand at Emma's elbow. "I don't understand why someone would want to torment Emma like this."

"I'll have the box and contents dusted for prints," Warner stated. "And we'll check with the florist again."

Kate found a paper bag and the policeman carefully put the box in it. He turned to Grant. "Mr. Wadsworth, I need to know where you were when your wife was shot at."

"I was at River Mill Steakhouse," Grant snapped.

"Can someone corroborate your story?"

Emma flinched when Grant's hand curled into a fist. "Yes. A co-worker and one of my clients."

"You were with Priscilla?" Kate said in an accusing tone.

"And Adam Bronson," Grant said, glaring at Kate. "We were closing a business deal."

"Anyone at the house today other than the three of you?"

"Martha, the housekeeper, came earlier," Kate replied.

"But she had to clean the jewelry store where I worked at five," Emma said. "And there hasn't been anyone else here since."

"And you, Kate?"

"I was baby-sitting Carly," Kate said.

"But you went to the store. Did anyone see you?"

Kate's eyes widened. "The clerk, I suppose, if she remembers me, that is."

"You or your wife own a gun?" Warner asked, his gaze on Grant.

"No," Grant said adamantly. "I'd never have one in the house with a child around."

Warner nodded his approval, his mouth almost quirking into a smile. "How about you, ma'am?" he asked, directing his question to Kate.

Kate bit her lip. "Er...no, I'm afraid of guns. Why?"

"Just checking." He gestured toward Grant. "I'll have a talk with Pete Landers. See if he owns a gun."

"You do that," Grant said between clenched teeth. Then he escorted Warner to the door.

A few minutes later Emma tried to eat the Chinese food Kate had picked up, but the meal was awkward and tense. Kate chattered on about how good the dishes were, and Grant was unusually quiet.

"Dan called and asked me out," Kate said idly.

"Are you going to date him?" Emma asked, pushing away the tasteless food.

"I don't know," Kate said. "He's really persistent. But I'm not sure I can trust him, especially now that I know he has an arrest record."

Emma saw Grant tense, but he didn't comment. Maybe he and Kate would put aside their bickering for tonight.

"I think I'm going to go lie down," Emma said. "Kate, I appreciate your keeping Carly, but maybe you'd better go home tonight."

Kate frowned, then pushed away from the table "All right. But I'll clean up the dishes before I go."

"Thanks for the dinner, Kate," Grant said. "I'll help clean up."

Kate smiled. "That's okay, Grant. Why don't you take care of Emma?"

Grant nodded and walked Emma to the bedroom door. Emma gazed into his eyes, Grant's hungry expression almost stripping her of her resolve. But exhaustion pulled at her muscles and she swayed slightly.

"Come on, you need to lie down," Grant said. He curved his arm around her waist and coaxed her into the room. Moonlight drifted through the bedroom window, dappling soft lines of light through the room and turning Grant's eyes to a smoky blue. His broad hands cupped her face and he gently lowered his mouth, kissing her with such sweetness she felt tears burn her eyes.

He slipped from the room with a whispered goodnight. Emma changed into a gown and crawled under the covers. The empty room closed around her like a tomb, draining the life and energy from her, sucking her into a pain-filled state of semi-sleep. She'd never felt more bereft and alone in her life.

"CARLY, YOU'RE AN ANGEL," Grant whispered. She snuggled into his arms, her tiny lips parting slightly as he slipped the bottle from her mouth. One chubby hand curled against his chest, and his protective instincts mushroomed. He hugged her to him, pressing his face to hers and inhaling the scent of baby powder and innocence, his anxiety over the danger surrounding Emma heightening his senses.

"I love you, Carly." He carried her through the darkened nursery to her crib. For an instant when he lay her down, she opened her eyes and stared at him, the trust and adoration so strong his chest swelled and tears filled his eyes. Then her mouth curved into a smile, and he swallowed, watching with an awestruck love as she curled her fist beside her curly blond hair and drifted back to sleep.

At least his daughter was sleeping peacefully, he thought, frustration mounting again. He could hear Emma in her bedroom, tossing and turning, and had to fight his primitive urge to go in and cradle her to his chest and hold her all night. But he'd promised he wouldn't touch her, not unless she asked, and earning her trust and love was more important than his physical needs. Then he heard a whimper and he turned, blinded by the light coming from the opened doorway. Emma's sweet scent drifted toward him, making him yearn to hold her.

"Grant?" Emma's voice came from the shadowed doorway.

"Yeah, I'm here." Her whispered sigh made his stomach clench. "Are you all right?"

She shook her head, the golden strands of her hair swishing on her shoulders, her slender body haloed in the moonlight. "I can't sleep," she murmured.

He moved slowly toward her, his hand outstretched, his arms open. She fell into them and clung to him. He guided her back to bed and helped her climb beneath the thick comforter. Unspoken needs materialized, stronger than the distance that separated them, stronger than the forgotten vows and promises of a lifetime. He removed his shoes, then stretched out on the bed beside her and took her in his arms. The minute she curled into him, her head tucked into the crook of his shoulder, he brushed a whisper of a kiss on the top of her head.

"Stay with me tonight," she said in a sleepy whisper.

"I will, sweetheart." His throat was thick with emotion. He hugged her to him, pulling her into the safety of his embrace, and he heard a soft sigh of contentment escape her lips. Then he closed his eyes, dreaming of the day he could do more than hold her, imagining stripping her gown and dropping hungry kisses all over her body. She was warm and as sweetly fragrant as a flower garden, as heady as the finest wine, and he wanted to devour every tantalizing inch of her.

But for now, lying beside her, holding her in his arms, and knowing that she'd taken a giant step toward trusting him was enough to keep him content through the night.

EMMA WOKE UP, feeling vaguely content and safe in spite of the lingering memories of the incident in the parking lot. When she opened her eyes, she saw Grant lying beside her. She felt comforted because he was there. Comforted, but embarrassed. The night before had been filled with nightmares. Then she'd found Grant in Carly's room, bent over her crib, murmuring sweet loving words, and she'd asked him to come to bed with her.

Peeking lower, she realized he'd removed his clothes except for his boxers. His chest was bare, and at the sight of his broad muscled shoulders, heat curled through her.

She ran her hand over his chest, reveling in the powerful muscles beneath her fingers. His scent invaded her senses, reviving desires she'd thought lost with her past. His lips parted slightly in his sleep and he mumbled something, then rolled to his side and slung his arm across her, his hand groping downward, finally resting on her hip. He groaned, a happy catlike sound, then smiled.

She closed her eyes, unable to fight the lustful sensations stirring in her abdomen as his leg brushed hers and his breath feathered against her cheek. When she looked at him again, she saw he was awake and staring at her, the early-morning sunlight flickering off cheekbones, his blue eyes filled with the sleepy haze of sensual awareness.

"Hi," he said in a husky voice.

"Good morning," Emma murmured.

He stared at her for a long time, his gaze intense. Then he pulled her close, and she snuggled against his chest. It felt incredibly sweet to lie with him, a little slice of heaven early in the morning.

"This feels nice," Grant said softly, his thumb caressing her shoulder. "I've missed mornings like this."

She nodded against him, loving the feel of his heart beating against her cheek.

"I've missed holding you, Emma."

"I'm glad you're here," she whispered, and closed her eyes, savoring the tenderness of the moment.

But the phone jangled and Grant groaned, giving her a look of regret as he reached for it. When she heard him say the detective's name, she headed for the shower. Desperate to gain control, she turned on the hot water and stepped under the showerhead, the bright bathroom light illuminating the scar on her thigh and bringing back reality. Even if she remembered her marriage to Grant, she was still too scarred to become intimate with him. He would be expecting the same woman he had married, the flawless face and body, not the scarred, ugly—

"Emma, are you all right?"

"Yes, I'm fine," she said, stepping out of the shower and jerking a towel around her. "I'll be out in a minute."

"I'll make some coffee."

By the time she combed her damp hair and dressed in a pair of blue sweatpants and a powder-blue shell sweater, Grant had breakfast and coffee ready. She avoided his gaze as she slid into her chair.

"Did you sleep okay?" he asked.

"Yes, and you?"

"Better than I have in a while," he admitted with a sexy smile.

She couldn't help but smile back at his mischievous honest reaction. "I'm glad. I know this is hard on you."

His smile faded slightly. "We're going to get through this, Emma."

She nodded, slicing into the steaming omelet. "Is Carly still sleeping?"

As if on cue, they heard the sound of Carly's early-morning gurgling and they both laughed. "I'll get her," Grant said. "She can have breakfast with us."

Like a normal family, Emma thought, as he came back and propped her in the infant seat between them.

"Hi, sweetie." She grabbed Carly's finger. "So you're hungry, too, huh? Did you smell Daddy's yummy eggs?"

Grant grinned rakishly and kissed Carly's forehead, then Emma's. "Thanks, Emma."

She looked at him. "For what?"

"For letting me hold you last night."

Emma nodded, the memory of his husky voice lingering between them during the rest of the morning. The sweet tenderness they'd shared during the night had created a bond that neither seemed to want to break.

"What did Warner say earlier?" Emma asked after they'd settled Carly on a blanket on the floor.

"Well, no witnesses to the shooting." He paused. "And Pete denies owning a gun."

A knock sounded at the front door and Martha bustled in. "Good morning, folks. I brought you some peach pie.'' She placed a plastic container on the kitchen counter. ''Dan said to send his best. He wants to stop by again and see you, Emma.''

''Sure, I'd like that,'' Emma said.

''Said he wonders if you might want to come back to work sometime.''

''I don't know. I'm certainly not ready right now.''

''Emma's going to stay home with Carly,'' Grant said, his voice level. ''We discussed it before you quit, Emma.''

Emma gritted her teeth in frustration, wishing there weren't so many holes in her life. Martha stopped to talk to Carly for a few moments, then tweaked her toes. ''I'm going to change your linens, Carly, so you'll have a fresh bed for your nap.'' Martha dashed off to the nursery with a wave.

Carly pedaled her arms and legs, cooing up at Emma. Emma lifted Grant's jacket from the chair and moved it out of Carly's reach. A small slip of paper and a matchbook fell from the pocket and she picked them up. A phone number was scribbled on the paper, and the matchbox was from a place called the Seascape Motel. Her pulse hammered wildly.

She remembered the red lipstick and Kate's comments. ''Grant, what are these?''

Grant took the paper and matchbook from her, then studied them. ''I don't know. Where'd you find them?''

''They fell out of your jacket just now,'' Emma explained.

''What?'' A frown drew his mouth down. ''They aren't mine. I've never been to this motel.''

Emma hesitated, unsure what to say. ''They were in your pocket,'' she said slowly, ''but you don't know where they came from.''

''That's right,'' Grant said, his voice growing defensive. He sat down beside her and met her gaze. ''Emma, I swear I've never been to this place. I don't know how those matches got in my pocket.'' He released a tired sigh. ''The last motel I went to was the one we stayed in before Carly was born. We took a weekend trip to Florida for some sun.''

Emma pressed her memory for the slightest hint of what he was talking about.

''And the time before that, we stayed in this little bed-and-breakfast in the mountains. We got snowed in. That was the weekend we conceived Carly.''

Emma shifted, dangling a toy in front of Carly, suddenly uncomfortable.

''I'll never forget the day we learned you were pregnant,'' he said, his voice filled with the fondness of memories. ''You bought this home pregnancy test. When I got home, you'd fixed a special candlelight dinner. Then I asked where the wine was, and you grinned and showed me the test. We drank orange juice, instead, and danced around the room to Celine Dion.''

Tears burned the backs of Emma's eyes as he continued reminiscing about their past together. ''Our wedding day was the happiest day of my life, then Carly was born, and I thought that was the happiest day.'' He chuckled and Emma felt like weeping. ''Of course I almost passed out when you delivered, but I was exhausted and hadn't eaten all day, thinking about your labor and all—''

''Grant, stop, please stop,'' she said, the forgotten memories torturing her.

''I thought you'd want to hear about the good times we had,'' Grant said, obviously hurt.

Emma turned to him, tears filling her eyes. ''I did,

but I don't anymore. I can't remember them and it hurts to hear you talk about them.''

Grant's face paled. ''If we can't share the past, where does that leave us? With nothing?''

Emma shook her head, her voice lost.

Grant stood. ''I'm trying to do this, to live here without touching you, Emma, to be with you, but *not* be with you, and it's driving me crazy. I want you so much it hurts.'' He grabbed his jacket, his voice rough. ''I love you, Emma, and I'm tired of you shutting me out.''

''But you keep pushing me to remember,'' she said. ''And I can't.''

He stormed to the door and gripped the doorknob, then bowed his head, his words tortured. ''God help me, Emma, but yes, I want you to remember. And I'm not sure how we're going to make it if you don't.''

Chapter Ten

He should have kept his emotions under control. Grant charged into his office, furious with himself for losing his temper with Emma. And for leaving her alone. Only, she wasn't quite alone, he reminded himself. Martha was there and the cop was stationed outside his house. He was so frustrated with this damn mess—

"Something happen at home?" Priscilla's voice drifted past his fury, nagging at his confused emotions.

He didn't try to hide his anger before he faced her. "Last night someone tried to shoot Emma when she came out of the doctor's office." He explained about the flowers and the note.

"Good heavens," Priscilla said, pressing one hand over her heart. She gave him a sympathetic smile. "That's awful, Grant. I can see why you're upset."

"I should have been there," Grant said tightly. "She could have been killed, Priscilla, because you forgot to tell me to pick her up."

"I'm sorry, Grant, I had no idea—"

"No, maybe not." He tried to calm his voice. "But now you know she's in danger and I can't take any chances, so don't let it happen again."

"It won't, Grant, I promise." Priscilla reached out to

pat his arm, but he pulled away. Once again he found himself omitting the details of Emma's amnesia. He wasn't sure why he didn't want the people at his office to know. Maybe Kate's suggestion that Emma had forgotten him because she wasn't happy with him still bothered him.

"Do the police know who shot at her?" Priscilla asked.

"Not yet." His jaw snapped tight as Pete marched in, his face crimson.

"You put those cops on me again, didn't you, Wadsworth? You have to find someone to blame for your wife's accident and you want it to be me!"

Grant squared his shoulders. "I don't know what you're talking about."

Pete poked him in the chest. "You had the cops dig up all the gory details of my wife's death, then they came over and drilled me for an hour, implying I had something to do with Emma's accident."

"Look, Pete—" Grant held out his hand to calm him "—I didn't send the police to your house. They came to me and told me about your wife. I don't know why you never mentioned it before—"

"I came to work here to get away from my past. I thought, new people, new place, maybe I could forget!"

"Pete, calm down," Priscilla said. "You're making a scene."

Pete's eyes grew livid. "My past is my own private affair," he said, his nostrils flaring. "So stop trying to pin your problems on me, Wadsworth. You're wasting your time."

"I'm sorry about your wife and baby," Grant said, meaning it.

"I don't want to discuss them," he said in an anguished voice. ''Not ever. Now you can tell the cops to leave me alone.'' Then Pete stormed out of the office, slamming the door so hard the window rattled.

Grant stared after Pete, feeling sorry for him, wondering if his own life was falling apart. Not only had he almost lost his wife, but now the danger surrounding his family was affecting his work and co-workers. When would it all stop?

''Don't worry about him, he'll get over it,'' Priscilla said, once again stroking his arm. Grant glanced at her ruby fingernails, then into her heart-shaped face, and saw the subtle hint of sympathy, the slight offering of feminine comfort—and the haze of sexual awareness glistening in her emerald-green eyes. ''Remember what I said, Grant. I'm here if you need me.''

He forced himself to see Emma's face in his mind. Her soft brown eyes, the honeyed strands of her hair shimmering in the sunlight, her slim enticing body lying on satin sheets…

She let you hold her last night, sleep beside her, a little voice whispered.

But his heart squeezed at the memory of her parting words. She didn't want to hear about the past, about the wonderful memories they'd made. And memories were all he had.

What if she didn't want to remember him? And what if she never told him she loved him again—never let him in her bed as her lover, her husband? Was a platonic relationship all they would have together? And if it was, could he accept it?

''I'M TAKING CARLY for a walk,'' Martha said, setting up the infant stroller. ''Thought I'd do it before it gets much later.''

"I'm sure she'll enjoy it." Emma covered Martha's hand with her own. "Thanks so much for coming, Martha. I don't know what I'd do right now without you and Kate." Emma noticed a long scar on Martha's hand, reminding her of her own imperfect skin. "What happened to your hand?"

Martha wrinkled her forehead, then made a *tsk*ing sound. "Oh, I cut myself slicing some zucchini. Bled like the dickens."

"It looks as if it's healing nicely."

"Yeah. Now I'd better get going or it'll be too chilly to walk the baby."

"I did some of those exercises the therapist showed me and I'm tired," Emma said. "I think I'll take a nap."

Martha bundled Carly into a thick sweater and cap and covered her with a blanket.

Emma kissed Carly's nose. "Enjoy your ride, sweetheart. Maybe soon Mommy will be able to take you out in your stroller."

After Martha left, Emma looked out the window and saw the officer standing guard.

A few minutes later she stretched out on top of her comforter and closed her eyes, grateful she could lie down and feel safe. Grant's scent still lingered on the pillow beside her and she hugged it to her chest, remembering how wonderful it had felt having him next to her all night. He'd been protective and understanding and he hadn't asked for anything, hadn't pushed her to make love. Part of her wanted the intimacy, but part of her was still afraid.

Of what? Of Grant?

Guilt suffused her for her lack of trust. This morning she'd reacted terribly when he'd started reminiscing.

She should have let him talk, allowed him to share the past. One of the stories might trigger her memory. But it had all been too much, what with the threats, the amnesia, the new feelings she had for her stranger husband. She closed her eyes and tried to imagine the events he'd talked about, their wedding, the night in the mountains, being snowed in, but soon the fatigue of the day drew her into blissful sleep.

Sometime later she jerked awake, a strange sensation overwhelming her. Outside the sun had faded and darkness shrouded the room. She listened for Carly, for Martha, for the familiar family sounds, but only silence greeted her. She must have slept longer than she'd intended. Dragging herself up, she reached for the lamp and flicked it on, but nothing happened. The bulb must have burned out.

Feeling jittery, she moved away from the bed, groping for the doorway, wanting to find Carly. She ran her hand along the wall and made her way into the hall, a streak of musty air teasing her neck and sending prickles down her spine. Panic arose in her, but she ordered herself to relax. She'd find a light in a minute and everything would be fine. Taking a calming breath, she pressed her hand on the wall for the light switch, but missed it completely and felt the stair railing at her fingertips. ''Carly, I'm coming. Martha, are you still here?''

Suddenly someone pushed her from behind and she stumbled, flailing her arms for control. Her foot hit the edge of the step and her injured leg gave way. She screamed as she lost her balance and went tumbling down the steps.

DETERMINED TO RIGHT THINGS with Emma, Grant pulled into the drive, his heartbeat accelerating when he noticed the guard was nowhere in sight. He jerked the door open and ran up the drive, storming into the entryway. Then he spotted Emma, lying on the floor, the guard kneeling over her. Martha rushed in from the back of the house, looking down in horror, Carly cuddled in her arms.

"Emma!" He raced over and dropped down beside her, his heart pounding when her eyes flickered open. "Oh, my God, are you all right?"

She nodded weakly, her pupils dilated. "Sweetheart, talk to me. Where are you hurt?"

"I'm okay," Emma whispered faintly. "I fell down the stairs."

He squeezed her hand, glancing at the guard. "What the hell happened?"

"I don't know, sir," the young man said, his face alarmed. "I heard a scream, then tried to get in, but the door was locked. So I jimmied the window on the side, came in and found your wife lying here."

Emma squinted at him in confusion. "Carly? Where is she, and Martha?"

"They're here," Grant assured her. "They're fine."

Martha slowly approached them, Carly wedged tightly in her arms. "Carly and I just got back from our walk. I came in the back door," Martha said.

"Ma'am, do you need me to call an ambulance?" the officer asked Emma.

She shook her head and tried to sit, wincing. "No, I'm fine."

"You don't look fine," Grant said. "I think we should have you checked over by a doctor."

"No." Emma accepted Grant's arm and pulled herself to a sitting position.

''Go slow now, take it easy, ma'am,'' the guard said. ''In case you get dizzy.''

Grant ran his hands over her face, her hair, down her sides, checking for injuries. ''Are you sure you're okay, Emma? I don't want us to take any chances.''

''I'm fine, Grant, really.'' Emma squeezed his hand. ''Just bruised.''

He nodded, his throat tight as he helped her to the sofa. ''What happened?'' He propped her leg on the ottoman, then knelt beside her.

She steadied her gaze on Grant. ''I woke up and it was dark. Something didn't feel right.'' She shivered. ''The room felt cold and too quiet, and the light on the nightstand was burned out. I wanted to see Carly so I went into the hallway…then someone pushed me.''

The blood drained from Grant's face. ''What?''

Martha gasped. ''Someone was in the house?''

''Are you sure, ma'am?'' the officer asked. ''I've been outside the whole time and I didn't see anyone come in.''

Emma's face crumpled. ''I know someone pushed me. I felt it.''

''I'll search the house and the outer premises. You guys stay here.''

Grant curved his arm around Emma while the officer hurried away. ''Shh, sweetheart, it's okay.''

A few minutes later the guard returned, clearly puzzled. ''Everything looks secure. I don't know how anyone could have gotten in.''

''What about the security system?'' Grant asked.

Martha cleared her throat. ''I'm afraid I turned it off when I left for our walk.'' Her voice quivered and she seemed visibly shaken. ''And I forgot to turn it back on. I'm so sorry.''

''It's okay,'' Grant said. ''What about the back door?''

''It was locked when Carly and I got back from our walk,'' Martha said, holding up her key. ''I wouldn't have gone off and left Emma without locking all the doors.'' Carly began to fuss and Martha took her away.

''Ma'am, maybe you *thought* you felt a push,'' the guard suggested to Emma. ''People get skittish in the dark, especially with everything else going on. Then you got nervous and slipped.''

Grant gave him an angry look, then asked him to leave the two of them alone. When the guard went back out to his car, Emma reached for Grant's hand, rubbing it for warmth. ''I know someone pushed me, Grant. I just know it.'' She pressed her hand to her temple, massaging her head. ''I'm not going crazy, am I?''

''No, of course not,'' Grant said, wondering if the stress could be getting to her. But one look at the fear in Emma's eyes and he didn't think she was imagining things. ''I'm sorry I wasn't here.'' Guilt once again assailed him as he brought her hand to his mouth and kissed her fingers. ''I'm so sorry, Emma. I shouldn't have left earlier. I had no right to get angry with you....''

She cupped his face in her hands. ''No, you've been wonderful, Grant. It's not your fault.'' A faint smile curved her lips. ''You don't understand. I get so upset because I want so badly to remember and I feel like I'm failing you when I can't.''

He sighed and shook his head. ''Sweetheart, I'm the one who's failing you. You don't know how helpless I felt when I saw them pull you from the wreckage. And then later in the hospital...'' His voice trembled and he bowed his head. ''I thought I was going to lose you. I thought Carly and I would have to go on without you and I…wasn't sure I could.''

''I'm sorry, Grant,'' Emma whispered, squeezing his hand. ''I wish this would all end. I keep hoping I'll wake up and remember, not be afraid anymore.''

''I don't want you to be afraid, not ever again,'' Grant said, his voice rough as he lowered his mouth to hers. She parted her lips, her shaky sigh an invitation, a declaration of her need. He drove his mouth over hers, plundering the warm recesses of her mouth with his tongue. Too long denied, he felt his control shatter. His hands groped around her, surging up her back, along her spine, pulling her tightly into his embrace. Her hands shook as they clutched his shoulders, but she kissed him back eagerly, her desire and passion as strong as his. Their hot breaths mingled, stoking the fire already burning between them. He swelled with arousal, aching with need. He cupped her breast and tasted the salty sweetness of the skin at her neck with his tongue. His urgency grew to a painful point from which he wasn't sure he could return.

One kiss led to another, their hands touched and comforted, their sighs and moans an expression of their pent-up needs, then he lowered his hand and caressed her thigh. Grant felt her sudden withdrawal. It was almost more than he could take.

''I can't,'' Emma whispered.

He remembered that Martha was still upstairs with Carly. ''Maybe later tonight, Emma. We can be together. I can hold you and show you how much I love you, how much I want you.'' His hand once again skated along her injured thigh, he hoped to soothe her, to assure her he wanted her. ''I want to take off your clothes, look at every inch of you to know you're still here, then make love to you until you're never afraid again, until you know in your heart we're meant to be together.''

But the tension in her face answered him before she could even reply. He hugged her, telling himself to be grateful she was still alive.

SHE WAS FALLING IN LOVE with Grant, Emma realized the next day. She had been ever since she'd come home from the hospital. A tear seeped from her eyes as she entered the doctor's building. Kate had driven her here, and Martha would pick her up. Martha was going shopping with her daughter for baby clothes and furniture today. Another memory lost to her, Emma thought sadly.

Last night had been another strained night, even more so after she'd stopped their lovemaking. Grant left her alone on the couch, his disappointment weaving through her like a thread of despair. She wanted him, wanted to feel him inside her, his love and passion making her whole. But the minute he'd touched her leg, an image of the jagged skin flashed before her eyes, and she'd panicked. Would he still love her? Would he still want her so passionately when he saw her scars?

She brushed at the tears, deciding she had to gain control of her life. And to do that she needed to face her fears. She prayed the police would find out who was harassing her soon. For she had to know if she was ever going to get her memory back.

She felt a moment's regret for not telling Grant about today's visit, but she needed to face the doctor and his diagnosis alone.

Five minutes later she was seated in Dr. Jacobs's office, her hands knotted as she waited. When he walked in, his serious gray eyes sent dread mushrooming inside her. He took several minutes preparing her X rays.

"I went over and over the tests we ran," he said, his tone steady, his intent gaze resting on her face.

"And?" Emma asked, unable to assimilate any more words.

He positioned his glasses on the end of his nose and shook his head. "I'm afraid the news isn't good, Emma. I'll show you what we found."

"I don't want to look at the X rays, Dr. Jacobs. I just want to know if my amnesia is permanent or due to psychological trauma."

In spite of her announcement that she didn't want to see the X rays, he pointed to them. "You see this section of the brain. It houses memory cells." He peered at her over his glasses and she nodded. "I'm afraid this section was damaged in the accident. The swelling has almost subsided, but there's this tiny area that...well, sustained permanent injury."

"So the amnesia isn't a result of emotional trauma?"

"No."

Emma let out a deep breath. "And I'm not going to remember my past? Not even with hypnosis?"

"I'm afraid not, Emma." He made a sympathetic sound. "Cases like yours are rare, but it happens. The physical damage you incurred in the accident was simply too much."

"You can't do surgery?"

"No, I'm afraid it wouldn't help."

Emma felt as if a vacuum had sucked the air from her lungs. Her mind reeled. Grant was so full of memories, had admitted he wanted her to remember. How could she tell him she never would?

Chapter Eleven

Grant prayed he would fall asleep, wake up and find that Emma's memory had returned. For the first time in his life the projects sitting untouched on his desk didn't spark his creativity or pump his adrenaline the way they normally did. He had three weeks to complete the scale model for the Little Raleigh project; he'd shaken hands with Bronson on the agreement. And his boss had arranged a final meeting with the president of Comp. Link for the Paris deal. The only emotion Grant could summon was apathy.

He toyed with a stack of miniature wooden pieces he used for designing the models, stacking them one on top of the other, but he was so frustrated his hand was shaking and they all came tumbling down. Just like his life was tumbling down around him. He stared at the strewn mass of sticks. He was simply biding time until Emma's amnesia and the threats were gone, so life could return to normal. He would take Emma and Carly on a family vacation, he decided. He and Emma would snuggle and cuddle while Carly napped and he'd make up for all the time they'd lost. He'd wine and dine her and make her fall in love with him again. He forced a smile and picked up the scattered sticks. Yeah, he had to think positively. Soon this nightmare would be over and he'd have Emma back, exactly like before. As soon as she regained her memory.

SHE WAS GOING to win Grant's love again, Emma decided. And she would start tonight.

She'd thought the news about her amnesia would upset her, and it had. Dr. Jacobs had suggested a counselor, and she'd agreed to give the woman a call. Then, uncaring that Martha and Carly were in the car with her, she'd cried the entire way home. Cried for Carly, for herself, for Grant.

She'd also realized in despair that she couldn't help the police find the person who'd caused her accident.

But with the news came a certain sense of peace. It was time to move on with her life. Thinking about the way Grant had cared for her over the past few weeks, she realized she wanted to be with him, to reestablish the bond they had once shared. She wanted to make their marriage real.

Tired of feeling out of control, she called Kate to baby-sit. Emma smiled as she hung up. Her relationship with Grant might be better after tonight. She immersed herself in a hot bubble bath scented with a jasmine fragrance, and soaked until her sore muscles felt languid. After her bath, she applied jasmine lotion to her legs, wincing at the puckered red flesh of her scar. When the doorbell rang, she hurriedly donned a long green robe. Martha stood at the door, signing for a package.

''This came for you, Emma,'' Martha said, carrying a big white box tied with a red ribbon to the dining table. ''It's from that fancy department store in town.'' Carly cooed from her swing, waving her hands, and

Emma paused to talk to her for a minute, her heart warming when Carly giggled at her.

"I wonder who it's from," Emma said, searching for a card. She had a moment's hesitation when she remembered the last box she'd received. Maybe she should call the police. Then she noticed the card. It read: *Wear this for me tonight. Love, Grant.*

Breathing a sigh of relief, she smiled at Carly. "Daddy sent me a present, sweetheart. Isn't that sweet of him?"

"He's a thoughtful man," Martha agreed.

Emma opened the box and gasped in surprise. "Oh, my goodness, it's beautiful!" She gently lifted the red satiny evening dress by its spaghetti straps. Both elegant and sexy, it had a low-cut neckline and beaded bodice, and was narrow enough to hug the hips and short enough to hang a few inches above her knees. She instantly imagined Grant picking it out for her. What had he been thinking when he'd chosen it? Was he planning a romantic evening for the two of them?

"It's lovely, dear," Martha said. "I'm sure you'll look nice in it."

"So, what do you think, Carly?" Emma asked, holding the dress up to the light. Carly cooed, her eyes sparkling as she watched the sequins shimmer.

Maybe Grant felt as badly as she did about last night, Emma thought. Perhaps he had reconciliation in mind, too. And maybe if she could overcome her insecurity about this scar, he wouldn't be staying in the guest room tonight. He'd be sleeping with her.

GRANT ENTERED THE HOUSE, determined to control his baser instincts and win Emma's trust and love. The minute he saw her sitting in the den holding Carly, his heart clutched.

"Hi," he said, approaching her slowly.

"Hi." Emma gestured toward Carly. "She's finishing her bottle. She tried some peaches earlier and loved them."

Carly batted her hand at the bottle as if she wanted to hold it and they both laughed, easing the tension. She wondered if he was going to mention the dress and decided not to bring it up. He was probably waiting to see if she'd wear it.

The phone rang, charging the air with renewed tension. Was it the threatening caller again? As Grant reached for it, Emma watched his face twist into a frown. When he hung up, he dropped onto the sofa with a loud sigh.

"What's wrong?" Emma asked, propping Carly against her shoulder and patting her back.

"That was Detective Warner. He said he's reached a dead end with the investigation, although they think the voice on the tape might be a woman."

Emma bit her lip in frustration.

"He had this theory about Pete, the guy I work with whose wife died. Pete drives a black Jeep, wants my promotion, and he recently lost his family. Warner thought Pete might have gone off the deep end, but Pete has an alibi for the night of your accident. And the paint samples on his Jeep don't match the ones found on your car."

"I see," Emma said, wishing the call had cleared everything up, instead of leaving more questions in its wake.

"Your boss, Dan, is clean, too. Hasn't had so much as a traffic ticket in the past four years." Grant propped his elbows on his knees and leaned forward, angling his face toward her. The urge to reach out and smooth away the worry lines around his eyes seized her by surprise. "Warner got the scoop on McGuire's arrest record—Dan was set up by the guy he was working for. McGuire was so naive he didn't realize the guy was using him to fence stolen goods until he saw his boss fudging the paperwork one day. When he caught on, his employer threatened Dan so he wouldn't tell, but he went to the police, anyway. His boss tried to frame him for the theft, but eventually the cops got to the bottom of it."

"I'm glad to hear he's legitimate," Emma said. "Especially since he's interested in Kate."

Grant nodded and stared at the floor, his mood dark. "But that means the police are back to square one."

Emma fought the helplessness, trying to focus on her earlier plans. Now that she'd stopped trying to force her memory, she saw the effect the stress was having on Grant. His face looked hollow and tired, he had dark circles beneath his eyes, and his whole body radiated with tension.

She stroked the ends of Grant's hair where it curled up around his collar. Startled, he swung his head around toward her again, his eyes wary. She smiled gently and traced her finger along his shoulder. "I know this is rough on you, Grant. You look exhausted."

"It doesn't matter," he said. "I just want you to be safe."

"I feel safe when I'm with you," Emma said softly.

Some emotion flickered in the depths of his eyes, guilt, concern, desire.

"I asked Kate to baby-sit tonight. I thought maybe the two of us could go out to dinner."

His eyes widened, the dark lashes fluttering up in

surprise. Had he forgotten about sending the dress and the note?

"You'd leave Carly with a sitter and go out with me?"

Emma nodded, touched by the wonder in his voice. "Of course I would. Why do you ask?"

He shook his head. "You were a little nervous about it before."

Emma smiled gently. "Are you saying I was one of those overprotective first-time mothers?"

A sexy smile lifted the left corner of his mouth, the irises of his eyes twinkling. "Yeah, something like that."

"Well, tonight I want to be with you." Emma's tone was more serious now.

"I'd like that," he finally said. Heat, dangerous, exciting and potent, darkened his eyes to purple. Then he ran a hand through his hair and stood. "Let me grab a shower."

"I have to change, too." Emma gestured at the baby food dotting her robe. "I knew better than to dress before I fed Carly."

Grant smiled, seemingly relieved at her attempt to lighten the mood. Then they both headed to their separate rooms to get ready for the night.

MAYBE SHE WAS REMEMBERING their love, Grant thought as he splashed aftershave on his face. And maybe tonight the two of them would make progress in their relationship. He buttoned his white Armani shirt and pulled on gray dress slacks, ordering himself not to get his hopes up. At least an evening out would be a change, maybe a beginning. And at least Emma seemed to be trying. How long had it been since they'd been out to dinner alone? He sighed. Too long. Since before Carly was born.

Way too long, he decided, as he opened the bedroom door and saw Emma standing in the middle of the den. A shimmering short red dress hugged slender curves and dipped precariously low at the neck to reveal a hint of cleavage. His breath caught in his chest. She was beautiful. Absolutely beautiful.

She'd brushed her shoulder-length golden hair until it shone. The diamond earrings he'd given her for their first anniversary dangled from her delicate ears. The thin straps revealed the creamy texture of her skin. Dark hose encased her long legs and dragged his gaze upward to the hem of the dress. Was she wearing a garter belt? His arousal was swift, and he itched to touch her, to hold her in his arms and slide those tiny straps down so he could kiss the skin at the base of her neck and then below.

But when she turned to face him and the light caught the twinkle of red satin, a strange horrible feeling engulfed him. Like déjà vu, a vision of another young woman wearing a shiny sequined red dress with spaghetti straps flashed into his head. *Faye.* He instantly saw her face, the tears streaking her cheeks at the homecoming party, the way she'd held her hand over her stomach when she'd told him about her pregnancy, her chest heaving with sobs. Then later, lying on the wet ground with blood dotting her face, splattered all over the red dress, the material ripped and smattered with mud and weeds... His hands started to shake and bile rose in his throat. Where had Emma gotten the dress? Had she gone shopping today? And why had she chosen red? She normally chose black or blue or green, darker, less flashy colors.

"Grant, don't you like the way it fits?" she asked, her brow furrowing.

"What?"

She gestured at the dress and swirled around as gracefully as possible, wincing only slightly with her injury. "I said, don't you like the way it fits?"

He shook his head. "Where did you get that dress?"

Her eyes widened in confusion. "What do you mean? You sent it to me this afternoon." She pointed to a white box on the floor in the dining room. "It arrived around five."

Shock jolted him into action and he closed the distance between them, taking her hand in his. "Emma, I didn't send you that dress." Nausea gripped his stomach, wrenching through him. The blood, red like the dress, was everywhere, underneath Faye's fingernails, on her silky hose... He shook his head in an effort to clear his mind of the images. "You have to take it off. Now." He gripped her hand, his voice urgent. "It's... just like the one that girl from my college was wearing the night she died. I'm calling Warner."

A horrified gasp escaped Emma's mouth, the color draining from her face. He started to reach for the zipper to jerk the dress off but caught himself when he saw her tremble. Then she reached for the zipper, frantically tugging at it, and his stomach roiled. He gently held her hands and turned her around, then slid the zipper down, his breath catching at the sight of her smooth back. Another shudder rippled through him as she walked slowly to the bedroom, the tension once again winding through the room and destroying their hopes and plans. He heaved an angry sigh. Damn whoever was doing this to him. And to Emma.

He picked up the phone, his mind reeling with bits

and pieces of the past few weeks as he tried to make some connection. The car accident—Faye had died in a car wreck. The dead roses—Faye had a blanket of roses on her casket at her funeral. The messages, now the red dress…

Whoever was threatening Emma must have known Faye Simmons. The person obviously blamed him for Faye's death, just as he'd blamed himself. But this person was crazy; he or she had actually bought a dress similar to Faye's and sent it to Emma, saying it was from him. Why did this lunatic want to hurt Emma?

Warner's voice sounded on the line just as the twisted logic hit him. Revenge—the lunatic intended to kill Emma to get back at *him.*

EMMA STUMBLED out of the dress, a shiver tearing through her. Someone had sent her the dress as a reminder of another woman's bloodshed. The realization repulsed her. Her hands shaking, she fumbled through her closet searching for another outfit, wondering if Grant still wanted to go out, wondering if *she* still wanted to. Would they be able to salvage the evening after this chilling incident?

She'd planned to have a nice dinner with Grant and subtly work up to telling him the truth about her amnesia. But he'd looked so shocked, so utterly appalled at the memory of the dead woman, she wasn't sure he could take bad news on top of it.

She spotted a sapphire-blue silk dress that reminded her of Grant's eyes and pulled it from the closet. It was sleek and sophisticated with a square neck trimmed in silver beads. Simple but elegant. Actually much more appealing to her than the red dress had been.

She gritted her teeth and slipped the dress over her

head, determination filling her. She was not going to let this crazy person destroy her life. At least not without a fight. She surveyed her reflection in the mirror, touched up her hair and went to find her husband. Even if he wasn't in the mood for dinner, she'd insist they go out. Then she would make him forget the horror of their situation and focus on the bright side. She was still alive and getting stronger every day, and memory or not, they still had each other. That is, if he still wanted her when he learned her memory loss was permanent.

ON THE WAY to the restaurant Grant tried to shake his black mood. But Warner's words kept haunting him, and he needed to be honest with Emma. "Warner took the box and dress to check for fingerprints," he said. "He thinks if he can trace the dress to where it was bought, it might lead us somewhere. The salesperson might even remember who bought it, then this whole mess could be over."

"I hope so." Emma wound her purse strap around her hand.

"He also agrees with me that whoever's doing this must have known Faye Simmons." Grant ran the fingers of his free hand through his hair, guilt weighing heavily on his shoulders. "Maybe someone who blames me for her death and is trying to punish me by hurting you."

"But you didn't have anything to do with her death," Emma argued. She reached for his hand and covered it with hers, making Grant's heart pump with renewed fervor. This was the second time tonight she'd actually made a move to touch him; she wasn't shrinking away from him anymore. "And I still don't see a connection," she said, her voice low. "Like you said, it's been over five years since she died. Why come after you now?''

''I don't know,'' Grant said, stumped. ''I really don't, Emma. But Warner's going to cross-check all the people I knew in college, including the kids at the party that night with the people we know now. Maybe something will click.''

Emma nodded, growing quiet. He put their favorite Bob Seger CD in the player and tried to relax as Seger's husky voice began to sing Emma's favorite, ''We've Got Tonight.'' As the music played, Emma's tension seemed to dissipate slightly. And when they reached the restaurant, she graced him with one of her heart-stopping smiles as he offered her his arm and led her inside.

''When did you make the reservation?'' Grant asked as a waiter escorted them to a candlelit lace-draped table in a corner facing a cozy fireplace.

''Earlier today,'' Emma replied.

The soft flowery scent of Emma's bath oil sent his senses sizzling. ''J. Bones was our favorite place,'' Grant said, a twinge of hope resurging. ''We came here for our anniversary. We even spent the night in the hotel here.''

Emma smiled and took her seat. ''It's beautiful. I've been thinking about a filet all afternoon.''

She always ordered the filet. He grinned, trying to forget about the earlier incident. Maybe this place, this luxurious restaurant and upscale hotel where they had spent a titillating anniversary night, would be the place that would bring back her memory.

''You look beautiful,'' he said, his gaze scanning the dress she'd changed into. ''That's one of my favorite dresses. You said you bought it because it reminded you of my eyes. You were wearing it the night I proposed.''

He thought he heard Emma's breath hitch, and he wondered if his obsession with their past history was going to upset her again. ''I'm sorry, Emma, I know you don't want to hear—''

''Shh, it's okay,'' she said softly. ''We have a past together, Grant, and it's not fair to not allow you to talk about it. I want you to relax tonight. We both need a break from all the tension lately.''

He smiled with relief. ''I want that, too, more than you know.''

Her eyelashes fluttered almost flirtatiously, and his senses came alive, awareness, need, hunger ignited, all strumming through the air, reminding him again of the Bog Seger melody they'd heard in the car. They ordered wine and steaks and let the conversation drift to inane things—music and movies and things they'd talked about when they'd dated.

In a way it was like their first date, Grant thought, wishing he'd brought her flowers or candy or something romantic.

''Elton John's coming to Atlanta in May,'' he said. ''I was thinking of getting us tickets if you'd like.''

''I'd love to see Elton John,'' Emma said. ''I know he doesn't dress as wildly as he used to, but his music is still great.''

Grant hesitated, not wanting to spoil the moment, but he had to be honest with her. ''We saw him at UNC when you came up one weekend. It was our first date.''

Her smile faded slightly, but he threaded his fingers through hers. ''We'll go and pretend it's our first date again, okay.''

She smiled at his effort and the ice seemed to be

broken. They sipped their wine and enjoyed the perfectly prepared steaks, their conversation less of a struggle as the evening wore on. "How about cherries jubilee for dessert," he suggested. "It's steeped in rum and they serve it flambé."

"Sounds wonderful." Emma glanced at the dance floor as the band began to play a litany of soft classic rock.

"I can see why we came here," Emma said. "This place has a wonderful atmosphere."

A woman carrying a basket of flowers wove through the tables, and Grant motioned for her to stop. He pulled out a couple of bills. "I'd like a white carnation."

He handed it to Emma, and her eyes sparkled with pleasure. "I know these past few weeks have been difficult for you, Grant. And I appreciate how wonderful you've been."

He swallowed, the guilt thick in his throat. "God, Emma, don't thank me. You wouldn't have been hurt in the first place if it wasn't for me." He tucked the flower in her hair and caressed her cheek with the pad of his thumb. Emma leaned into his hand.

"Don't blame yourself," she said softly. "It isn't your fault, Grant."

He shook his head, his voice lost in the turmoil in his head. After the last incident he couldn't escape the truth. He knew it *was* his fault, but Emma squeezed his hand and he remembered they'd decided to enjoy the night, so he sipped his wine, then brought her hand to his mouth and kissed it.

"You look lovely tonight, Emma. I appreciate the fact that you made the reservations here."

"I told you I wanted to be with you." Her gaze of approval flicked over him, sending shards of wicked sensations through his body. It had been so long since he'd been with her, since he'd held and poured his love into her body, that he wondered if he was mistaking the gleam of sexual interest in her eyes for love. Maybe she was starting to have feelings for him. Or remembering the old ones…

The waiter came with their dessert, a showcase of flaming cherries in a syrupy rich sauce with whipped cream. He placed it between them, making a show of extinguishing the flame. The dessert was meant to be shared. Grant dug into the whipped cream with his spoon, then lifted it to her mouth, teasing her with the pillowy white concoction. Then she treated him to cherries covered in tangy rum sauce, licking her lips as she watched him savor the sweet heady flavors.

Her eyes glowed with appreciation for the dessert, and his were mesmerized by the soft tilt of her chin, the slight curve of her button nose, the glowing cheeks that dimpled every time she smiled. He'd almost forgotten what it was like to see her happy and free of worry. When the last bite of cherries sat temptingly on the plate, she scooped it up and he bit off the end, his tongue lapping at the syrup. He imagined dribbling the cherry juice over her naked body and licking it off. Her breath hitched as if she'd read his mind, then a tiny subtle moan of desire erupted from her throat that flamed his body with raw desire. He turned the spoon and she licked the syrup off after him, her slitted dark gaze pinned to his mouth. Heat raced through him, and her brown eyes darkened to black pools he felt himself drowning in.

A soothing love song drifted from the piano and he held out his hand. "Would you like to dance?"

She hesitated and he remembered her injured leg.

"You can lean on me, Emma," he said quietly.

The vulnerability shadowing her eyes eased slightly and she nodded. He led her to the dance floor and she practically glided into his arms, as if she'd always been there, as if she always would be. He wrapped his arm around her waist and pulled her against him, sucking in a breath of her jasmine fragrance, elated at the way she fit perfectly into his hungry embrace. He guided her around the dance floor, their bodies swaying slowly in perfect time to the piano, the heat between them swirling into a fire. She lay her head against his chest, and he was sure she heard his heart pounding with hunger, his blood sizzling through his veins. When she nuzzled into his embrace, he thought he was going to explode with want.

But he held his libido in check and simply stroked her back, the curve of her waist. He whispered sweet nonsense words at the nape of her neck, reveling in the tiny shiver that rippled through her when he kissed the sensitive spot behind her ear. Her body brushed against his, her hands massaged his arms, found their way to his hairline, where she toyed with the strands, her tentative touches like scorching coals to his cold and lonely soul.

By the time the song mellowed and the next one began, he was so tormented with lust and want he thought he wasn't going to be able to walk back to the table. Then Emma leaned up and kissed his cheek, and after all they'd been through, the sweetness of her trust nearly brought him to his knees.

The music drifted into an instrumental, and he felt her pull slightly away and look into his eyes. "I...I booked us a room," she said so low he almost didn't hear her.

"You what?" He searched her face.

"I want us to be together tonight, Grant, but—"

He heard the slight quaver in her voice and his heart pounded. "But what?" Her chin trembled just the tiniest bit and his gut clenched. He wanted her so badly he thought he'd explode. "I'm not pushing you, sweetheart. I can wait—"

She pressed her finger to his lips. "I know you're not pushing me, but I want to be with you." Her voice dropped to a strained whisper. "But I have scars now, Grant." She lowered her head. "I'm not the same. My leg—"

He crushed her to him and closed his eyes, the sound of her uncertainty slicing into him like a razor. "Don't you know it doesn't matter?" he said in a voice so rough with emotion he was afraid she didn't catch the words.

But she must have because he saw tears fill her eyes. "It's the reason...I stopped you the last time," she whispered. "It's not pretty, Grant, the skin is red and—"

He silenced her with a gentle kiss, shame hitting him hard for not realizing before the reason for her reservations. He cupped her face in his hands, vaguely aware the music had stopped playing and they were still in the middle of the dance floor, swaying and hugging one another, their bodies mating in the rhythm of a seductive slow dance. "You are the most beautiful woman I've ever known, Emma, and you always will be. You're my wife, and I love you. Don't you know by now how much you mean to me?"

A tear slid down her cheek and he caught it with his lips. "Don't cry, sweetheart. I love you and nothing, I mean *nothing,* can change that. Especially not a scar."

She pulled back and looked into his eyes. "I don't want to disappoint you, Grant."

He chuckled, a husky sound filled with desire. "Honey, I know you don't want me to tell you about the past, but if you could remember how shamelessly I chased you, you'd know you couldn't disappoint me. Not ever."

"But it's different now," Emma murmured. "I'm different."

He cupped her face in his hands. "No, you're the same woman I begged to go out with me, the same one I actually serenaded in front of the dorm..."

"You serenaded me?" she asked, her lips quirking into a tentative smile.

He nodded. "I sang that Seger song to you. The guys in the dorm laughed their heads off."

"Tell me what else you did," she said, the dim light softening the shadows beneath her eyes.

"I used to play soccer on an intramural team." He ran his hand down to her waist, pulling her into him as they swayed to the strains of an Eric Clapton melody. "Later you came to spend the weekend with Kate. It was my big chance to impress you, only I sprained my ankle at the beginning of the game—"

"And you didn't get to play?"

He chuckled again. "No, I played all right. You'd just gotten there, so I wouldn't let them take me out."

"You played the game knowing you had a sprained ankle to impress me?"

"Actually I found out later it was fractured. I was on crutches for three weeks."

Emma threaded her fingers into the tips of his thick hair. "That's really romantic, Grant."

"It was really dumb, but it should tell you how much I wanted you then."

She grew silent, her expression once again worried, but she held him more tightly. He felt a sense of longing so deep it hurt.

"But it was nothing compared to how much I want you now, Emma. Or how much I love you." He brought her hands to his chest as he'd done before. "At the hospital I told you that you might not remember me in your head, but you'd always be in my heart, didn't I?"

She nodded, smiling slowly, then he curved his arm around her and she leaned into him as they walked slowly back to the table. He signed for the check, she retrieved her purse, and they barely made it to the hotel room before he lowered his head and took her mouth with all the urgency he had penned up inside. Before the night ended, she was going to know how strong his love was, and she would be his wife again, in every sense of the word.

EMMA LET HER HEAD drop back as Grant took possession of her, body, mind and soul. His kisses sent her into bliss, his hands caressed and loved and stoked her fire, his hunger a need she wanted to fill, again and again and again. In the far recesses of her mind, a tiny voice said she should have told him about her permanent memory loss, but the raw heat burning between them consumed her logic and the splendor of his lovemaking doused her worries. There would be time for talk later. After she'd sated his desire.

And hers.

She tore at his clothes, hungry to feel his bare chest with her fingers, and reveled in the way he caressed her breasts through her clothes. His hands cupped her bottom, pulling her into his arousal, and she felt him hard and hot and boldly pushing against her. She cradled him in her thighs and he moaned, sliding his hands up to remove her dress. She raised her arms, closing her eyes when he tossed the satin to the floor, and she felt his hands and mouth touching her bare shoulder and neck.

"You're so lovely," he said. "Look at me. Emma. I want you to see how much I love you."

She opened her eyes and saw him feasting on her with his eyes, devouring every inch of her with his hot wanton looks, and she suddenly felt wanton and wicked and beautiful. He cupped her breasts over the lacy blue bra and then, with a flick of his fingers, unsnapped the front clasp and sent the bra falling to the floor. Her small round breasts ached for him, her nipples hardened to twin peaks of need. A sexy smile of self-satisfaction lit his handsome face. "You do want me, don't you, Emma?"

She nodded, moved beyond reason.

He touched her nipples with his thumbs, slowly rotating the peaks until she moaned. "Say it," he whispered. Then he licked his finger and brought it back to one nipple, teasing it mercilessly.

She gasped. "I want you, Grant."

His breath hissed out, a guttural sound of male want that sent chills skating over her body. Then he brought his mouth to her nipple and licked, first one, then the other, until her belly burned with arousal and her legs quivered. He braced her back with his hand and dipped his head to suckle the tips, making loud sweet hungry sounds that made her swell with need. Then he rained kisses up and down her abdomen, his tongue flickering at the edges of her garter, nipping at the seam of her panties near her heat, then dove beneath the edges to tease her inner thighs. One finger slid inside her, tormenting her with long slow strokes, and her legs gave way, tremors of passion rocking through her.

He scooped her into his arms, tore off her garter and hose, then shucked his slacks and briefs in one quick motion. He was strong, his bronzed body a picture of virility, like a Roman soldier bared for the trusting eyes of his woman, and she reached out to draw him near. She threaded her fingers through his hair, then found him with her hands and nearly came apart in his arms when she felt his hot flesh swell in her hands.

''Emma, I don't know how long I can last,'' he whispered in a rough voice. ''And you're so ready.''

She cupped his buttocks and dug her fingernails into his skin, pulling him closer. ''I know, Grant. I need you.''

He lowered his head, pushed her thighs apart and tasted her with his tongue, the sweet wonderful sounds of hunger he whispered making her convulse with pleasure. Then he rose above her, teasing her softness with the strength of his manhood. She groaned and felt the fine tremors of satisfaction lapping at her.

''I love you, Emma.'' He lowered his mouth to hers, parted her lips with his tongue, tantalizing her breasts with his fingers, then slipped into her. He said what he wanted from her in such a husky lust-filled voice that the fiery sensations stirred within her middle. The fire rose to a crescendo, rocking through her with the most intense pleasure she could ever imagine. And just before she cried out his name and he came inside her, she told him she loved him.

Chapter Twelve

Making love to Emma once had only whetted his appetite for more. Like an imprisoned man suddenly set free, Grant felt exalted and so damn humble he didn't know what to say. She'd said she loved him. Whether she'd remembered any part of their past life or not, he didn't know. And he was afraid to ask, afraid to break the closeness their silent words of intimacy had forged.

They made love again and again during the night, and now with early-morning sunlight streaming through the lacy sheers and Emma lying in his arms, the soft weight of one breast in the palm of his hand, he didn't think he'd ever be completely sated. She murmured something unintelligible, her sleepy eyelids barely fluttering open as she reached for him and drew him into the erotic sanctity of her bosom. He lay in her embrace, his head nestled against her warm flesh. He stroked the delicate skin of her thighs, mentally wincing when he contacted the scar she'd been so reluctant to reveal to him.

Tenderness welled inside him, and he rained kisses in a fiery path down to her belly, the curve of her hip and over the puckered skin. He instantly felt her stiffen. Her hands dug into his hair and she pleaded with him to stop. "No, let me love you," he whispered. "I need you, Emma."

She whimpered, but he brought his hands up and covered her fingers with his, rubbing his tongue across her sensitive skin and flicking it lower until he tasted the heady sense of her need. She made a soft sound, half plea to stop, half plea to end the torture he'd only begun. But he took his time, loving her, letting her know with his intimate touches and his whispered words, with his fingers and his tongue, how erotic he found her body.

Her hips bucked upward as he drove his mouth against her, her sweet feminine scent spiraling through his nerve endings, exciting him into a hardness only she could fulfill. And when she cried out her release, her body quivering with passion, he rose to look at her. She was awake now, the pupils of her eyes soft and dazed with longing, and he smiled with a male satisfaction that swelled in his manhood. She tucked her bottom lip between her teeth as if embarrassed, and he instantly nipped at it with his mouth, plunging his tongue into her mouth, letting her taste her own desire and feed his. Her fingernails scraped his shoulders, her hands moved down his back to cup his buttocks. Finally one hand closed around him, and he couldn't stop the guttural groan that erupted from deep within him.

She smiled, her eyes raking over him as wickedly as his tongue had taken her body, then she pressed him over onto his back. He caught her hands and kissed her fingers, sucking on the tips as she lowered her head and flicked a tongue over his nipple. The ends of her silky hair tickled his chest and he sucked in a harsh breath, battling for control. Then she delved lower, into his navel, then lower still, until her tongue touched the tip of his manhood.

His legs quivered, his hips jerked up in primal response, and her breath whispered erotically against the juncture of his thighs. "Emma..."

"I told you earlier I wanted you," she said in a husky edgy voice that reminded him of the first time they'd made love. Then he lost all coherent thought as she buried her head against him and loved him with her tongue. Her hair whispered against his belly, her fingers teased the hair on his legs and groped his thighs, holding him still for her pleasure, and her heated sighs of passion turned him on as much as the act itself.

The warm wetness of her mouth cradling him inside, the flicker of her tongue, the sweet wantonness of her hunger almost drove him over the edge. And when he thought he would burst in mindless pleasure, she lifted her head and moved above him, straddling his thighs. He groaned as he filled her, saw her eyes mellow and close as she rotated her hips and took the full length of him. Unable to resist touching her breasts, he rolled her erect nipples with his fingers until she cried out and rocked herself harder and faster, accepting him thrust for thrust as she strained around him. He slid one finger down and stroked the sensitive nub between her legs, and she threw her head back and cried his name.

He bucked upward, filling her until she whimpered with pleasure, until he was lost inside her. Her body quivered again with the strength of her release, then she collapsed on top of him, her breathing erratic, the strands of her golden hair draping over his chest like silk.

HAD MAKING LOVE with Grant always been this cataclysmic? And emotional? With no memory to compare it to, it was as if this was their first time. Blinking back the moisture in her eyes, Emma stroked the dark hair on his chest, traced circles over his hard flat stomach, drinking in the heady scent of him and their lovemaking on his skin. If they'd had problems before their marriage, she was sure they could have used their lovemaking to solve them. She'd never known or even thought sex could be such a splendid experience, so totally enthralling that she could forget the dangers around her, but the past twelve hours had proved otherwise.

Only the bright slivers of sun washing the room brought her back to reality. She needed to tell Grant about her visit to the doctor. She hoped the intimacies they'd shared through the long soulful night would enable him to bear the news. For a fleeting second she contemplated lying, keeping the truth to herself. But that wasn't an option. Whether or not she remembered falling in love and marrying this man, she knew she was falling in love with him again. And she owed him the truth. They would deal with it together.

"Grant?" she whispered.

His reply was long in coming, and he turned toward her, nuzzling his morning beard against her cheek before he answered. "Yeah?" Even as he spoke, one large hand covered her breast, teasing her senses and momentarily making her forget what she wanted to say.

She ran her toe up and down his muscled calf. "That was wonderful."

His chuckle tickled her neck, the hairs on his chest brushing against her arm and side tantalizingly. "Baby, it was so good I don't know if I'm going to be able to walk for a while."

Emma smiled, secretly pleased to hear him sound so content. "Well, we could stay here until you're feeling better."

"If we stay here, I'm gonna love you again." He pulled her hand to show her how easily he could reach excitement again.

She swallowed, her own impulses rising in response. "Your body is heavenly."

He chuckled again and put his tongue in her ear. "And yours is like heaven and hell mixed together. Wonderful and fiery and hot and sinful at the same time."

Touched again by his bedroom voice, she turned and looped her arms around his neck. He slid his hands over her breasts, cupping her, then lower to her buttocks and pulled her into the cradle of his thighs, gently making circles on her hips with his fingers.

She looked at him. His blue eyes were gleaming, his smile was wicked and wonderful, and his hands danced erotically across her body. "I need to tell you something," she murmured, praying the time was right.

"Yeah, like we were meant for each other," he said.

Smiling, she wiggled her hips, a shiver rippling up her spine when he swelled and surged against her thigh. "I do think we were meant for each other," she said in a soft voice.

He stilled, the teasing in his expression mellowing as he studied her face. She realized she'd given him a flicker of hope and chided herself for her wording.

"Grant, I saw the doctor yesterday."

Tension tightened his muscles, then worry ripped the earlier contentment off his face completely. "Was it a checkup, or weren't you feeling well?"

"I asked him to run tests to find out if my memory

loss was permanent.'' She squeezed his shoulders, willing him not to pull away. ''I was going to try hypnosis if it was psychological.''

The look in his eyes frightened her almost as much as his silence. ''And?''

She kissed his cheek, then his lips with as much feeling as she could render without bursting into tears, then curled her hands into his hair. He still hadn't moved. She forced herself to look into his face and watch his reaction. ''He did X rays and showed them to me. He said it...the amnesia is physical. Hypnosis is out.''

The barest of nods was his only response. Emma exhaled shakily.

''So he'll do more tests later?''

The strained sound of his voice made her wind her legs around his, an unconscious move to keep him from bolting. ''He may, but he says most of the swelling around my brain has receded. He...'' She paused, begging him to understand. ''Grant, the news isn't good. He doesn't think I'll ever regain my memory.''

THE AMNESIA WAS permanent.

Grant's body fell slack as the realization sunk in. The arousal he'd had only moments earlier disintegrated, and his breath hissed out between clenched teeth that had dug into his jaw so hard he tasted blood.

The last twelve hours, the incredible lovemaking, Emma's initiative in making dinner and hotel reservations, her announcement of love—all had come on the heels of her discovery. Why? Because she felt sorry for him?

He searched her face, where the elation she'd felt earlier had transformed once again into concern. Had she made love to him out of some kind of pity? Or misplaced loyalty?

No, she said she loved him. But how could she when she didn't remember that love or anything about their past?

"Grant?"

The worry in her voice jerked him out of his jumbled thoughts, and he saw the questions haunting her eyes. "I'm sorry," she whispered. "I know it's not the news you wanted to hear, and I know how much you wanted my memory to return."

He realized he'd completely let go of her when her hands caught his and she squeezed his palms. "Please don't pull away," she urged in a pained voice. "What we shared last night was...was so wonderful, Grant. I know I don't remember our past, but—"

"You knew last night that you never would," he said, anguish lacing his voice.

Tears blinded her eyes and he could see the pity in them. "Yes, I knew," she said in a voice edged with sorrow.

"Why didn't you tell me then, Emma?" He jerked to a sitting position. Anger, despair and the reality of what he'd lost all converged on him, colliding with his worst fears. Emma would never remember their love, would never be able to feel the same about him as he did her, and without her memories how could she forgive him for causing this psycho to hurt her? Like sand slipping through an hourglass, he was losing the love of his life. And it was all his fault, because someone blamed him for Faye Simmons's death. "Did you go through all this...just to soften the blow?"

She drew back, pulling the covers up to her neck, covering the secrets of her body she'd given to him so wantonly only minutes earlier. He silently cursed himself for putting that hurt look on her face, but he didn't understand how she could have slept with him without telling him.

"I told you I wanted to be with you," she said, her voice quivering. "And I meant it, Grant."

Then she whipped the covers off the bed and stood, trembling, and looking so damn vulnerable his heart contracted. "See, I told you I was afraid I'd disappoint you. I guess I was right." Then she wrapped the covers around her tightly, rushed into the bathroom and slammed the door. He lowered his head and cradled it in the palms of his hands, the test results and the guilt over the danger around Emma all crashing down on him. He couldn't be upset with her; hell, it was his fault she'd been hurt, his fault she didn't remember him or their marriage or their baby, his fault he was losing her. Seconds later he heard the shower running and what he could only imagine was the sound of her crying, and he felt like the biggest heel in the world.

But how could they make their marriage work if his wife couldn't even remember saying their vows?

EMMA EMERGED from the bathroom, knowing her swollen eyes and blotchy cheeks were a testament to her emotional outpouring. She couldn't blame Grant for his reaction—she'd been in shock when she'd first heard the news about her amnesia—but after their night of passionate lovemaking, she'd hoped they could weather the truth together, not allow it to drive them apart.

He was completely dressed, holding his keys in his hands, his face a mask of remorse when he spotted her. "I'm sorry, Emma," he said in a voice so controlled she could tell it was painful. "I need some time to digest this."

She instantly remembered the way she'd gasped his name in the throes of ecstasy and couldn't meet his eyes. "We'd better go home and check on Carly," she said.

He nodded, his movements stiff and jerky and his comment about the sex being so good he'd be unable to walk flitted through her mind. Her hands itched to touch him, but she curled them around her purse straps. A muscle ticked in his jaw as he opened the door, and she wanted to throw him down and ravish him until he laughed and called her name in mindless ecstasy again and again, until he agreed that the past no longer mattered.

But he wore a solemn tight-lipped expression as he politely escorted her to the car, his flat gaze prolonging the agony as they climbed in and drove home. His silence was like a sword wedged between them, cutting through the trust and affection they'd built over the past few days.

And when she reached out for his hand as they walked up the driveway to their house, he silently pulled away. She felt like crying again. Somehow she had to make him see that it didn't matter if she remembered their love before, because she was in love with him now. And the future was all that mattered.

THE PAST TWENTY-FOUR hours had been hell, Grant decided when he got out of bed and showered the next morning. He hadn't been able to return to the guest room, but he hadn't been able to make love to Emma again, either. He'd waited until she fell asleep, then slid in beside her and listened to her breathing while he tried to figure out how to handle his emotions.

Frustrated, he dressed for work, wondering if he should call Martha or Kate to keep Emma company today so he could go to the office, instead of working at home. And he'd have to ask Warner for another guard for the house. Irritated, he headed to the kitchen to make coffee. But first he called Warner.

"Do you have any news?" Grant asked without preamble.

"We've looked at all the files on the Simmons case. Can't locate any of the girl's family. So far, the only people who went to school with you and live in this vicinity are your sister-in-law and that woman you work with, Priscilla." Warner clicked his teeth. "There was a guy named Billy Hogan, but he turned up dead a couple of months ago. Stabbed with a butcher knife."

"Someone else who knew Faye was killed?"

Warner cleared his throat. "He was found in his house. He and his wife had a reputation for fighting, so the police arrested her. But she's been saying she didn't do it, so I'm checking into it. Matter of fact, I'm on my way out the door right now to meet with her."

Grant hung up, the hair on the back of his neck standing on end as he considered the implications. Another person who'd known Faye in college had been murdered. Had Billy Hogan been one of Faye's boyfriends? Chilled to the bone, Grant went in search of coffee and found a steaming pot waiting on him, with a note from Emma.

"Carly and I have gone with Martha to the store. I thought maybe we could take Carly for a picnic if you have time today. I think some fresh air and family time would be good for all of us."

He crushed the note and sighed, grateful Martha had accompanied Emma and wishing a simple picnic would cure the problems in their marriage. He cursed himself for being so cynical. The doorbell cut into his thoughts and he went to answer it, suddenly jittery about Emma being out of the house. But Priscilla stood on the porch, her briefcase in her hand. ''Mind if I come in?'' she asked, shivering as a gust of wind ripped through the trees, rustling the leaves and scattering them across the lawn.

''Of course not.'' He gestured toward the foyer and watched as she shrugged out of her jacket, sweeping her red hair off her shoulder with her fingers. ''What's up, Priscilla? Didn't you get my message?''

''Yes,'' she said with a faint hint of disapproval. ''But I really think you should come into the office, Grant.''

''I've been getting my work done,'' he said defensively.

Priscilla's green eyes narrowed. ''Oh, honey, what's wrong? You're still mad because I forgot to tell you about picking up Emma.''

Grant shook his head, too many other problems crowding his mind.

Priscilla moved closer to him, one manicured finger lifted. ''You look like you haven't slept in days, Grant. Has something else happened?''

He shook his head again. ''I have a lot on my mind right now, Priscilla. Just give it a rest and let me focus on work.''

A sympathetic smile tugged at the corners of her ruby-red lips, then her fingernail tapped against his coffee cup. ''Why don't you pour me some coffee and tell me about it? Maybe I can help.''

"I don't think anyone can help," Grant muttered beneath his breath, too tired to play games with Priscilla. He didn't care about the promotion anymore. "But come on and I'll get you some coffee."

"Is Emma here?"

"No," Grant said, leading her to the kitchen. "There's no one here but me."

Priscilla squeezed his arm. "Then let's sit down and talk."

Grant took one look at the genuine concern on her face and lost his resolve. After all, now they knew Emma's amnesia was permanent, he'd have to tell the people at the office. He might as well start with Priscilla.

"YOU'RE AN ANGEL, Martha," Emma said as Martha lifted a sleeping Carly from the car seat and carried her to the house.

"I'll put her in her crib," Martha said, "then help you get that picnic ready."

Emma gave a smile, wondering if Martha could read its lackluster quality. A black Lexus coupe sat in the driveway. Opening the front door for Martha, she heard voices coming from the kitchen, so she tiptoed, careful not to disturb Grant in case he was dealing with a client. Even with the renewed tension between them, he'd insisted on working at home to protect her, and she refused to encroach on his business.

She heard a woman's voice and hesitated at the kitchen door, her stomach knotting when she heard the woman ask about her and Carly.

"So Emma's never going to remember you?" the woman asked, her voice sympathetic. "No wonder you've been so upset. What a terrible ordeal for both of you."

Emma peeked through the doorway and spotted a gorgeous redhead sitting at the kitchen table with Grant, her hand covering his, their heads bowed close together.

"It has been. The police still don't have a clue as to who's been threatening her," Grant said, his voice rough with emotion. "I should have told you before about the amnesia, but I kept hoping things would work out."

The woman made a soft whispery sound and squeezed Grant's hand, her red fingernails walking up his arm to massage his shoulder. Emma's breath caught in her throat. Who was this woman?

"It's been so frustrating, Priscilla," Grant continued.

Priscilla. The woman who worked with Grant, the one who'd told Emma she should be more supportive of Grant's career.

"I've tried to remind her about our past, but it upsets her. Now there's no hope, and I don't know what I'm going to do." Grant's voice grew shaky. "She doesn't remember our wedding. Hell, she doesn't even remember giving birth to Carly." He lowered his head, his dark hair tumbling over his forehead, and Emma's fingernails dug into the wooden frame of the doorway. Did Grant think she couldn't be a good wife and mother without those memories?

She stepped farther into the doorway, aware they were so absorbed in each other that neither of them heard her.

"I'm just not sure about our marriage now. I always thought Emma and I would be together forever, but now I don't know."

Tears blurred Emma's vision and she swiped at them,

anger mingling with hurt when Priscilla, arms open for an embrace, reached for Grant. He hesitated, then fell into it, wrapping his arms around her.

The picnic basket slipped from Emma's hand and clattered to the floor. Grant instantly pulled away from Priscilla and stood, his chair scraping the floor in his haste, guilt flushing his face. Kate had hinted that Grant's co-worker was interested in him on a personal level, but she hadn't believed it. Now she wondered if Kate had been right.

Chapter Thirteen

"Uh, Emma, hi." Grant knotted the napkin in his fist, grateful to see Emma home safe, but unable to believe she'd walked in at the very second he'd given in and allowed Priscilla to comfort him. He'd been so damn unhappy...but now Emma was looking at him with this shuttered expression. How much had she heard him say?

Priscilla stood, brushing her short black skirt with those red inch-long fingernails and pasting on a bright smile that looked fake even to him. "Hi, Emma, you probably don't remember me. I'm Priscilla Weston—I work with Grant."

He cringed at the way Priscilla enunciated the words slowly, as if Emma was hearing impaired or mentally challenged.

"Hello," Emma said warily. Her gaze shot back to him, and he saw the unspoken accusations.

"Priscilla came by to check on one of our projects," Grant heard himself say inanely.

"Oh, is that what you were doing?"

"Well, yes, among other things," Priscilla babbled. "We miss Grant at work. You really should encourage him to return to the office. We have two very important deals pending, and Grant's input could mean his promotion and—''

''Priscilla,'' Grant interrupted, ''Emma doesn't need to worry about my business—''

''Is she right?'' Emma asked.

He hesitated, the question taking him by surprise.

''Is she right?'' Emma repeated, then moved into the room, her limp more noticeable probably because Priscilla instantly zeroed in on it. Insecurity flickered briefly in Emma's eyes, and he remembered her concerns over her scar. His throat suddenly felt thick.

''This is the second time Priscilla has told me this,'' Emma continued. ''Haven't I been supportive of your career in the past, Grant?''

He opened his mouth to refute her, but she silenced him with a wave of her hand. ''Tell me the truth,'' she demanded. ''Don't lie to me because I was in an accident or because I have amnesia. I don't want your pity, Grant.'' She squared her shoulders. ''And I don't want your guilt, either.''

Admiration and love and guilt all warred within him. And also sorrow for all they'd lost. ''You have always been supportive,'' he answered honestly. ''Although there were times you wanted me to be home more. I wanted to get ahead. I was determined to have a successful career even if I had to work seventy hours a week.''

''It takes that kind of dedication at first,'' Priscilla said. ''You don't understand—''

''Is that why you turned to her, because she understands those needs?'' Emma asked, her voice calm compared to the stream of emotions glittering in her eyes.

Fury swelled in his chest. ''I haven't turned to Priscilla for anything but work.'' Grant raked a hand through his hair. ''No matter what your cynical sister has told you, I've always been faithful to you, Emma.''

''Emma, don't—''

''Priscilla, let me handle this,'' Grant snapped. ''I think you should leave.''

Priscilla shot him an angry look, then snatched her briefcase. ''Fine, I'll see myself out.''

Seconds later the door banged shut behind her and Grant's breath hissed out as Emma sank wearily into a chair. He moved toward her, his hands outstretched, needing to make her understand, but once again she silenced him. This time with a look of hurt so deep he felt his stomach knot.

''This isn't working, Grant.'' She dropped her hands in her lap in a gesture of defeat. ''I heard what you said. I thought making love would bring us closer, but since I told you about the amnesia, you've been more distant to me than you were the first day you brought me home.''

''I'm sorry, Emma. The news was a shock.''

''I know,'' she said, compassion in her voice. She turned tear-filled eyes up to him. ''And I realize you feel guilty, even though I don't want you to. I also know you want things to be the same as they were before the accident.''

''Can you blame me for that?'' he asked, hating the anguish in his voice.

''No,'' Emma whispered. ''I'd like that, too. But it isn't going to happen.'' A tear slid down her cheek. ''We both have to accept that.''

''I know.'' Grant felt as if his heart had been torn out. ''I'm trying.''

Emma nodded, then said with heartfelt determination,

"I know that, too. Maybe it would be better if we had a few days apart."

His shocked gaze swung to her. "What are you talking about? You're not going anywhere, not with that lunatic still out there somewhere."

"We haven't heard from him in days. He may be long gone—"

"No, Emma," he said, panicking as he remembered the conversation with Warner. "I'm not leaving you alone."

Her lower lip quivered, but she stood and backed toward the door. "Then I'll take Carly and stay at my sister's for a few days. I can't stay here with you, not after the things you said to that woman about our marriage."

THE NEXT FEW DAYS were horrible. The once homey house creaked with loneliness, so Grant poured himself into his job, all the while rationalizing that at least Emma was safe at Kate's. The psycho couldn't know where she was, but he'd insisted on a patrol car outside Kate's house, anyway.

He finished the scale model and made the final set of blueprints for the bid on Comp. Link, trying his best to ignore his co-workers. Pete's antagonistic attitude and Priscilla's smug comments, no matter how subtle, grated on his nerves. And the fact that Kate was probably doing her damnedest to turn Emma against him only drove the knife in deeper.

Of course Kate had reason now to dislike him; he had hurt Emma. He'd made love to her, then shut her out when she'd told him the truth about her amnesia. How could she forgive him when he couldn't forgive himself?

He got up from his computer and headed to the lounge for coffee, vaguely aware that two of the office assistants were staring at him, then began whispering. He frowned, wondering what gossip they'd started this time. Rumor had it that he and Priscilla were cozying up after hours. He'd done his best to avoid contact with Priscilla, hoping to diffuse the ill-found gossip.

Later, as he sipped his coffee, Pete dropped into his office. Spreadsheets lay scattered everywhere, and he'd tacked a stack of blueprints to his drafting table. Grant decided to find out if Pete had been spreading the gossip.

"We have to talk," Pete said, his tone serious.

"I've been thinking the same thing," Grant said, striving for calm.

Pete folded his long body into a chair. "All right, you go first."

"If you've been spreading rumors concerning me and Priscilla—"

"I haven't been spreading rumors," Pete objected. "If anyone's hinting there's something going on, it's Priscilla. According to her, she was at your house comforting you, and your wife walked in and saw the two of you in an embrace. Now your wife has left you."

Grant froze. Pete's rendition certainly told what happened, but the facts were skewed. Or were they? And by whom? Priscilla or Pete?

"Listen, Landers, it's not what it sounds like." Grant ran a hand through his hair, sighing loudly. "I was upset. For God's sake I just found out my wife has permanent amnesia. Priscilla simply gave me a hug."

Pete's eyes narrowed. "And your wife saw it and left you?"

Grant couldn't explain to Pete, no one would understand his guilt. "She's staying at her sister's for a few days," he explained. "She needed some space and she thought I did, too."

"I'm sure Priscilla has been really kind about offering to fill up the space?"

Pete's snide voice fueled his anger more. "She's been understanding, yes. But there's nothing going on between us except work." He waved his hand around the office, his anger and frustration focused on Pete. "Now let's talk about the real issue between us. You keep slipping in to take my place on business deals so you can snap up the promotion I've earned."

"What?" Pete circled the desk and grabbed Grant's collar, his face livid. "You, man, are way off base. I don't give a damn about taking your job from you."

Grant grabbed Pete's hand and jerked it loose. "That's the reason you stay here till all hours of the night?"

Pete's eyes widened in surprise. "Who told you that?" He paced across the room, a cynical laugh escaping him. "Let me guess. Priscilla?"

"It doesn't matter who told me. The fact is you're trying to undermine me."

"That's ludicrous. I'm trying to help you with the deal because you have a personal crisis."

"What do you care about my personal life? You're jealous of my place in the company."

Pete shoved his hands into the pockets of his slacks. "You're right, I am jealous of you," he finally conceded, his voice low. "But it's not your job I want, Wadsworth, it's your *life.*"

A frisson of fear bolted through Grant. Did Pete mean he wanted to kill him?

Pete's sarcastic laugh echoed off the immaculately

decorated walls. "I want your life, Wadsworth—your wife and baby." He sank onto the leather love seat and bracing his elbows on his knees, dropped his head into his hands. "You have it all, but you don't appreciate it."

Grant's chest felt tight. "That's not true."

Pete slowly raised his head and tears sprang to his eyes. "You don't know what's it like to lose your family, to have your wife there one minute and gone the next." He snapped his fingers. "And to know your baby died and there's nothing you can do to bring them back."

Grant remembered the note. *I lost my loved one and so will you.* Pete was obviously distraught. Could he be disturbed enough to take revenge on Grant? Then he remembered the suspicion that the killer knew Faye Simmons. Pete had been in California at the time, a couple of thousand miles from Faye.

Pete's agonized voice shook him back to the moment. "I look at you and I see myself two years ago, working hard, neglecting my family." Pete tugged at the cuff of his left sleeve. "Jeanie kept asking me to come home early, to take off for the weekend with her, but no." He shook his head. "I said there'd be time for us to take vacations and go on picnics and all that stuff later." His bitter laugh filled the room. "Work always came first."

Conversations Grant had had with Emma before the accident skated through his mind. Pete's attitude mirrored his own.

"Then one night she fixed this candlelit dinner. She was going to surprise me and tell me about the baby." His voice grew scratchy and he scrubbed his hand over his eyes. "But I didn't show. Instead, I went out with a client."

Grant swallowed, already guessing the rest of the story. Pete continued, his voice pained as he relived his nightmare. "Jeanie was so upset she decided to go to her mother's, but it was raining and—" his voice dropped off "—she never made it. A drunk driver hit her and she wrapped her car around a telephone pole. Died before I could even make it to the hospital."

The agony in Pete's voice diffused Grant's anger. He could only partly comprehend Pete's loss—he still had Emma. Or at least he had, until he'd been such an idiot.

Pete looked up, his eyes red and miserable. "When I went back to the house after I left the hospital, I found this little gift waiting for me. All wrapped up in this silly wrapping paper with a goofy elephant-shaped rattler taped to it." His voice cracked. "It was a tiny pair of baby booties." He held his fingers a couple of inches apart, indicating the size. "They were blue, and she'd bought this itty bitty Braves cap because she knew how much I like baseball..." A low sob tore from Pete's chest.

Grant's hand trembled as he placed it on Pete's shoulder. "I'm sorry, Pete. I didn't know."

"Yeah, I'm jealous of you," Pete continued hoarsely, squeezing the bridge of his nose with his thumb and forefinger. "I've been harping on you to stay home with your wife, 'cause unlike me—" he raised his face and stared at Grant "—you have a chance to get it all back."

Grant's eyes felt gritty. He sucked in a harsh breath.

"Sure I'm here working all the time," Pete said with a shrug as he dried his eyes. "Work is all I have. I didn't realize how much my family meant to me till I lost them. I can't stand to go home to that empty house."

Grant understood the feeling too well. And Pete was right—he *could* do something about his situation. He had a chance with Emma. Memory or no memory, she was his wife. He still loved her and he damn well needed to show her.

"THANKS FOR LETTING ME stay here, Kate. I think Grant and I both needed some time apart." Emma wiped a drop of milk from Carly's cheek and kissed her tenderly.

"You two are always welcome." Kate scooped Carly into her arms and patted her back. "I could happily keep Carly all the time."

Kate tickled Carly's stomach with her nose. Carly cooed and batted at Kate's head.

"I'm sure Carly could sense the tension," Emma said, "but I still wonder if I did the right thing." She shrugged. "I feel like I deserted him."

"Sounds as if he was the one backing off," Kate said, bouncing Carly on her lap. "He couldn't deal with your permanent memory loss, so he pulled away emotionally."

Emma chewed her lip. "I suppose. I know it was a blow to him."

"It can't be easy for you, either," Kate said.

"It is hard," Emma admitted. "But I'm trying to look at this ordeal as a second chance. Grant has been wonderful to me since he brought me home, and I've fallen in love with him all over again."

Kate looked shocked. "You told him that?"

"Sort of." She gave Kate a forlorn look. "I told him I loved him, but I'm not sure he believed me."

"He'll come around in time," Kate said. "He really cares about you, sis. He stood by your bedside day and night after the wreck."

"I remember his voice," Emma said. "Soft and soothing. His pleas made me fight to come back."

Kate finger-combed Carly's fine hair. "I know you have problems, Emma, but still, I can't help but be jealous. You have the perfect family."

"I know. And I want us all to be together again." Emma shivered, remembering the other voice in the hospital, the one from the person who'd wanted to kill her.

Kate wagged a finger at her. "Uh-oh, you've got that stubborn look about you."

Emma laughed. "I'm not going to lose Grant over this. I'm going to win him back."

The doorbell rang. Kate went to answer and escorted Dan McGuire in.

"Hi, Emma," Dan said. "I didn't know you were going to be here."

"I'm catching up with my sister," Emma said.

"She's staying overnight. Grant had business to take care of," Kate said. Emma shot her a grateful smile for glossing over the truth.

"I hope you're feeling better, Emma." Dan's easy smile made her relax. There was no way her old high-school friend would hurt her.

"I am. I'm barely limping now."

"That's good. Did Kate tell you she finally agreed to go with me on a buying trip?"

"No, she didn't, but that's great," Emma said, noticing Kate's blushing face.

"Yeah, I thought I'd stop by and see if I could talk her into dinner."

Kate immediately made an excuse, but Emma shook her head. ''You two go ahead. Carly and I are going to turn in early.''

''I don't want to leave you alone,'' Kate argued. ''Not until the police catch that creep.''

''He has no idea I'm here. If he did, I would have gotten some kind of weird message by now,'' Emma said, handing Carly a toy bear. ''I feel perfectly safe in your house, Kate, especially with that policeman outside.'' She ushered them toward the door. ''Besides, it'll do me good to be alone. Maybe I can come up with a plan to win my husband back.''

Before Priscilla sinks her claws into him, Emma added silently. Grant might have remained faithful to her so far, but she recognized the signs of a lioness on the prowl—Priscilla obviously wanted Grant, and she'd probably resort to almost anything to win him.

A shudder coursed through her. Would Priscilla resort to killing her?

ALL AFTERNOON Grant stewed over his conversation with Pete. Whereas once he'd disliked the man, now he felt sorry for him. Pete had been through hell. Grant couldn't blame Pete for drowning his sorrows in work; hadn't he been doing the same thing this week with Emma gone?

He pushed open the front door of his house, the squeaking almost eerie as he waited for the sounds of his family to greet him. The wonderful sounds of Emma's voice and Carly's cooing that made the house a home, not just empty rooms. But the silence closed in around him, reminding him Emma and Carly were gone. When he flipped on the light, he froze. Someone had been in the house. His heart pounded as he listened. Was that someone still there?

As he scanned the living room, a sick feeling rose in his stomach. The wall of family photographs had been destroyed. Shattered glass from the frames littered the floor, and pictures had been torn into shreds. Then he glanced at the mirror above the fireplace and staggered against the wall when he read the message scrawled in lipstick: *It is time for Emma to die.*

SOMEONE WAS IN HER ROOM.

Emma opened her eyes, her heart fluttering into her throat. Darkness bathed the room. A shadow loomed above her, large and powerful, and she opened her mouth to scream. The sound died in her throat when the shadow pushed a pillow over her face and pressed. She kicked and writhed, bucked, and tried to swing her fists. The pillow was pressed harder. She clawed wildly, but finally the pressure over her mouth and nostrils would no longer allow the intake of air. Darkness began sucking her in and her limbs went limp. Her attacker was winning....

Chapter Fourteen

As soon as Grant phoned the police, he dialed Emma. The phone rang and rang, and he paced the room, wondering why she wasn't answering. Maybe she was already asleep. Where was Kate?

Warner showed up within minutes and ordered a team of officers to dust for fingerprints.

"I'll be surprised if we find anything." Warner's gaze rested on the message scrawled with lipstick. "Have you talked to your wife?"

Grant shook his head. "I phoned but there's no answer."

"I'll call the guard outside her door, make sure he checks on her."

"Thanks." Grant sighed with relief. He had a bad feeling about things. The destruction this time seemed so much worse, as if the person had gone completely crazy.

The sick feeling rose in his stomach again and he tasted bile. He needed to hear Emma's voice for himself to be sure she was all right.

EMMA REFUSED TO LEAVE her baby behind. And Grant...he would never know how much she loved him.

A surge of renewed energy kicked in. She shoved her attacker, sending him toppling backward. Then she screamed, slid to the end of the bed and hit the floor at a dead run. Her attacker lunged after her, but she barreled through the door yelling for help.

Seconds later the door to the apartment opened and the light came on. Kate dashed toward her, flushed and out of breath. "What's wrong, Emma?"

"He...someone...tried to kill me," she gasped. "Where's Carly?"

Kate grabbed Emma's hand and they ran into the room where Carly was sleeping. Someone pounded on the apartment door and Emma picked the baby up, holding her tightly against her chest.

The pounding grew louder. "Police, ma'am. Let me in!"

"Thank God," Kate said, heading for the front door. Emma glanced into the bedroom where she'd been attacked and saw the curtains flapping in the breeze. Her attacker must have escaped through the opened window. "I think he's gone." She sank onto the couch, trembling.

Kate checked the peephole, then let the policeman in.

"Call Grant," Emma pleaded as the tears began to stream down her face. "Kate, please call Grant."

GRANT SAW THE ALARM on Warner's face and his heart almost stopped beating.

"What's wrong? Is Emma okay?"

Warner hung up and gestured toward the door. "She's all right, but she wants you, Grant. Someone attacked her."

Ten minutes later Grant raced into Kate's first-floor apartment, his fear almost choking him. He pounded on the door, yelled his name and the door swung open. Kate greeted him soberly and moved aside. Emma was sitting on the sofa in a thin cotton robe, her hair tangled, her cheeks pale, her eyes wide with shock. She clutched Carly in her arms. The policeman stood in the corner looking grave. He instantly apologized to Warner.

"Sir, whoever it was came in a back window. I couldn't see him from the car."

Grant cast him a furious look, then strode toward Emma. Still holding Carly, she stood up and stepped forward into his arms. He held both her and the baby, his eyes suspiciously moist.

"You two are coming with me," he said against her hair. *And I'm not ever letting you go again.*

AN HOUR LATER, after Emma had given the details of her attack to Warner, the police escorted them to a hotel. The questions Warner had asked bothered her, in particular, who'd known she was at Kate's? Grant, of course. Martha. And Kate. And Priscilla and Pete. Also Dan McGuire, who'd been at Kate's earlier. But none of them would want to kill her, would they? Then she remembered her earlier suspicions about Priscilla. If Priscilla wanted Grant for herself…

Kate checked into a separate room while Grant booked a suite for Emma, Carly and him. After they settled Carly in a crib, he turned down the bed and faced her. She tried to give him a brave smile.

Since he'd arrived at Kate's, Grant hadn't left her side. He'd held her and encouraged her during all the questions, and from the expression on his face, her story scared him as much as it did her. When she'd asked to go home, he'd told her about the break-in at the house.

Exhausted, she stumbled toward the bed. Grant

caught her and pulled her to him. She wondered if she'd ever stop shaking.

"Shh, it's okay now, sweetheart. We're safe here."

"I just want you to hold me," she whispered.

"I'm going to hold you, Emma, all night. I'm never going to let you go again."

He helped her remove her coat. Beneath it she still wore her nightgown, and he insisted she lie down, then he shucked his clothes except for his boxers, pulled her into his arms and brought the thick comforter up over them. She heard his chest heaving for air and realized he was struggling with his own emotion; she ran her hand over his biceps wanting to assure him she was fine. "I'm glad you're here, Grant. When I thought he was going to k-kill me—"

"Shh, don't," he said hoarsely.

She squeezed his arm, then traced her finger over his cheek. She felt moisture on his face and realized he was crying. "All I could think about was Carly and not seeing her again..." Her voice broke and she felt him swallow hard against her cheek. "And you, Grant. I kept thinking that I might never see you again, that you might never know how much I love you."

He rocked her in his arms. "I love you, too, Emma," he whispered roughly. "I love you, too."

As soon as Emma heard the words, the tension drained from her and she closed her eyes. As long as Grant loved her, everything would be all right.

HE WAS GOING to make everything up to Emma, one way or the other, Grant thought, stroking her hair as she slept fitfully beside him. He was going to prove to her how much he loved her. She whimpered and snuggled closer and he held her protectively, the anger and fear churning together, roaring through his veins. He couldn't sleep. There was no way, not tonight, not when he'd almost lost her. Again. If he had to quit work to keep her safe, he would. He could always find another job, but he could never fill the empty place in his heart or bed with another woman. Because there was only one woman for him. His wife, Emma.

To hell with her memory loss. The past didn't matter. It was the future that was important. And he was damn sure going to spend his with Emma.

"GRANT, ARE YOU SURE you can't convince Emma to stay with Kate again so you can make this meeting?" Priscilla whined on the other end of the phone line. "You said the police will have a guard posted at your house."

"I'm sure, Priscilla. Pete can handle it."

"I thought you hated for Pete to sit in with your clients. Do you want to lose this account to Pete?"

"Look, Priscilla, things have changed. I almost *lost* Emma four times and I'm determined to not let that happen again." He smiled at the bathroom door, wondering if Emma would mind if he joined her in the shower. "Besides, I want to spend time with her. We're going to work things out."

"You are?" Priscilla sounded shocked. "You mean she's moving back in with you?"

"I mean we're trying to put our marriage back together," Grant said, uneasy with Priscilla's attitude. Ever since Warner had asked who had known Emma was at Kate's, something had nagged at the back of his mind. Pete and Priscilla had known. But Priscilla had been coming on to him, and she'd left angry the other day.

"Grant?"

"I think our marriage will be stronger this time," he said, jerking himself back to the conversation.

Priscilla hesitated. "Are you sure that's what you want, Grant? You know we'd make a great team." Her soft sigh hinted at a more personal relationship. "I wish you'd give us a chance. We have a lot more in common—"

Grant had to set her straight. "I love Emma. She's my wife."

"I see," Priscilla said in a clipped tone. "Well, I think you're making a mistake, Grant, but I guess Pete and I can take care of business."

She was miffed, Grant realized as he hung up. Maybe Priscilla had read more into their relationship than he'd intended. But he couldn't worry about her. He had plans to make. He wanted to spend the week wooing his wife. By the time Saturday rolled around, she'd have some wonderful new memories to replace the horror of the past few weeks. And she'd be back in his bed forever. And he hoped he'd be back in her heart, where he belonged.

"HE'S SENT YOU a carnation every day?" Kate asked.

"Yes, isn't it romantic?" Emma sighed dreamily, trying to focus on her budding romance with Grant, instead of the guard posted outside her door. "Monday we went to a movie. Tuesday we went to dinner at this new steak house. Wednesday we drove up to the mountains for a picnic."

"Wow, he's really pouring it on strong."

"He said we were going to start a new memory book." A blush climbed Emma's throat, and she realized she was practically gushing. ''What about you and Dan? How's it going between the two of you?''

A wry smile crossed Kate's face. ''Actually it's going pretty well. When he found out about your attack, he was upset. But he was also worried about me. So he's been staying over.''

''You're sleeping with him?'' Emma asked, surprised.

Kate shrugged. ''Hard to believe, but we're not. I'm still kind of leery, but he's so sweet. He said he didn't mind waiting.''

''That's really great, Kate,'' Emma said, hugging her. ''He must really care about you.''

''It's weird,'' Kate admitted. ''All this time I've been so jealous of you and Grant.''

''You have? And here I thought you didn't like me.'' Grant strolled in, dipped his head and kissed Emma. She wrapped her arms around his neck and met him with enthusiasm. When they finally pulled apart, Kate gave an exaggerated sigh of disgust. ''See, that's what I mean. It's enough to make a girl green.''

Emma laughed, and Grant, sinking down beside her, slung his arm around her shoulders. Kate stood, her expression serious. ''I know I gave you a hard time, Grant. I guess I was jaded after my divorce.''

''I can understand that,'' Grant said quietly. ''I'm sorry for what Todd put you through.''

Kate hooked her thumbs in the belt loops of her jeans. ''There's...something I didn't tell you guys,'' she said hesitantly. ''You see, I found out about a year and half ago I can't have children.''

A soft gasp escaped Emma. ''I'm sorry, Kate,'' Emma said softly. ''That must have been hard for you when Carly was born.''

Kate eyed Carly's playpen, twining her hands together. "Yeah, and Todd didn't take it too well." She shrugged. "Of course I must admit I fell into a depression, and I kept pushing him away. I just couldn't be with him...then he found someone else."

"That's awful." Emma stood up and gave Kate a hug. "But it's not your fault. He should have stuck by you."

Kate brushed at a tear. "I see that now. Especially after watching the way the two of you have handled the ordeal you've been through."

"He was a lowlife, Kate," Grant said, hating the man for hurting Kate. "You're better off without him."

Kate nodded. "Well, I just wanted you two to know, so you'd understand why I acted so weird for a while. I even got desperate and considered adopting a baby by myself—that's why I wanted Dad's money." She tucked a strand of hair behind her ear. "But I'm doing better now. And I'm happy for you two."

"Thanks, Kate," Emma said, reaching out to squeeze her sister's hand. Carly whimpered from the bedroom. "Hey, if you ever want to talk, let me know. I'm here for you, Kate." Then she went to get Carly.

Grant got up and put his arms around Kate. "We're both here for you," he said in a scratchy voice.

"I'm really glad Emma has you, Grant. I hope one day I have a man like you."

The comment struck him as odd. But he patted Kate's back, trying to be sensitive to her needs. "You'll find someone someday. Don't be so hard on yourself."

Her eyes got a strange faraway look. "I know. And I still may adopt a child someday."

"Good, you'll make a wonderful mother. Carly sure adores you."

Kate smiled, the bitterness he'd sensed the past few weeks dissipating. "Thanks for saying that, Grant." She released him and reached for her purse. "I'm going to meet Dan for dinner. I've decided to give him a chance. Maybe there's one other good guy out there besides you."

Grant shrugged. "I hope it works out, Kate. I'm glad you're moving on with your life. It's the best way to get over your ex." Kate nodded, then picked up her purse, but the snap came unfastened and the contents spilled out onto the sofa table. In the middle of the smattering of cosmetics lay a small pistol.

Grant froze, remembering her comment to the detective about not having a gun. The bullets from the gun that had shot at Emma were from a .38. He didn't know much about firearms, but it was possible Kate's was the same kind. Then Kate snatched it up and stuffed it back in her purse and left so quickly he didn't have time to ask her about it. Even stranger, she hadn't offered an explanation.

"I CAN'T BELIEVE you rented a carriage for us." Emma leaned into Grant's strong shoulder as the horse and buggy took them on a leisurely stroll around the downtown area. Moonlight spilled through the mossy trees, and the stars twinkled merrily as if promising the night would remain clear. Heat lightning streaked the sky somewhere in the distance, and Emma shivered, snuggling closer to Grant and kissing his neck.

"This feels like heaven," Grant said, tipping up her chin to taste her mouth.

Emma savored the feel of his lips, the clip-clop of the horse's hooves and the swaying of the carriage lulling her.

''Did we ever do this before?'' Emma asked, glancing around at the glittering lights of the skyline. Water gurgled and bubbled from a fountain at the entrance to the downtown park. She could imagine Carly running and playing in it in the heat of summer when she was older.

''No.'' Grant stroked the palm of her hand. ''I told you we were going to create new memories. The past is the past.'' He angled his head and brushed his lips across her forehead, then teased the delicate shell of her ear. ''The future is what's important. And I intend to spend it with you.''

Tears burned in Emma's throat, but she swallowed them back, knowing they'd had enough emotional upheaval recently to last a lifetime. Instead, she graced him with a sexy smile and kissed his finger. ''I love you, Grant. Thank you for...for all this.'' She gestured around her at the quaint ambience of the carriage and the romance of their evening ride.

''I'd do anything to keep that smile on your face,'' he whispered.

The corners of her mouth lifted automatically as he tickled her neck with his tongue. ''You are a devil, you know that.''

''Yeah, and the night's still young,'' he murmured in a sexy whisper.

Emma cupped his face with her hands and gazed into his eyes. ''Make love to me tonight, Grant.''

EMMA ROLLED OVER and turned herself into Grant's arms, completely disarmed by the uninhibited way she'd allowed Grant to make love to her. No, she hadn't allowed it—she'd practically begged for it.

"That was incredible," he whispered, nuzzling his face into her hair.

"I can't believe how I am with you," she said.

A sexy chuckle rumbled from deep within his chest.

She pulled back and looked at him, and he kissed her soundly again.

"I know, darlin'. Why do you think I married you?"

Emma stared at him in shock, but the sincerity in his eyes was so sweet she hit him on the chest and giggled. "You *are* a devil."

He laughed again, rolled her beneath him and straddled her, dipping his head to kiss her. "Yeah, and the night's *still* young." Her laughter died when she felt the evidence of his arousal already jutting at her.

The next morning Grant got up quietly and let Emma sleep. He'd given in and scheduled a lunch meeting with Priscilla and a new client, but he would come home after work. He planned to swing by the jewelry store on the way home and buy Emma a new locket. Maybe Kate could take the one from Dan. He wanted Emma wearing *his*.

He found Emma stretching, her eyes still sleepy when he went back into the bedroom. "I'll be back after lunch," he whispered. "You can wait for me right here if you want."

She laughed softly. "What about our daughter, dear?"

"Martha's watching her. She'll be here for a while." She wrapped her arms around his neck and kissed him so greedily he was tempted to crawl back into bed. But if he didn't make this meeting, Priscilla would probably come and drag him to the office. "The guard's outside. Don't go anywhere, okay?"

A slight frown momentarily replaced her smile, then she nodded, and he whispered goodbye.

EMMA FELT DECADENT sleeping in, although she admitted she hadn't actually slept all that much. Stretching sore muscles, she pulled on a robe and went to find Carly. Grant had been so romantic all week with all his surprises, maybe she'd plan one for them today.

She found Martha in the kitchen, washing the dishes. Kate was holding Carly.

"Hi, sleepyhead," Kate said. A blush burned Emma's cheeks, but Kate simply laughed. "I came to see how you are. And, of course, to see my darlin' niece." Kate kissed Carly's nose. "You know I could raise this one like she was my own."

Emma smiled and turned to Martha. "I was wondering if you could do a little shopping for me this morning."

"Sure. What do you need?"

"I'm planning a surprise for Grant. I want to make a special dinner for us." Emma quickly scribbled a list.

"Would you like me to baby-sit Carly at my place?" Kate asked.

Emma remembered Kate's admission about not being able to have children. "Sure, if you don't mind, Kate. But what about Dan?"

"He'll come over and we'll order pizza or something."

"Great," Emma said. She handed Martha the list and some cash and waved her out the door.

"As a matter of fact, why don't I take Carly to the park while you get dressed? Take your time."

"You're a doll, Kate." She helped Kate gather the stroller and a diaper bag, then after checking to make sure the guard was still posted outside, headed to the shower, her plans taking shape in her mind.

Feeling more optimistic than she had in days, she took a long hot shower, letting the warm water wash away her tension. Then she stepped from the shower and gasped in horror. She was staring right into the muzzle of a gun.

Chapter Fifteen

"MR. WADSWORTH, your wife's on line two."

"Thanks, Bernice." Grant thumbed through his itinerary and punched the extension, surprised Emma had called. "Hey, sweetheart, you miss me already?"

"Grant...I've been thinking..."

Her voice sounded strained, a far cry from her earlier optimistic tone. Every nerve cell in his body went on alert. "Are you all right, Emma?"

"Yes," she said, but the slight quiver to her voice alarmed him even more. "But I've been thinking about us, and it's not going to work."

"What?"

"I... All this tension is getting to me. I need some time alone."

His hand tightened on the receiver. "What are you talking about? Last night—"

"I'm going away for a few days," she said, cutting him off. "Please, if you love me, just let me go."

The line clicked into silence. A wave of hurt turned into shock, then disbelief. Things had been going so well. Why would Emma change her mind? And where would she go? Kate's?

Reeling with confusion, he quickly redialed his number, tapping his foot impatiently on the floor as it rang repeatedly. Dammit, either she wasn't answering or she'd already left!

Cursing under his breath, he slammed down the phone and headed to Priscilla's office to tell her he couldn't make the meeting, that he had to find Emma.

He was surprised to see it was empty. Where the hell was she? They were supposed to meet the new client in twenty minutes. Had she said she'd meet him at the restaurant? He grabbed a notepad, then swept the top of the desk searching for a pen. Muttering a curse when he couldn't find one, he opened her desk drawer, raking the contents until he located one. But something jutted out from the edges of a blue folder. Curious, he opened it, startled to find an old college photo of him, one similar to a picture he had at home. Odd. Where had Priscilla gotten the photo?

Memories clamored through his head—the mutilated photographs on his floor after the break-in. Warner's comments—the only two people you knew in college who live close by are your sister-in law and that woman you work with. He sank into Priscilla's desk chair, his chest tight. He had to be wrong even to think such a horrible thing, but he searched Priscilla's desk, anyway, and found a small envelope of floral receipts. His stomach churned. Were they from the florist who'd sent the dead roses to Emma? He didn't remember. And there was no mention of what Priscilla had ordered. Was it a coincidence?

He remembered Priscilla's less-than-subtle attention, the sly coy remarks he'd let pass without notice, the offers of comfort that had hinted at more. He'd been flattered she thought him attractive, but was it a *fatal* attraction? And what did she have to do with Faye Simmons? Could they have been related? Friends?

Too many questions bombarded him, and he knew he had to have some answers. He rushed to his car and grabbed his cell phone, then dialed home as he raced to the restaurant. But once again, no one answered. Surely Emma had gone to Kate's. He tried Kate's number, but no one answered there, either. If Priscilla was responsible for hurting Emma, he would find out, then he'd find Emma and bring her home. He'd make her believe in them as much as he did.

Exhaling a shaky breath, he wiped the perspiration from his forehead and steered the car onto the highway. Cursing a blue streak at the traffic, he pounded on his horn and wove in and out of the rows of cars, yanking the car into the parking lot of the Ritz, then jogging inside.

He saw Priscilla waving from a mauve lace-draped table and tried to collect himself, scrutinizing her as he made his way across the crowded dining room. In college Priscilla had been ambitious. He'd heard she'd even slept with one of the professors to better her grades. She'd said she and Grant would make a great team. Her green eyes raked him as he approached, and doubts assailed him. How many times had she come on to him and he'd turned her down without realizing what he was doing?

"Hi." Priscilla captured his hand and squeezed it. Her hand was icy cold. "I'm glad you made it, Grant."

"You said it was important." He gestured at the table for two. "I thought a new client was meeting us here."

A sly smile lit her face as she sat down and sipped her wine. "Actually it's just the two of us today."

He arched an eyebrow, hoping he was wrong about

suspecting her of foul play. She poured him a glass of wine from the bottle in the wine cooler and handed it to him. His fingers tightened around the stem but he didn't take a drink. He needed to play it cool and try to coax the truth from her. "So, what are we discussing?" he asked casually, settling into the chair opposite her.

"I told you I've been worried about you," she said.

"And I told you things were going better with Emma."

Her smile slipped slightly. "I'm not sure how you can say that if she still doesn't remember you." She tilted her head, her auburn lashes fluttering seductively. "But I remember you, Grant, way back in college." She took another sip of wine. "I always knew you'd succeed and—" she took his hand and traced her finger along his palm "—I knew we'd make a great team."

"But we never really went out, Priscilla. How could you know those things?"

"Because I watched you—in class, at the sorority house with the other girls."

"You mean with Faye Simmons?" he asked, fear making his voice sound hard.

She straightened, looking stunned by his question. "Yes, her and the others. And then Emma came along and I thought I'd lost my chance. Until I landed this job at the firm." She slipped a hotel key into his hand and he stared at it, momentarily stunned. When he finally raised his gaze to meet hers, the cutthroat business look he'd come to know in her eyes had transformed into cutthroat seduction.

"You can't be too surprised," Priscilla said softly. "I've been pretty obvious these past few weeks. When Emma was hurt and the two of you were having problems, I thought you'd realize how wrong you were for each other.''

''So you thought you'd step in and take her place?''

The pupils of her eyes dilated. ''I could, Grant. I could give you everything she gave you, and more.''

Disgust ate at his calm, but he tried to mask it. ''Look, Priscilla, did you take the job at the firm just to be near me?''

A brief glint of anger shot through Priscilla's eyes. ''It's one of the reasons,'' she admitted.

He studied her face. ''Did you do something to hurt Emma? Are you the one who's been threatening her?''

Priscilla's gasp of horror took him off guard. ''How dare you accuse me of such a thing? Just because I want you doesn't mean I'd try to kill your wife.''

Grant relaxed his hand and let the key clatter onto the table. ''Then...this whole seduction, you...''

''This whole seduction is because I want to sleep with you, and I want us to open our own company.'' Priscilla's tight smile was steeped in fury. ''With your skills and my marketing ability, we'd make a good team.'' She hissed out an angry breath. ''Both in the bedroom and the boardroom.''

''Look, Priscilla, I'm sorry, but Emma called and sounded upset. Then I found a picture of me in your desk—''

''You were snooping in my desk?''

''I was looking for a pen—''

''I'm not the only one who had a crush on you in college. Half the girls in the sorority did! Why aren't you asking all of them if they tried to kill your precious Emma?''

''What are you talking about?''

"Your sister-in-law, for example. She had the hots for you before anyone else even knew you existed."

Grant's jaw went slack. "Kate?"

Priscilla twisted her mouth into a nasty snarl. "Yes, Kate. She kept photos of you posted all over her closet door. She was furious when her little sister came for a visit and you started drooling over her."

"Oh, my God."

"She told everyone how much she hated Emma for taking you away, how her little sister always got everything she wanted."

Grant jerked up, nausea rolling through him. "I have to go."

Priscilla opened her mouth to speak, but he backed away, his insides quaking. Could it be true?

He rushed to his car, twisted the key in the ignition and took off, frantically dialing his home, and Kate's as he drove. Still no answer at either. Snatches of comments Kate had made played over and over in his head. *I've been so jealous of you and Grant... I found out I can't have children... I love Carly like she's my own... I hope one day I find a man like you.*

Kate had wanted all their father's money and had been furious when Emma refused her. She'd lost her husband. She'd lied about having a gun. And he'd taken Kate's name off the list because he'd never suspected her.

A cold shiver engulfed him—Emma had actually stayed with her sister thinking she was safe. But that same night someone had almost killed her for the fourth time. Kate had been at the hospital, too. And she'd been at the house when someone tried to push Emma down the stairs. Why hadn't he seen the connection before?

He slammed his fist on the steering wheel and raced

to his house, praying that Emma would be there when he got home, that she hadn't already gone to her sister's and walked into a trap.

"WHY ARE YOU DOING this?" Emma cried. Her plea was lost in the cotton rag that had been stuffed in her mouth. She struggled against the blindfold over her eyes and the ropes digging into her arms, panic gnawing at her insides.

"Shut up and walk," the agitated voice said.

The blunt muzzle of a gun jabbed Emma's back, and she stumbled, a whimper of terror rising in her throat. Tangled briars and weeds scraped her arms and legs, and she almost fell on the cold ground, but a hand jerked her up and shoved her on. A tree branch slapped her in the face and leaves hissed beneath her feet. She paused to try to figure out where she was, how she might escape. She was in the woods somewhere. Near the river? She could hear the sound of water rushing over rocks.

"I said walk." Another hard push jolted her forward, and she hit the ground on her knees. The sharp point of a stick sliced though her jeans and dug into her skin. She cried out again, but the gag muffled the sound, and she heaved, tears spilling onto the dirt.

"You took everything from me, everything I should have had. And you're going to pay for it now."

The image of dead bodies discovered months or years later in some deserted stretch of woods flashed though her mind. Nausea rose in her throat, and her hopes faded with the sound of thunder that suddenly rumbled above her.

She was going to die in some muddy bug-infested thick of the woods, and Grant might never even find her.

GRANT RUSHED into the house, yelling Emma's name. But the empty house greeted him with an overpowering silence. Where was the guard who was supposed to be watching the house? Had Emma dismissed him?

Then he spotted a note on the coffee table with a picture taped to it. A picture of Faye Simmons with the words *Remember me* scrawled below it.

Where was Emma? And what did Kate have to do with Faye Simmons? Unless...unless Kate had drugged Faye and caused her accident.

He didn't have time to waste, so he rushed to his car and raced to Kate's. His heart pounding, he jumped out and ran to her apartment, then banged on the door with a vengeance. When no one answered, he dropped his head against the door and yelled in frustration.

Seconds later he pulled himself together, massaging his head with his fingers, trying to decide where Kate might have taken Emma. *Remember me.* Faye had died at the river. He was desperate. That was the only place he could think of—Kate had taken Emma to the same place Faye had crashed.

Oblivious to the sweat pouring down his face and the cars honking at him, he drove ninety miles an hour toward the old bridge. Remembering Kate's gun, he grabbed his cell phone and called Warner, relaying his suspicions.

"Your wife's sister told Officer Parrish to go home. Said she and the housekeeper would be with Emma all day." Warner cursed. "I'll meet you at the river."

THUNDER CLAPPED as Emma was prodded across a wobbly bridge, the wooden slats creaking beneath her feet. The stench of mildew and rotting wood assaulted her already churning stomach, and she staggered, hitting a broken board that snapped and plunged to the river below. She could hear water crashing against rocks and rushing downstream as she fought to keep her balance. Rain began to pelt her arms and mingle with the tears pouring down her cheeks.

The gun dug farther into her back, and she put her foot carefully in front of her. She stumbled and almost fell because of a gaping hole in the flooring. A sob fought its way into her throat. She swayed, straining for any sounds of other people, someone who might rescue her. A crow cawed somewhere in the distance.

And she knew this time she was going to die.

THUNDER CLAPPED as Grant bolted from his car. He decided against the trail and slogged his way through the heavy underbrush leading to the bridge. He hadn't seen any cars, so he'd parked at the secret place he and the guys had discovered years ago, a shortcut to the old bridge where Faye had died. Rain pounded his head and shoulders. He squinted through the downpour, dove around a tangle of vines and moss-covered stumps, then paused by a tall poplar. His hands clutched the trunk with such force the bark scraped his palms and drew blood. But he barely noticed: His gaze froze on the horrible sight in front of him. Emma stood in the middle of the dilapidated bridge, rain pelting her skin and hair, her hands tied behind her, a gag in her mouth, her eyes blindfolded.

Anger unlike anything he'd ever experienced tore through him. He had to force himself to move slowly to the bridge, not go raging through the woods to rescue her. Kate had a gun; she could pick him off in a second, and then what? He listened for sirens as he scanned the area for Kate. His head jerked around at a mewling sound coming from one end of the bridge. Then he saw her. A lone figure huddled in a hooded raincoat, her hand trembling as she held a gun on Emma.

He moved forward on the balls of his feet so as not to make a sound, but his foot hit a tree limb that snapped and went flying in the air. The figure in the raincoat turned, and his lungs almost collapsed with shock. It wasn't Kate who had Emma at all.

Chapter Sixteen

''Martha?'' Grant said in shock.

''Stay right where you are, Mr. Wadsworth,'' she ordered in a cold bitter voice.

He saw Emma stiffen, trying to locate the direction of his voice. He had to let her know where he was. ''Don't move, Emma,'' he said. ''I'm here.'' Then he stared at Martha, willing himself to be calm, to stall until the police could arrive. ''I don't understand, Martha. Why are you doing this?''

She waved the pistol in the air, her eyes wild as she paced back and forth between him and Emma ranting, '''Cause it was *you.* You took my baby away, you killed her, and you have to pay for it. You have to suffer.''

She was irrational, her confused state scaring him almost more than the gun. Emma was soaked and trembling and frightened, but she didn't appear hurt. Thank God.

''What are you talking about?'' Out of the corner of his eye he kept Emma in his sight as he slowly inched toward the housekeeper. ''What baby, Martha? How did I ever hurt you?''

''You wouldn't marry her. No, you had to finish

school. You had to meet some finer richer girl to play house with.'' She pointed the gun at Grant, her hand wobbling up and down. ''You didn't even care about the baby.''

Grant held out a calming hand. ''Martha, tell me what baby you're talking about.''

''My grandbaby!'' Martha shouted. Rain slashed across her face and dripped down her chin, the streaks of lightning highlighting her wrinkled skin, making her appear even more sinister in the harsh darkness. ''Faye's child. She was yours, but—''

''Faye?'' Grant's mind reeled. ''You're Faye's mother?''

Martha nodded, and a low sob erupted from her. ''She was my only girl and she died. Died 'cause she was having your baby and you didn't want it. You wouldn't do right by her—''

''But that's not true,'' Grant said, working to steady his voice. ''Martha, Faye and I were only friends. I swear, we talked a few times, and she told me about the baby, but it wasn't mine.''

''You're lying!'' Martha swung the gun back toward Emma. Emma seemed to sense Martha's rising hysteria and shrank back, almost tripping on one of the loose boards.

''Don't move, Emma,'' Grant said, barely able to breathe.

''Shut up,'' Martha yelled. ''She's the reason you wouldn't marry my girl. You wanted someone with money—''

''No, Martha,'' Grant said calmly, his heart racing. ''I told you Faye and I were only friends. I helped her with an assignment or two. We talked. But that's all. The baby wasn't mine.'' His chest ached with the breath he'd been holding. ''Emma had nothing to do with Faye. You have to let her go.''

Martha shook her head, another sob escaping. ''I saw your name, yours and that nasty Billy Hogan—''

''You killed Hogan?'' Grant asked, trying to sound rational while his heart pounded double time.

''That's right. He was sorry and no good.'' She laughed shrilly. ''After Faye died, I found her journal. She wrote about the baby, wrote about you, how you were going to be an architect. That's how I found you, and I swore I'd make both you guys pay for what you did to my girl...''

Grant exhaled sharply, hoping Emma didn't believe these ludicrous lies. ''Martha, I don't know what Faye wrote in the diary, but I promise you if she'd been pregnant with my baby, I would have stood by her. She dated a lot of guys—'' he hesitated, not knowing how much to tell the woman ''—and when she came to me, she didn't know what to do. She said she wasn't sure who the baby's father was—''

''That's a lie!'' Martha shrieked. Thunder crashed again and lightning shimmied across the sky. He stared at Emma, desperately wanting to drag her off that bridge, knowing any minute Martha might go wild and shoot Emma, if lightning didn't strike her first.

''I'm afraid it is true,'' he said. ''Faye didn't think she was pretty. I told her she was. I tried to be her friend, really I did,'' Grant said, still hoping to calm Martha.

''Stop it!'' the woman screamed. ''Stop saying those things about Faye! She was beautiful.''

Emma's slim body was shaking so badly he thought she was going to collapse any minute and go plunging into the frigid river.

"I know she was, but Faye was afraid to tell you about the baby, Martha," he said. "She didn't want to upset you. She loved you so much, Martha."

His calmly spoken words seemed to sink in, but then the wildness returned to her eyes and she stepped onto the bridge. She jerked the blindfold from Emma's eyes and pulled out the gag. His heart leaped into his throat. Fear and shock registered on Emma's face, but she took a deep breath and looked at him, such love and trust in her eyes that he nearly fell to his knees. God, he had to do something to save her. There was so much he had to tell her. He had to show her how much he loved her. He had to ask her to marry him again.

"She hated Billy. If you weren't the baby's father, then why'd she write about you like she loved you?" Martha asked, her deathly calm frightening him even more.

"I don't know," he said honestly. "Like I told you, we were friends."

"Martha," Emma interjected softly. "If Grant had fathered Faye's baby, he would have done the right thing," Emma said. "Think about it. You've gotten to know him over the past few months. Hasn't he been wonderful with Carly? And look how he's stayed by me during all this. He's not a man who shirks his responsibilities."

Martha's face contorted in a snarl. "He should have taken care of my grandchild." She turned to Emma and raised the gun to her face. "But he didn't. That's why you have to die. Then I can take Carly and raise her as my own."

"That's the reason you've been doing this?" Emma asked, her voice a hoarse whisper. The rain slackened to a sprinkle, but water still dripped down her face. "So you can take Carly?"

A hideous laugh filled the air. "I dropped hints that he was unfaithful, but you ignored them. Didn't even see that lipstick until they searched your car. I thought you'd die in that wreck, but no, you went into a coma. I tried to finish you off in the hospital—"

"You were there? You tried to kill me?" Emma's voice quavered.

Martha nodded. "Yes. But he came back to see you, sat by your side all the time. Damn him, he should have stayed with Faye."

"And you tried to shoot me and later shoved me down the steps at the house?" Emma asked. "Then you broke into Kate's and tried to smother me again."

Martha's head jerked up, the rain hood falling back, exposing her soggy gray hair. "Yeah, except you won't die," Martha wailed.

"But why did you bring me out here? Why not just shoot me at home?"

"I knew they'd find you at home. Your sister would be back any minute and they'd know it was me. I wanted time to get away with Carly!"

"Why didn't you just kill me?" Grant asked. "I'm the one who knew Faye. Don't hurt Emma. Faye wouldn't want that."

Emma gave him a beseeching look, but he had to lure Martha's attention away from her. It worked. Martha whipped the gun around toward Grant. "'Cause I wanted you to suffer the way I had, to know what it was like to lose someone, your baby girl..." Tears filled her tormented eyes, and Grant almost felt sorry for her.

"Is Carly the grandchild you've been shopping for?"

Emma asked, and he realized she was trying to distract Martha so he could edge closer to her.

Martha nodded, the lines beside her eyes softening. "Carly's going to be the grandchild I should have had years ago. I fixed Faye's room up for her. Little pink and blue teddy bears on the wall. She'll love it."

Grant's stomach churned as the pieces fell into place, all the while edging closer to Martha.

"So Faye was the daughter you said lived in Atlanta, the one who was pregnant?" Emma asked.

"She would have lived in Atlanta one day, would have had a fancy job, a great place to live, just like I said she did, all those dreams I had for her," Martha said in an oddly distant voice. "And she would have gotten married and given me grandchildren, and I would have loved them."

A shudder rippled through Grant. Martha had completely distorted the facts surrounding her daughter's death, and he'd become the scapegoat.

"I'm sorry she died," Emma said softly. "I know you miss her, Martha. But think about Carly. You love her, and she'll miss me if you kill me."

"She loves me already," Martha said, her teeth clicking as she vigorously nodded her head. "She loves me and she'll forget all about you."

He was a hairbreadth away from her now. "You can't kill Emma," Grant said, grateful when Martha swung around to face him, giving Emma time to pick her way off the bridge. "Faye wouldn't have wanted that, Martha. Faye would have been disappointed. She thought you were so good, so perfect. That's why she didn't tell you about the baby, she didn't want to disappoint you."

His arguments seemed to be working. Martha's hand wavered.

''You don't want Faye watching you from heaven, seeing you blame an innocent woman for her death, hurting an innocent baby by taking her mother away from her.''

The wildness in Martha's eyes melted as she turned her face to the sky. She let out an anguished cry, then pointed the gun at herself. Emma gasped and Grant dove, knocking the gun from her hands. Martha fell to the ground. Then she curled within herself and lay on the wet boards sobbing, despondent, until the police arrived.

GRANT GRABBED THE GUN, and Emma fell into his arms as soon as he untied her hands, laying her head against his muscled chest and hearing his heart pounding. They were both alive, here together, and that was all that mattered.

''Are you okay? Did she hurt you?'' His hands were everywhere at once, feeling to see if she was injured.

Emma shook her head, tears of relief clogging her throat. ''I'm okay, Grant, really.''

He cupped her face and looked into her eyes. ''I don't know what I would have done—''

''Shh, I'm here and I'm fine,'' she said, her voice shaky.

''Where's Carly?'' Grant asked, and she realized he'd probably been frantic about the baby, afraid Martha had done something with her.

''She's with Kate,'' Emma said quickly. ''Kate took her before Martha pulled the gun on me.''

''Thank God.'' He brushed the rain and tears from her face, pushed back her damp hair and kissed her.

Warner walked over, nodding toward the police car

where he'd secured Martha. "You two want to come to the station later and give me a statement?"

"Yeah. Thanks, Detective."

Warner tipped his hat. "I'm just glad it's over."

Emma stared at the blue swirling lights, wondering if it would ever be over for the sick woman in the car. "She'll receive some therapy, won't she?"

"You can bet on it," Warner said. Then he strode back to the car, climbed in and drove away.

Emma breathed in the crisp clean smell that follows a heavy rain. Grant cupped her face in his hands and covered her mouth with his, kissing her reverently. "I was so scared, so afraid I was going to lose you. I don't care about the past. Nothing matters except—"

"Shh," Emma whispered, wanting for once to be able to comfort him. "When you showed up, I knew everything would be okay, Grant." She brushed his mouth with a kiss, trying to tell him with her eyes how much she trusted their love. "I knew because I love you so much."

"And I love you, too, Emma. I never want us to be apart again."

"Never. You're not only my husband, you're my friend, my lover, my hero."

A slow sexy smile curved his mouth as he fell to one knee. They both laughed when mud squished around his jeans-clad leg. Then he clasped her hand in his and kissed her fingers. "Will you marry me, Emma?" He grinned rakishly. "Again, that is."

Her heart fluttered like the butterfly that suddenly glided out from behind a pine. "Yes, Grant, I'll marry you."

He stood and swung her into his arms, kissing her face and neck. Emma smiled, tears in her eyes, but he wiped them away and kissed her, then whispered a promise. ''This time, sweetheart, we're going to have a wedding you'll always remember.''

* * * * *

Coming next month, be sure to look for Rita Herron's warm and wonderful Harlequin American Romance debut:

HIS-AND-HERS TWINS #820

On sale March 2000!